FORSAKEN

A DJINN WARS NOVEL

CHRISTINE POPE

Dark Valentine Press

FORSAKEN

ISBN: 978-0-9883348-7-8
Copyright © 2016 by Christine Pope
Published by Dark Valentine Press

Cover design by Lou Harper

To learn more about this author, go to
www.christinepope.com.

FORSAKEN

CHAPTER ONE

THE GROUND RUMBLED UNDER HER FEET. OUT OF instinct, Madison Reynolds hugged the side of the building that had once housed a check-cashing place, her eyes scanning the area for any signs of djinn activity. As far as she could tell, she was alone, the city blocks stretching empty around her in every direction. She hadn't seen another human soul for more than a year. The djinn were a different story, but she'd learned to avoid them, to look for the telltale billows of smoke in the sky or the rustling of strange winds or an unexpected trembling of the ground.

But this—this hadn't felt like one of those tremors, although the movement of the cracked pavement beneath her feet sent adrenaline spiking all through her body, telling her to take cover immediately. Once she realized she hadn't seen any djinn in the vicinity, her heartbeat slowed a little, and she tried to make herself analyze what she'd just experienced.

The Albuquerque area wasn't all that seismically active; they'd had a minor quake here and there in the past, but nothing like the shaking she'd just experienced. It was the kind of shock that could have brought down unreinforced buildings, and it felt as if it had come from farther to the west, past the train station.

Madison hesitated. Her curiosity was urging her to head toward the source of the temblor, just to see what the hell was going on, but she knew that the farther away she got from home base, the more dangerous her return trip would be. Then she wanted to laugh at herself. She'd gone a good deal farther than this in the past, tempting fate as she ranged through the empty spaces of what used to be New Mexico's largest city, using the near-silent electric bicycle that had been part of her shelter's stock of survival equipment.

For the first few months after the world was forever changed, she'd kept hoping that maybe she'd find someone. Could the combination of the Heat and the arrival of the djinn who followed that dread disease really have killed off every single man, woman, and child in the greater Albuquerque metro area?

So far, the answer to that question appeared to be yes.

But there had been that one group she'd spotted less than a week after the Heat had struck. Madison had ventured out from her refuge, thinking that if she was immune, then logic suggested there must be others like her. At that point, the djinn were still only a legend from fairytales and stories to her, not a real and all-too-formidable threat, and so she hadn't thought she was risking herself by going out into the city to look for other survivors. She'd armed herself, though; she knew that any survivors out there could very well be desperate, unsure as to what had really happened, scrounging in the empty spaces of the city for any food that might have survived the collapse of the power grid.

And she'd seen the group of people, a mix of men and women, as she huddled in the shelter of an alley. They'd all looked tired and frightened.

Well, all except one of them. The man in the lead had appeared to be in his late forties, with short-cropped dark hair and cold, dark eyes. He wore Army fatigues, although Madison hadn't been close enough to make out any insignia. Something about his expression chilled her, and although she'd thought she would be happy to see another person—as long as that person appeared more or less friendly—that man had scared the crap out of her. Instead of going out to greet the little group of survivors, she'd remained in the alleyway's shadows, watching as they went by. One of the women had been strikingly pretty, with long warm blonde hair, and for the barest second her gaze had flickered toward the alley where Madison hid. But then she'd shrugged and moved on with the rest of her group.

Ever since that time, more than a year ago now, Madison couldn't keep herself from wondering what had happened to them. She supposed it was possible they had found a refuge somewhere, but she somehow doubted it. The djinn had been merciless in hunting down the pitiful remnants of Albuquerque's population that had survived the Heat.

Now she paused, glancing up at the sky, then back to the empty streets around her. Nothing moved, except a sun-bleached newspaper rattling up against the curb, blown there by one of New Mexico's ceaseless winds.

Then it came again—a shock so strong that again she had to steady herself against the wall of the check-cashing place. Across the street, a piece of brick fell off the building's façade and shattered on the sidewalk.

She frowned. That tremor hadn't felt so much like an earthquake as some sort of heavy demolition equipment at work. But there was no one left who could be using that kind of equipment. Most days, Madison was pretty sure she had to be the only human being left alive in New Mexico, if not the entire world.

Her curiosity wouldn't let it alone. Loosening her pistol in its holster—not that a gun was probably of much use against a djinn—she slipped out from the alley where she stood, and headed west toward the source of the disturbance.

Qadim al-Syan was not happy. True, he hadn't been punished outright by the djinn elders for his actions back in Santa Fe, where he'd been complicit in the kidnapping of Zahrias al-Harith, the head of that city's contingent of djinn and their Chosen. Qadim's involvement was due almost entirely to his sister Lyanna's machinations and her ridiculous obsession with Zahrias, and though Qadim had changed his mind at the end and had even assisted the Santa Fe djinn in reclaiming their kidnapped leader, apparently that hadn't been enough to redeem himself. He soon realized that the Council would have their own subtle revenge.

The djinn had taken this world from the humans when it became clear that they could no longer be trusted to be its stewards. Although Qadim had not been one of those who concocted the illness the humans had referred to as the Heat, he also had not done any-thing to prevent it from being made, or released upon an unsuspecting population. Like most of his people, he had wearied of the otherworld where they had all been banished for countless millennia, and was glad enough of the prospect of getting his own piece of land here on Earth once the humans were gone.

That land had not been denied him...but the Council had had their little joke.

"We have decided upon your grant," Ashtar had said, green eyes glinting with an amusement she did not bother to hide.

"Yes?" Qadim had come to their palace in the otherworld at the Council's summons, hoping that if he presented a meek enough aspect, they would believe he was not at all proud of what he had done to help his sister Lyanna in her foolish quest to regain Zahrias al-Harith's love, and that he regretted any pain he had caused.

None of that was precisely untrue. Qadim had regretted his actions soon enough, fearing that they would prevent him from receiving the land he thought was his due. And he regretted that al-Harith's woman, Julia Innes, had been so besotted with Zahrias that she wouldn't allow herself to explore what it might have been like to be with him instead.

But as far as regretting the kidnapping in the first place...that was a very different story.

Ashtar's emerald-hued eyes had seemed to bore into him as he stood there before the leaders of his people, as if she could see into his soul and read the truth there. However, while the Council were all very powerful djinn, each with his or her own particular gifts, Qadim did not think the woman before him possessed the ability to spy on his very thoughts. "We have decided that you would do best in the place the mortals called Albuquerque."

Anger had flared in him at her words, although he had somehow managed to keep himself from retorting that he did not think he would do very well there at all. Because of his sister's obsession with Zahrias al-Harith, who dwelled in Santa Fe, Qadim had acquired some familiarity with the region humans had once called New Mexico, and so he knew that while the state had vast tracts of undeveloped land, some of it quite beautiful, Albuquerque was the very opposite of undeveloped, a sprawling cityscape crowded with ugly architecture and all the artifacts of human technology he so despised. It would require years to be made over into anything resembling a livable place, even when using his talents as an earth elemental to reshape that territory.

But he had also known that he couldn't argue, that he had to bow his head and pretend to be pleased by the Council's magnanimity. At any rate, he had his sister's fate to remind him that this could have been much worse. Because of her plotting, and because she had threatened al-Harith's Chosen, Lyanna would be exiled forever in the otherworld, with its barren, rocky landscape and roiling skies and acrid air. She would live in the intricate palace she had constructed, true, but she would not be allowed to breathe the sweet air of this world, to revel in its blue skies and green hills.

Yes, there were far worse things than being stuck with Albuquerque.

He'd bowed and smiled, and made his escape as soon as he could. And then he'd come down to Earth, to what had once been the most populous city in New Mexico, to see what possibly could be done.

The task did seem monumental. Almost as far as the eye could see were buildings in all shapes and sizes, the contorted black ribbon of a highway interchange, the sprawling airport with its abandoned planes rusting on the tarmac. Yes, the outline of the mountains to the east was pleasing, and at sunset they turned a glorious reddish-pink shade, but everything that lay between there and here would have to go.

His power was of the earth, and so at least Qadim could use the earth itself against the monstrous structures of steel and glass. He'd decided it would be best to start in the heart of the city and work outward from there.

The first building he inspected, however, surprised him. From the outside, it was nondescript enough, a multi-story tower of sand-colored concrete, but within were furnishings as intricate as those one might find in a djinn palace, with grottos of various designs, and carved screens and hand-painted tile. Its name was emblazoned on one of the abandoned menus in the empty restaurant.

Hotel Andaluz.

Qadim thought he should make this his base of operations, his temporary home, so to speak, until he could construct a palace of his own. He brought to the hotel such items as he thought would be necessary to his comfort, and took up residence in the suite on the top floor. After that, though, it was time to get to work.

Next to the hotel was a parking structure. By some great good luck, it was mostly empty. Perhaps the people who would have normally parked there had stayed home because of the Heat, praying that the disease would pass them by. But it had spared very few, and those who had survived had been hunted down soon enough.

Qadim had taken no part in those hunts, even though the invitation had been extended to him on more than one occasion. While he had agreed that humanity was—for the most part—a festering boil that needed to be lanced, he knew he would take no pleasure in tracking down the few remaining survivors, pitiful creatures that they were. He saw no honor in hunting those who had no special abilities that might save them. So he had always demurred, even though his refusal to participate in those hunts had raised a few eyebrows here and there.

"What," Hasan al-Abyad had said once, "are you rethinking your decision not to take on a Chosen? For I can see no other reason, besides believing that a human female is a worthy companion, why you would not want to join us in exterminating these mortals. It is great sport."

"Oh, no," Qadim had replied with a chuckle, although once again he failed to see the sport in murdering defenseless humans. "I cannot see the point in tying myself down to a single woman for all eternity, especially a mortal."

"But she would not be mortal any longer, once you had chosen her."

"True, but you know me, Hasan. When have I ever spent more than a few decades with any woman? If I could not bear to spend any more time than that with a djinn, why would I wish to do so with a human?"

Hasan had laughed at that remark, and agreed it did not make much sense, and that had seemed to be the end of the matter. Truly, Qadim hadn't understood why a djinn would want a human at all, when their own women promised so many delights.

That is, until he had met Julia Innes. Her beauty was such that it would have stood out in any company, mortal or djinn. And she was as strong and passionate as she was beautiful. Zahrias al-Harith didn't deserve her, for Qadim knew she would be bored with him soon enough. He was far too rigid, too concerned with honor. She would have found eternity far more amusing at Qadim's side.

But she had made her choice, and there was nothing he could do about it, save brood over her folly from time to time, and think that she had made a foolish choice. As for himself, well, he had never wanted for female companions, although he worried now that a woman of his own kind might not be too terribly impressed with his new holdings, would rather be with someone who had been given miles of beach in California, or a mountain eyrie somewhere in the Swiss Alps.

In the meantime, he supposed he must do what he had to.

The parking garage came down in a flurry of dust and pulverized concrete. There was very little in it he thought worth salvaging, except perhaps some of the metal infrastructure that had given it strength. Qadim used his power as an earth elemental to extract that metal, to draw it out of the concrete and have it form into neat bars, which he lined up along the sidewalk next to the hotel. He also made sure that the foundations of the buildings were smoothed over and covered by soil, since he would need all of it for what he had planned.

Having the parking garage gone helped somewhat, but its collapse only revealed more buildings on the other side. Frowning, he wondered if he should continue the demolition in that direction, or whether he should destroy the tall building directly across the street from the hotel.

He went out and stood in the middle of Copper Avenue, surveying his surroundings. There seemed to be something of an open area abutting the building in question, so he walked over and took a look around. Yes, there were plants in large pots. Some of them even seemed to have survived their year of neglect, and he noted that he should do what he could to revive them, since his connection with the earth also gave him some small gifts in encouraging the growth of plant life.

Beyond that little arcade was a small park with red rocks and grass, and that should definitely be preserved. But the building itself served no useful purpose.

Again the earth shuddered, and the building collapsed much in the same way the parking structure had. Qadim made sure that all the debris fell away from him and the park where he stood. When it was all gone, the space felt far more open, the bright sun pouring down and making the red rocks and the grass around them more vibrant.

Yes, that was much better.

Madison paused in the lee side of a building that had once housed Albuquerque Health Partners and stared, not sure she could believe what she was seeing. Kitty-corner across the street was the Convention Center... or at least what was left of it.

Chalky dust still filled the air, but she could see clearly enough. The enormous building that had once stood there was basically gone. For some reason, the garden area outside was still intact, unharmed except for the fine white dust drifting over it.

Then her heart seemed to skip in her chest, because standing in the middle of the grass in the garden was a man.

No, not a man, her mind quickly corrected her. *A djinn.*

His back was to her, so she couldn't see his face. But he wore long flowing robes in shades of gray and black. She'd seen other djinn wearing more or less the same sort of thing, although in brighter colors. His hair was long and nearly as dark as his robes, rippling in the breeze. Even at this distance she could tell he was extremely tall, maybe six and a half feet or more.

He hadn't sensed her. Maybe he was so focused on the destruction of the building that he wasn't paying attention to his surroundings. Madison had never been entirely sure how close a djinn needed to be before he could tell that a human was in the vicinity. Most of the time, though, they hadn't picked up on her presence until they were within ten yards or so. Which meant they weren't omnipotent. If she kept her distance, she was safe. Well, unless they actually saw her, and she'd always taken care to prevent that from happening.

What this djinn was doing here in Albuquerque, blowing up buildings, she had no idea. The elementals she'd evaded during the past year had clearly been on the hunt, chasing down the city's few survivors, but that didn't seem to be this djinn's objective. As she took a quick glance down Copper Avenue, she realized that the parking garage next to the Hotel Andaluz was gone as well. That must have been the first "earthquake" she'd felt.

So did he intend to knock down every building in the vicinity? That would take a while.

He turned then, and she was able to catch a faint glimpse of a strong profile with a long nose, his chin and cheeks partially obscured by a closely trimmed beard. At the same time, she shrank back against the wall, praying that he hadn't noticed her hiding there and staring at him.

Apparently not. He crossed the street and disappeared inside the Hotel Andaluz, and she let out a breath. She knew it was time to go. Her luck had held so far, but pushing it would only get her into a world of trouble. This strange djinn and the mystery he represented would have to wait for later.

She hurried back the way she'd come, staying in the shadows, heart racing the whole time. Deep down, she knew she really didn't need to have ventured out here at all, that she'd done so to fill a far different need than mere food or water. After all, the shelter had enough supplies stockpiled to last for five years or more. These prospecting missions were her only way of keeping herself from dying of boredom.

The last thing she wanted to admit to herself was that they were a test as well. She'd survived when so many countless others had died. Getting through yet another expedition in dead Albuquerque was a way of proving to herself that she deserved to live.

Or maybe it just proved that the universe wasn't quite done with her yet.

CHAPTER TWO

THE BOMB SHELTER WAS LOCATED UNDER THE PROP-
erty that had once belonged to Dr. Clay Michaels, her
father's boss at Sandia National Laboratories. Madison's
father had never talked much about his work. It had
something to do with nuclear weapons safety, but that
was all she knew. He couldn't discuss his work because
it was classified, and Madison never asked. She knew
better.

Despite the secrecy surrounding his work at Sandia,
Dr. Michaels had always felt like another uncle to her,
one she actually got to spend time with, since both her
parents had come to Albuquerque from elsewhere, her
mother from Sacramento in northern California, her
father from Chicago. Madison had few opportunities to

see her relatives, except on the rare occasions when her parents had made the effort to travel out of state.

But Clay had treated Tom and Sarah Reynolds, Madison's parents, like the brother and sister he'd never had, and Tom and Sarah had only been too happy to reciprocate. At least, until Sarah got sick and wasn't up for entertaining, or much of anything else.

Madison closed the shelter's hatch behind her, making sure it was locked securely. The shelter had all sorts of failsafes in place to guard against radiation, chemical weapons, and biological contaminants, but none of that was really necessary now. There hadn't been a nuclear attack; no one had rained down sarin gas or weaponized anthrax. That the Heat had been some kind of biological weapon, she was sure, but obviously she was immune, or she would have died more than a year ago along with everyone else she'd ever known or loved.

Still, she followed all the procedures, locking the outer hatch, double-checking the decontamination filters before she headed into the shelter itself. The electric bike had a charging station just inside the final door, and she plugged it in before heading toward the kitchen. Her mouth was dry, maybe from inhaling too much of that dust.

Just what the hell had that djinn been up to? The only destructive behavior she'd seen djinn indulge in before had been directed solely at humans. Even now, many months after she'd seen the man who was apparently Albuquerque's only other survivor meet a violent end at the hands of those otherworldly foes, her sleep still rang with the screams of those who'd been brutally murdered.

She opened the refrigerator in the kitchen and poured a glass of filtered water from the pitcher she kept in there. The first swallow made her feel a little better, but her heart was still beating hard, far more than the slight exertion necessary to pilot the electric bicycle would have required.

When exactly had been her last djinn sighting? Sometime in March, she thought. Ever since then, Albuquerque had been a ghost town, and now it was early October. She knew she was the only person left within the city limits, or surely she would have seen at least a hint of another survivor's presence.

The only reason she wasn't dead was the shelter where she now stood. Bunker. Whatever you wanted to call it, the place had been designed to withstand a nearby nuclear blast, chemical warfare, civil unrest, or any other of a long list of additional catastrophes. Madison had no real idea how much the shelter must have cost, but she knew it had to be a lot. Maybe more than a million dollars. One wouldn't have thought a scientist at a government laboratory could afford that kind of extravagance, but Clay Michaels never had any children or anything much to spend his money on. From the street, his house had looked modest enough...if you didn't know what was hidden underneath the backyard.

Madison left the kitchen and headed toward the media room. Cable TV and streaming services were things of the past, vanished along with the world that had created them, but Clay had made sure that the shelter's media servers were stocked with all sorts of film and television classics, as well as an eclectic assortment of music. In addition, he'd done a credible job of backing up a number of scientific journals and reference texts, along with what appeared to be a data dump from Wikipedia as it had existed right before the Heat wiped out the internet, in addition to databases from a number of noted universities.

It was from studying those resources that Madison had eventually realized those human-looking but inimical creatures stalking the streets like a squad of angels of death were djinn.

At first she'd had no real idea what a djinn even was. Genies were something from *Aladdin,* not men of intense beauty with doom in their eyes. But after entering keywords in a variety of combinations into the shelter's database, she'd come to the conclusion that these entities had to be djinn. They had control over air, or earth, or fire. Probably water, too, but standing bodies of water were in short supply in Albuquerque. The strange beings could pop into existence from nowhere before they rained death upon any unlucky humans they might find.

Her research also explained why the djinn would want all humans dead. They desired this world, believing it had been denied them in favor of giving it to the human race.

Well, it was theirs now.

She sat down on the couch and set her glass of water on the coffee table in front of her. If anyone had been shown a snapshot of this room and not been told where it was, they probably would have said it was an image of a high-end model home, or maybe a very expensive hotel. The sofa was leather, the coffee table burnished juniper lovingly carved to preserve the twisted shape of the original wood. Alabaster sconces held in place by old bronze fittings hung on the wall, bracketing original oils by local artists.

Actually, several of the paintings in the shelter were hers. And not ones she'd created after she'd hidden herself away here, but *plein air* pieces Clay Michaels had bought from her to decorate the space. She'd always wondered if he'd done so because he truly appreciated her art or whether his installation of the paintings here was more or less the equivalent of a parent sticking his child's stick figure drawings on the refrigerator door.

As she stared without really seeing at an oil of the Rio Grande gorge near Taos, all brooding purples and grays and blacks, she couldn't get the image of the djinn she'd just seen out of her mind. If she'd been thinking, she would have pulled the slim camera she carried with her everywhere from her pocket and taken a couple of quick snapshots, if only to reassure herself that he actually was real and not something a mind fevered with too much loneliness might have conjured up.

Well, she'd have to settle for the next best thing.

She had sketchbooks and pencils and charcoals stashed away in most of the shelter's rooms, although one of the secondary bedrooms was the only place where she had an actual easel set up so she could work with her beloved oils. Now, though, a sketchpad would be enough. Madison picked up the one she'd left on a side table and then selected a charcoal pencil from the stoneware cup she used to store her drawing supplies. His looks cried out for charcoal, with his long nose and heavy dark hair and sweeping night-colored robes.

The profile first, with its severe but elegant lines of brow and nose and chin. She had to obscure that chin with the shadow of his beard, but it couldn't quite hide the shape of his jaw. Whether she was remembering those details correctly, she didn't know for sure. She'd been so startled by his being there at all that all she had was the sudden, shocked imprint of his appearance on her mind's eye, and that was what she consulted now, sketching quickly, the face and figure of the djinn taking shape on the paper beneath her charcoal pencil.

When she was done, she paused for a moment so she could stare down at her handiwork. Was he actually that handsome? Madison supposed he must be, or close to it, anyway; there wasn't much point in romanticizing a member of such a murderous race.

But although she'd consigned his appearance to paper, she still wasn't any closer to discovering what in the world he was doing here.

She stared down at the sketch for a long moment, then murmured, "Who are you?"

She didn't say the next words out loud, but they echoed through her mind just the same.

And what do you want?

Qadim crossed his arms and surveyed his handiwork. The buildings in a quarter-mile radius had all been leveled, including a cinema and a train station. Now the Hotel Andaluz stood proudly alone, a faded American flag still flapping above the entrance. That was better, and enough work for one day. If he was diligent, perhaps in a year he would have cleared enough to make all his efforts worthwhile.

Fighting back a scowl, he slapped the dust from his robes and went inside the hotel. Although the power had been out in Albuquerque for more than a year, a djinn had no need of something as limiting as electricity. All djinn had the ability to influence matter and energy, although their alignment with one of the four elements gave them additional talents when it came to interacting with earth or air, water or fire. At any rate, his inborn powers were enough to light the sconces on the wall, to let water flow once more down the waterfall in one of the grottoes that ringed the lobby area.

There had been some looting in the city before the last of the survivors were picked off, but none of them apparently had thought to come here. The food in the refrigeration units had long since spoiled, and Qadim disposed of it with a flick of his finger, but the wine cellar had survived completely unscathed. He poured himself a glass of shiraz and went back out to the lobby so he might sit in the grotto with the waterfall and congratulate himself on a good day's work.

The Council had most assuredly wished to punish him by making this town his new home, but he doubted they'd known of the existence of this hotel. Otherwise, they might have made a different choice.

The soothing sound of flowing water filled the silence, and he let his eyes close halfway as he sampled the wine, the dark fruit of the vines, the spice of the oldest grape in the world. He'd been drinking wines made with this grape for millennia, although it had been called something quite different back then.

Perhaps this wouldn't be so bad after all. In time, once he'd transformed this barren cityscape into a garden, he should be able to find someone to share it with him. Djinn had long memories, but even so, he thought that eventually his disgrace would be forgotten.

In the meantime, though, he thought he could enjoy himself well enough and learn to embrace his solitude.

Sleep had been one of the most difficult parts of her solitary existence in the shelter. At first Madison's sleeplessness had stemmed from worry and grief, and nothing more. Her mind hadn't wanted to grasp the enormity of what had happened to her, to the entire world. It had all happened so fast—within a few days of the first reports of the mysterious disease known as the Heat, the world had ground to a halt, its people dying in numbers so overwhelming that it was almost impossible to grasp the situation.

At the time, she was living in an apartment about fifteen minutes away from the house where she'd grown up. Unlike a number of her fellows in her master's program, she actually had been making a living from her art, although most of her income came from illustration work rather than the landscapes she loved so much. But that was all right; the freelance work still proved she could make it, that her decision to get a master's in studio art hadn't been complete insanity.

The Heat had begun to strike at the population while she had her head down, feverishly trying to finish a commission for a card set, an expansion pack to a *Magic: The Gathering* sort of game. When she was under deadline like that, she didn't turn on the TV or go on social media. She barely checked her email, and that was only because she didn't want to miss anything work-related. So although the disease had already begun to take its toll, only two days after it was detected, it wasn't until she got a phone call from her father late on the second day that she realized anything was wrong.

His voice had been hoarse and weak. She hadn't heard him sound like that since her mother's funeral. All he'd said was, "I need you," before the phone went silent again.

She'd put down her paintbrush and hurried out the door, not even bothering to throw on a jacket. Traffic had been oddly light, but she really didn't think about the number of vehicles on the street, was only intent on getting to her father's house as quickly as possible.

He was lying on the couch in the living room, his dropped cell phone on the floor next to him. Madison had picked it up and put it on the coffee table, then knelt by his side. Her father was a tall man, and he didn't quite fit on the sofa, his legs slipping down to touch the carpet. His face was flushed and sheened with sweat, his breaths a shallow pant.

Had she ever seen anyone that ill? Maybe her mother when she was in the last stages of her battle with cancer, but this was an entirely different kind of sickness. Even from a foot away, Madison had felt the waves of fever heat coming from her father's body.

Of course she'd grabbed her phone to call 9-1-1, but all she got was a fast busy signal, indicating that the circuits were overloaded. Her entire body tensed at the sound, even as her mind shied away from acknowledging what that busy signal probably meant.

And then he'd whispered her name.

"Madison."

She'd bent toward him, while at the same time worrying what in the world she was going to do, and whether he was contagious—even as she scolded herself for harboring such a selfish thought—and who she should call now that emergency services didn't seem to be responding. "Dad?"

He pointed toward the cell phone she held and shook his head. "No use," he whispered. His eyes were wide, so wide that she could see the whites all around the irises, even though those whites weren't really white at all, but choked with angry-looking red veins. "All gone."

"What do you mean, 'all gone'?" she asked, a terror she could barely comprehend beginning to well up in her.

"Everything," he said simply, the word barely more than a breath. "Madison...."

"What, Dad?" Her own voice was nearly as hushed, but that was more because of the tears she could feel rising, choking her vocal chords.

"Go...shelter."

Of course she knew about the shelter. Clay Michaels had treated her family as if they were his, and so he'd told them about the secret bunker twenty feet below the surface of his backyard, the entrance cleverly hidden in the bottom of a gazebo surrounded by roses. When she'd first learned of the shelter, around the time she was sixteen or so, she'd thought Clay was being just a little paranoid—after all, the Cold War was long over—although she'd kept her opinion to herself.

"I need to get you to a hospital," she told her father in reply. How she'd manage to do that, she had no idea. Yes, she'd inherited her father's height, and kept herself in shape by hiking or working out on the elliptical in her apartment when she didn't have time to get out and about, but that didn't mean she'd be able to lift a man who was six foot three and weighed around two hundred pounds.

"No hospitals," he replied weakly. "Gone. Nothing...go to the shelter."

"Dad—"

His eyes shut then, and a strange rattle came from his throat. Hearing it, her blood went cold, but she forced herself to reach out and take his wrist, so strangely, frighteningly hot, the skin slick with sweat.

She couldn't feel a pulse. Forcing in a breath, she moved her fingers to his throat, praying that she'd be able to feel the stronger beat of his heart there, but there was nothing to feel.

Nothing. Just as he'd said.

She knelt there for a long moment, her eyes burning, dry. Somehow she knew if she started to cry, she'd never be able to stop.

The night was so still. From far off she thought she could hear the wail of a siren, but otherwise, the only thing echoing in her ears was the thudding of her own heart.

"I'm sorry, Dad," she said at last. Thinking her failure at getting through to 9-1-1 earlier had to have been a fluke, she tapped the screen on her phone again. This time she didn't even get that fast, angry busy signal. There was nothing. Dead air.

She'd wanted to fling the phone at the wall in denial, but she didn't. Instead, she set it down and forced herself to confront what she must do next.

No one would be coming to take her father's body away. She'd climbed the stairs to the second floor, thinking she could fetch a sheet and bundle him up in it, then take him away from here, to the plot in the cemetery where he'd always planned to be laid to rest next to her mother. How in the world she'd manage to bury him, she didn't know, but it seemed horribly wrong to leave him here, even though he'd told her he wanted her to go to the shelter.

His last wishes warred with her sorrow, with her need to do right by him, and she didn't know what the hell she was supposed to do.

When she descended the stairs to the living room, though, she couldn't see her father's body anywhere. Relief came to her out of nowhere. Maybe she'd just thought she couldn't find a pulse. Maybe he'd snapped out of that strange fever, and everything would be okay.

As she approached the sofa, however, she could see by the light of the floor lamp next to it that the cushions were all covered in fine gray dust. What the—

A horrible suspicion came over her, one she didn't want to acknowledge. But she also knew deep in her heart that her father had been dead, that his heart had stopped beating a few minutes earlier. He hadn't gotten up and walked away. And he'd been burning with such a terrible fever....

Her free hand, the one not holding the sheet she'd just gotten from the linen closet, went to her mouth. A strangled sound came from her throat, like a whimper throttled before it had a chance to really begin. And then she was turning and running out the door, hurrying to her car so she could turn on the radio. Not the satellite music she usually listened to, but a local news station.

What the hell was going on?

She'd halfway feared no one would be broadcasting, but a man's voice came through the speakers. He sounded young and scared, and Madison had a feeling he wasn't a reporter at all, but maybe someone who worked at the station.

Maybe he was on the air because everyone else was already dead.

"Emergency service are no longer responding," he said. "They told us to stay indoors and away from other people, but that doesn't seem to make any difference. If the Heat gets you, it's over."

The Heat, Madison thought. *That's what killed my father.*

"There's no contact from Washington," the young man went on. His voice cracked on the last syllable. "No contact from anyone. I think they're all gone."

Gone. That word again. She didn't want to hear it ever again.

After viciously stabbing the power button for the radio, she pressed down on the accelerator, weaving in and out of cars that seemed to have stalled in traffic. Or maybe the people driving them had dropped dead behind the wheel, leaving behind little piles of gray ash.

Her father had told her to go to the shelter, so that was where she'd head. Part of her thought that maybe she should go home first and pack some belongings, but that would be going the exact opposite direction of Clay Michaels' home out on the border of Kirtland

Air Force Base. Besides, he'd said the place was fully stocked with clothing, food, toiletries.

Weapons.

Of course, were weapons even necessary if everyone else was dead?

A hiccupy little sob forced its way out of her throat, and her eyes blurred with tears. But she kept driving. For one crazy instant, she had the idea that maybe she should go to the radio station, find the person who had been broadcasting there. No, that was stupid. She'd be going far out of her way, and from what he'd been saying, he could very well be dead by the time she got there.

Fingers white-knuckled around the steering wheel, she made herself drive on.

Some instinct made her park her car around the corner from Clay's house. The last thing she wanted was to attract any attention. His street was dark, though. Two houses showed some kind of dim illumination from within, but that was the only sign of life.

Madison got her purse and the Mag-lite flashlight she always kept tucked under the passenger seat of her Nissan Rogue, then hurried down the sidewalk to Clay's house. It, too, was dark. She didn't know what to think of that. Maybe he was already hiding in the shelter, hoping against hope that Madison and her father would make it there.

Or maybe he'd succumbed to the Heat, the same as everyone else.

It was entirely possible that this was a fool's errand, that at any second she'd break out in a sweat, her body flushing with a fever so hot it burned its victims to dust.

But she kept walking anyway, the flashlight clutched in her hand. She hadn't turned it on, though, was carrying it more as a handy weapon than anything else. Using the flashlight for its real purpose would only attract the attention of anyone on the block who hadn't yet succumbed to the horrible disease.

She went in through the side yard, not bothering to go into the house. There shouldn't be anything inside she needed anyway. Her real destination was in the backyard.

The gazebo glimmered faintly white within a garden of carefully trimmed rosebushes. Madison went around to the back and then squatted down next to what looked like a control system for the sprinklers. It had a keypad, and she typed in the code her father had taught her.

Rosebud.

A little joke, and maybe a reference to the "hide in plain sight" nature of the shelter itself. In the next moment, a piece of the lattice at the base of the gazebo slid aside, and she remained crouching so she could slip under the floor of the structure and into the hatch that revealed itself there. Three turns, and it was open as well.

Inside was a corridor that sloped gently downward. LED bulbs burned overhead, lighting her way.

"Clay?" she called out. "It's Maddie."

Only silence in reply, and she swallowed. Well, the shelter was huge, stretching nearly to the property lines. How Clay had managed to build this place without his neighbors noticing, Madison had no idea. She'd have to ask him.

If he was here.

In a way, she didn't know what would be worse—for him to have died along with everyone else, or for him to have survived so they'd be forced to share the bunker for the rest of their lives. She'd always looked on him as a sort of uncle, but would he see her as a niece...or as a woman who could help him repopulate the earth?

She pushed that thought aside, knowing she was allowing her mind to go down all sorts of crazy pathways because it was a good way of distracting herself from what had just happened to her father...to all of Albuquerque...to maybe the entire world.

The corridor widened as she descended, and she came to the final hatch, the one that would allow entrance to the actual living quarters themselves. As she opened it, she called out again.

"Clay?"

Nothing. She went inside and methodically walked from room to room, calling his name periodically. But he never answered. The shelter was clearly empty.

She didn't know what she'd been expecting. Sometimes Clay Michaels had seemed nearly invincible, but apparently even he couldn't withstand the strange virus that had swept through the city's population.

Fighting back panic, she headed to the room she knew had been designated as hers. It held a queen-size bed, a dresser, and a small table and chair in one corner. A door opposite the one she'd just entered led to a Jack-and-Jill bathroom.

She looked in the dresser and found stacks of jeans and T-shirts, as well as a drawer filled with underwear still in its packaging and several bras with the tags still attached. Creepy. Or was it? She'd left some things behind when she moved out of her father's house. For all she knew, he'd used the sizes on those items to make sure the proper items waited for her here in case the worst happened.

Same thing in the bathroom—soaps and cleansers and moisturizers in all the brands she liked, an electric razor still in its box. Ditto for an electric toothbrush and a blow dryer with a diffuser that wouldn't cause her long, curly hair to frizz.

All the comforts of home, she thought, and a weird little giggle rose to her lips. She pushed it back, because otherwise she worried she might break into hysterical laughter then and there.

Since she didn't know what else to do, she went to the media room and turned on the television. Even though this bunker had been prepared in the event the apocalypse occurred, it still had cable. Half the channels were blank, though, or showing reruns of sitcoms no one cared about. MSNBC had a camera fixed on an empty desk, as if someone had been sitting there but was now gone. For all Madison knew, the cameraman had dropped where he stood, but the feed kept rolling and probably would continue to do so until the power failed.

It wasn't until that moment that she realized this was real. The Heat hadn't hit only Albuquerque, or even just New Mexico. No one was safe anywhere.

She sat there all night, watching as the channels dropped out one by one. From time to time she dozed, then jerked awake, praying that she'd open her eyes and see Clay standing there, exuding his usual quiet confidence. By morning, she thought she would have been happy to be his Eve to her Adam, if only it meant that she wouldn't be alone.

But he never came. And the next night she slept in the room that was supposed to be hers. And the night after that. All the cable stations were blank. Moving the radio along the FM and AM bands produced only static. Fear coiled in her belly, but she couldn't give in to it. Not while waking, anyway. She would fall asleep and then wake screaming from nightmares where she was surrounded by a faceless horde, only to have them shiver into dust and blow away as she watched. Or the ones where her father would take her by the hand, and an unnatural heat would race up her arm, and she herself would begin to fall apart into nothing.

She screamed herself hoarse, but there was no one to hear her. By the time the fourth or fifth day rolled around, she realized dully that, for some strange reason, she was immune to the disease which had killed everyone else. Otherwise, she would have been dead her first night here.

The thought brought her no real relief.

Even now, after so many months in the shelter, sleep was something she indulged in because she knew she had to, not because she felt all that refreshed when she awoke each morning. While she understood intellectually that the air she breathed was filtered and scrubbed and cleaner than anything she would have been breathing back in her apartment, sometimes she felt as if she would choke if she couldn't get any fresh air.

Those were the times she'd venture out into the upper world. The first had been about a week after she came to the shelter. She'd watched movies and TV shows, played games on the computer, read—anything to fill up the empty hours. What she'd really wanted, though, was to paint. She'd sketched a little with the ballpoint pens and computer paper she found in what had been intended as Clay's office, but that wasn't the same as the soothing process of mixing her own oils, planning the composition, spending hours on just one section until it was right. If she had to spend eternity in this place, then she needed something more meaningful than reruns of *The Big Bang Theory* to keep her occupied.

Besides, if everyone was dead, what difference would it make if she went out and raided a few art supply stores?

At first, she'd thought about taking her car, just because it would have been easier to bring back all the supplies she needed. For some reason, though, that didn't feel right. A bright red compact SUV maneuvering along Albuquerque's deserted streets would be far too conspicuous.

So she'd taken the electric bike, which was fast and silent, and laboriously hauled it out from under the gazebo, then headed out into town. There was a store called Artisan up on Monte Vista that wasn't too far from Clay's house, so she decided it would be her first stop. It was during that expedition that she'd seen the band of survivors pass by, and had done nothing. Even now she wondered what would have happened if she'd gone with them, wherever it was they'd been headed.

But she hadn't, had instead hidden until they were gone, then made her way inside Artisan. The front doors were unlocked, and she worried that the store might have been looted. Aside from the cash register standing open, though, she hadn't found any sign that anyone had come in and helped themselves to the shop's wares. She supposed that art supplies were pretty far down the chain when it came to the necessities required for surviving the apocalypse.

Carrying pre-stretched canvas on an electric bike was tricky, and so she'd only grabbed a couple small ones, no bigger than sixteen by twenty inches, along with a bag of paints and brushes and some pencils and charcoal, just for when she didn't want to be working with oils. The trip back had been harder than she'd thought, and she'd had to stop several times to adjust everything she was hauling.

One of those stops probably saved her life, because it was then that she saw her first djinn. She'd paused in an alley between a liquor store and a pawn shop so she could redistribute her loot, and then heard a strange tearing sound coming from somewhere above, almost as if the sky had been ripped open. At the same time, the street echoed with the sound of running feet.

She had to look, because that sound meant someone had to be alive. Someone who could erase the painful solitude she'd been living in for the past week.

Pounding down the center of Washington Street was a Hispanic man probably a few years older than she, maybe close to thirty. Sweat soaked the T-shirt he wore, even though the day was fairly mild, and he kept casting terrified glances upward.

Puzzled, Madison looked up as well, wondering what in the world could possibly have him so frightened. And then she saw—well, at first her mind didn't want to grasp that unthinkable vision, couldn't comprehend what she was seeing.

Hovering approximately twenty feet above the ground were two men. That is, they looked like men, and at the same time couldn't possibly have been, not with the way they hung in the air with no visible means of support. They had black hair that whipped around their faces in an unseen wind, as did the flowing garments they wore—some kind of open robes over blousy pants. Their bodies were magnificent, their faces something she would have liked to paint...except for the expressions of maniacal delight they wore.

They threw back their heads and laughed, and then they dove.

Madison barely ducked her head in time. Even so, blood sprayed across her face in a warm mist. One terrified whimper escaped her throat before she cut it off, knowing somehow that she would share the same fate as that stranger in the street, if those two unnatural men should happen to hear her.

She used his shrieks of agony to cover her escape, taking off down the alley and then pushing the electric bike to its very limits so she could get away as quickly as possible. Even when she reached the shelter, a good two miles away, she kept glancing upward, certain that they must have tracked her there.

But the skies remained empty. She hadn't dropped any of her supplies, probably because she'd been terrified that those two impossible creatures who looked like men would hear the clatter the canvases made as they hit the pavement.

And she'd stood in the shower afterward for nearly an hour, willing the hot water to rinse away every last trace of blood spatter. It couldn't get rid of those screams, though. They kept ringing in her ears.

A month passed before she gathered the courage to venture out again. By then the fires she'd seen raging on the UNM campus had burned themselves out, and the skies were clear, the ultra-hard, bright blue of a New Mexico autumn. The air had begun to pick up a slight bite, and Madison had shivered in her T-shirt. The shelter was always kept at a perfectly controlled seventy-two degrees, and so she hadn't even stopped to think about what the outside temperature might be.

Exactly what had driven her forth again, she couldn't say for sure, except she had to know. The horrible events of the day when she'd gone out to fetch her art supplies had taken on the quality of a nightmare, and she began to wonder if she'd imagined the whole thing.

But she saw them again—or rather, two other beings who resembled the first two superficially but who she thought were different people. This time they were up on Menaul. The screams she heard that time were more or less the same, although it sounded as if more than one person was their target. She'd fled back to the shelter, shaking, wondering how on earth the world could have gone any more insane than it already was. After she'd recovered herself somewhat, though, she went to the computer and started going through the database, trying to put a name to those creatures she'd seen.

And that was when she first read about the djinn. Her mind didn't want to believe such a thing could be possible, but she'd seen it for herself. Was their presence any crazier than a disease that could kill almost the entire population of the planet and leave behind only dust?

Since she'd managed to escape the djinns' notice, she became a little bolder after that. One time she even made the trek to her old apartment to claim some items she'd been missing—a few favorite pieces of clothing, a locket containing a photograph of her parents on their wedding day, both of them sunny and happy and completely unaware of what lay ahead for them. A coral and turquoise cross that had once belonged to her mother. Madison wasn't religious, but she remembered her mother wearing that pendant, and she wanted it with her now, after the world had ended.

Otherwise, though, her expeditions kept her closer to home, and often she popped out just long enough to snap a few photographs, something that would provide her with more material for her paintings. Winter came, and went. In early spring she saw one of the djinn doing a casual sweep of the city, his blue silk robes blowing in the wind as he circled overhead like the world's largest, deadliest raptor.

But he was the last.

Except the man she'd seen today.

She stared up at the ceiling, which was faintly lit by the warm glow of the Himalayan salt lamp on top of the dresser. It didn't matter to her whether the lamp really worked—it was supposed to put out negative ions, or something like that. What mattered was that it held the darkness at bay, allowed her to shut her eyes and know that she would be able to awake in the morning.

This time as she closed her eyes, the proud, hawk-ish profile of the djinn she'd spied on earlier floated behind her eyelids. And again she wondered,

Who are you?

CHAPTER THREE

BY THE AFTERNOON OF HIS THIRD DAY IN Albuquerque, Qadim had cleared nearly a half-mile radius around the hotel he had designated as his new home. He could see the contours of the land better now, where it rolled and where it was flat. The soil was terribly depleted from years of human interference, however, and so he brought in new topsoil and seeded it with native grasses and plants and trees, sending them the nutrients they needed to grow. He would have preferred a landscape of green, rich grass, so different from the barren surroundings he'd left behind in the otherworld, but he knew it would never survive here in this high desert environment, and he would not do what humans had always been far too eager to do—plant according to their own aesthetics, and not based on what the land could support.

At night he would go out on the rooftop bar with a bottle of wine and watch the blackness all around. Not one light in the city, not one sign of life. Of course, he had expected nothing else. Hasan al-Abyad and the others of his ilk had made sure that no mortal survived their sweeps.

But overhead were the brilliant desert stars, and soon there would be moonlight as well, for the thin crescent that hung in the sky grew a little plumper with each passing day. The night wind might be cold, but a djinn did not suffer extremes of temperature the way a human might. At any rate, he would endure a little chill to be able to enjoy such a view.

The only problem with these solitary enjoyments was just that—they were solitary. He wished he had someone to share these evenings with, someone with whom he could discuss his grand plans for the city, but such a wish would most likely go unfulfilled. The women of the djinn tended to be independent, and would have their own lands to watch over, now that his people had come down to settle this world. They might form temporary alliances if it suited them, but he feared he did not have very much to offer. He was beginning to love this land, true. However, that did not mean the women of his people would feel the same way, especially if their own land grants occupied much greener pastures. But while he could admit these truths to himself, he also could not ignore a deep, underlying dissatisfaction with his current situation. He wished he could have someone to share this world with him.

When he roused himself from bed the morning of the fourth day and stepped through the side entrance to the hotel, he was surprised and not altogether pleased to see Hasan al-Abyad standing there on the small bit of sidewalk Qadim had not yet demolished. He'd decided to leave it intact for now, as it provided something of a frame for the building, a line of demarcation between the hotel's concrete walls and the open area that now grew with waving grasses and low junipers, manzanita, and mesquite, along with spiky yucca and the odd cross-shaped cactus the humans had referred to as "cholla."

The other djinn had his arms crossed on his chest and appeared to be surveying Qadim's handiwork. Then he turned and surveyed his companion, brows pulling together as he took in his fellow djinn's attire. After only a day of demolitions, Qadim had decided that his flowing robes and bare feet were not all that practical, and he had looted a few local stores to get the items he required.

Apparently Hasan was not impressed by the denim pants or work boots or dark T-shirt. With an ironic smile pulling at his full mouth, he said, "It seems you have traded one desert for another, Qadim al-Syan."

"Perhaps," Qadim replied, nettled, although he did his best not to show it. "I am only giving this land back to itself."

"How very noble."

Since it seemed that Hasan was in no hurry to explain his presence, Qadim added, "To what do I owe the honor of your visit? I did have a number of matters I wished to attend to today—"

"Planting more cactus?" There was the slightest suggestion of a sneer in Hasan's voice, and again Qadim began to bristle. But then the other djinn said, "I wanted to ask if you had noticed anything...unusual... while you were out and about in the city."

"Unusual?" Qadim asked, and raised an eyebrow. "What do you mean?"

"Any human activity. I've sensed it from time to time, but it never lasts for long, and when I come to investigate, I find nothing."

More than once Qadim had wondered precisely what it was about humans that had turned Hasan into such an avenging zealot, had made him focus all his energies on making sure not a one of them survived. They had been poor stewards of this earth, true, but they were gone now, except those few who had been lucky enough to be Chosen.

Or the mortals who inhabited the colony at Los Alamos, a town protected from ravaging djinn such as Hasan al-Abyad by the devices of the mad scientist

Miles Odekirk. Perhaps the mere notion of their continuing survival was enough to inflame Hasan, to keep him moving over territory that had been cleared long ago when he should be watching over the lands the Council had given him.

"You find nothing because there is nothing," Qadim said calmly. "I have walked the streets of this city, and they are empty. I stand on the rooftop of this building"—he lifted a chin to indicate the hotel behind them—"and I see miles and miles of darkness. No light, no movement, the only living things the birds and the insects, and the odd snake or two. Certainly no humans."

"But I have felt—"

"Forgive me, Hasan," Qadim cut in, "but I believe your zeal has led you to believe in that which no longer exists. Should you not be tending to your own lands? Where have you settled?"

"In a place they called Chama, to the north of here. But there is not much to do there, except watch the trees grow."

At least Hasan had a forest, instead of this great flat valley ringed by mountains and hills. Perhaps the elders had rewarded him more richly because of his service in hunting down New Mexico's last humans. It was difficult to say for sure, because they had always seemed indifferent to the fate of the remaining mortals—except when it came to the Chosen. Those particular humans, consorts of the djinn who had selected them from humanity's few Immune, were sacrosanct. Everyone else, however, was considered fair game.

"I am sure you will find some way to occupy yourself," Qadim said. "Perhaps it is time for you to find a woman who also enjoys watching the trees grow."

The other djinn grimaced. "And ruin all that peace and quiet? My last liaison was some trouble to me, and so I have no great desire to find her replacement. But thank you for the advice."

Qadim could not quite understand that sentiment. Women were always worth the trouble, in his opinion. But he said nothing, only inclined his head, and hoped they were nearing the end of the conversation. He had work to do.

Hasan seemed to detect his restlessness, for he said, "I will trouble you no more on the subject. If you do hear or see anything, however—"

"You will be the first to know." Whether that promise was entirely the truth, Qadim didn't know for sure. After his dealings with Julia Innes, he had a rather different view of the human race from what he'd held previously. In the unlikely event that any survivors still hid somewhere here in Albuquerque, he'd be inclined to let them go—and tell them to hurry to Los Alamos, where they would be safe. In fact, he thought he would probably help to get them there; this world had seen enough death. Also, something about the fanatical gleam in Hasan's eyes bothered Qadim more than he wanted to admit. They had known one another for countless centuries, but his old friend seemed lately to be skirting on the borders of madness.

But of course he would say nothing of any of that to Hasan. Best to avoid conflict, and let him be on his way to this Chama place, wherever that might be.

The djinn nodded, then rose from the pavement before blinking out of existence—on his way back home, presumably. All djinn traveled in such a manner, the miles involved mattering very little. There was no real need for Hasan to float off the ground before disappearing, but it was an affectation of some air elementals. With any luck, he would see no reason to return anytime soon.

For now, though, Qadim knew he needed to get to work...and also be glad that no humans were left in Albuquerque to become Hasan's victims.

She'd resisted the impulse for as long as she could. Deep down, Madison knew it was crazy to go back to the Hotel Andaluz so she could see what that lone djinn was up to. He didn't even know she existed. The smart thing to do was stay here in the shelter and hope that whatever he was doing, it wouldn't take long. Then maybe the city would be hers again. After all, it had only been a few days since she first spied him.

But his presence nagged at her. She still couldn't figure out why he'd bothered with knocking down those buildings, unless that was his way at getting back at humanity now that all the actual people were gone.

Only one way to find out, she supposed. Besides, what was the point in having fate on your side if you didn't tempt it every once in a while?

She made sure the electric bike was fully charged, just in case a sudden burst of speed was required. And she wore a Ruger 9mm at her hip, even though she hadn't fired a gun in nearly two years and had no idea whether she could hit the side of a building, let alone an avenging djinn.

Could a bullet even stop a djinn?

The day was bright and sunny, and Madison blinked as she emerged from underneath the gazebo, then quickly put on her sunglasses. Despite the bright sun, the breeze felt cool, blowing down from the Sandia range to the north and east. A few clouds dotted the sky.

In all, everything looked picture-perfect as Madison emerged from the side yard and began to pedal down the street. Well, not exactly picture-perfect, she supposed. The front yards of all the neighborhood's homes were choked with weeds. Cars sat on cracked driveways and slowly rusted while the stucco of the houses began to spiderweb with their own cracks. She wondered how long it would take for the whole city to slowly crumble apart and be reclaimed by the desert. Years? Decades?

Once she'd determined that the garage at Clay Michael's house was empty, she'd moved her own beloved Nissan Rogue inside, but she'd never driven it since. The small SUV was far more conspicuous than the electric bicycle that had become her mode of transportation. Besides, gas didn't last forever, was losing its potency every day, and the abandoned vehicles on the streets made maneuvering difficult. The electric bike was a far better solution, and the power would never run out, thanks to the bank of solar panels on the roof of the house.

By this time she knew all the best ways to get downtown, the routes that slipped through alleys and hugged buildings. There were still stretches where she had to go more or less out in the open, but that was when she used the abandoned vehicles on the street to her advantage, keeping as close to them as she could as she moved from car to car. The wind blew in her face and tugged a few strands of curly hair loose from its elastic, and oddly, the sensation gave her courage.

She'd escaped so many times before. She knew she could do it again.

A little more than half a mile from her destination, however, just after she passed beneath the raised concrete ribbon of Interstate 25, she hit the brakes and came to a skidding stop. Because what used to be the beginning of downtown's sprawl...wasn't.

In its place was a vast open field covered in blowing grass, some of it waist-high. Dotting that improbable grassland were low junipers and the odd cross shapes of cholla cactus, along with artful groupings of desert trees and red rocks, similar to the plantings that used to thrive in the middle of Interstate 40 as you approached Albuquerque from the west. And in the very center of the field that hadn't been there a few days ago was the blocky outline of the Hotel Andaluz, the ten-story structure sticking out of the plain like the proverbial sore thumb.

Madison resisted the urge to rub her eyes. Somehow she knew that wouldn't change what she was looking at. Downtown was...gone. In the distance she could see the outlines of some buildings, but the heart of Albuquerque's city center had apparently been erased from the face of the earth. As far as she could tell, the open area occupied approximately a half-mile sweep, with the hotel as its epicenter.

The destruction floored her. Actually, could she even call it destruction when something alive and growing had been put in its place? What she saw before her shouldn't have been possible, because the plants that now populated the grassland would normally have taken months or even years to grow.

Something very strange was going on here.

Her instincts told her that she had to leave. She didn't see any sign of the djinn whose handiwork this all had to be, but that didn't mean much. This open, oversized meadow didn't offer any shelter at all, except for a few juniper trees that might have been tall enough to conceal both her and the bike. In a place like this, she could be spotted from a mile away.

Then she saw something moving off to her left, something tall, its long, dark hair blowing in the breeze.

Oh, shit.

At once she turned the bike around and started pedaling like a maniac, giving the electric motor an extra boost. Its max speed was limited to twenty miles per hour, although she knew she'd coaxed more than that out of it going downhill after she'd disengaged the motor, the only way to make the damn bike move faster than its designers had intended.

Was it enough to outrun a djinn? But the world's fastest human had been clocked at something like twenty-eight miles per hour....

He didn't see you, she told herself. True, she'd only gotten a glimpse of him, but it seemed to her he'd been looking in the other direction, away from her. If that was true, then she had a fighting chance. And in a minute or two she'd be safely back within streets and buildings that still existed, and she could give him the slip then...if she even needed to.

The sound of footsteps pounding behind her sent her heart into her throat. Looking back could quite possibly slow her down, but she had to know.

He was there, bursting through a patch of waist-high grasses before emerging onto the pavement of Central Avenue. Incongruously she noted that he appeared to have traded his flowing robes for a pair of jeans and a dark green T-shirt. But she couldn't risk more of a glance than that, had to keep going, no matter what.

"Wait!"

His voice was deep and resonant, even when calling out to her. For some reason, she was surprised that he spoke English. This time, she didn't look back. She'd already slowed herself down by stealing that first glimpse. A grim smile tugged at her lips, though, even as terror lent strength to the legs pumping away on the bike's pedals.

Did he really think that she'd stop just because he asked her to? She'd seen what happened to humans when djinn caught up with them.

Familiar pavement was once more under her bicycle's tires. Madison couldn't sigh in relief, though, because all her breath was being used up to force the bike to speeds for which it had never been designed.

He was still behind her, though—she could hear his booted feet churning away at the street's surface. For a second she wondered why he hadn't taken to the air to pursue her, but then she remembered how he'd lifted his hands and the earth had shaken. He was an earth elemental, not a being of air. Quite possibly he couldn't fly at all.

Please God, she thought. If this was a footrace, she might have a real chance at getting away from him.

She jinked down Walter Street in the hope that the sudden movement might throw him off. But no—those implacable footsteps still sounded behind her. At least they *were* behind her, though. He was fast, but he was no Olympic sprinter.

Avenida Cesar Chavez was coming up fast. Should she head over there and hope to lose him in the sports complex with its stadiums? No, too many open parking lots. It was probably better to cut over on Gibson, even if that meant overshooting a bit and having to come up at home base in a "soft underbelly" approach. At least that way she could zig and zag through narrow residential streets. She knew the area, and he didn't.

She hoped that would be enough.

Dodging abandoned cars, she cut a sharp left onto Gibson and kept going. The problem was, so did the djinn. An ordinary man would probably have begun to get winded by now, but the sound of his footfalls never flagged. She made another of those abrupt left-hand turns onto Indiana Street, tires squealing. Actually, she could feel the bike skid beneath her before it caught again and kept going.

Her heart still seemed to be sticking in her throat, so it really didn't have anywhere else to go after that near-miss. And soon she'd have to make a decision, because by this point she was only a quarter-mile away from Clay Michaels' former house and its backyard bomb shelter. Risking a quick glance down at the gauges, she saw that pushing the bike to its limits had drained the battery far more quickly than usual. Should she use up all the charge left in the bike for one final burst of speed in the hope that she'd get there enough ahead of the djinn that she could lock down the shelter and keep him out? Maybe should she take another detour and pray that she'd lose him far enough away from the house so he'd never be able to find her.

Neither option seemed particularly appealing. And a second glance confirmed that there just wasn't enough battery left for her to lead the djinn on a wild goose chase through Albuquerque.

Shit. *Shit.*

She all but stood on the pedals, pumping away, lending her own energy to bolster the bike's flagging resources. This time she did risk a look back, just because she needed to know how much of a lead she had on him. It already had been a good hundred yards or so, and now the gap seemed to widen slightly. Good, but not good enough.

Come on, come on, she urged the bike, even though at this point it was as much her own energy as the bike's battery that pushed it forward.

As she yanked the handlebars to turn down onto Sandia Court, the bike slid for real under her. Madison could feel it going, knew there was no way to prevent it from falling. The best she could do was go limp and pray she'd be able to roll with it and get to her feet before the djinn caught up with her.

From behind her, she heard a sound of dismay as she hit the pavement. Pain flared in her shoulder, and she couldn't seem to pull air into her lungs. But she'd broken a bone in a skateboard fall when she was twelve, so she knew what that felt like. She didn't think she'd broken anything this time, even though her shoulder hurt like a mother.

Which meant she needed to keep going. The house was so close....

Wincing, she pushed herself to her feet and stumbled forward, ignoring the throbbing sensation in her shoulder. She could deal with that later. Plenty of pain meds in the shelter's first aid cabinet.

But when she got to the curb, she tripped over the uneven pavement, which had been forced upward by a tree root, and fell onto the sidewalk. This time the agony was so intense that she couldn't prevent herself from crying out, even as she tried to push herself up by one hand and get back to her feet.

Too late. Strong arms went around her and lifted her from the sidewalk. She had an impression of deep-set dark eyes staring down at her and a clean, warm scent, like sun-dried grass, before her head fell back against the swell of his bicep and the world swirled down into darkness.

CHAPTER FOUR

His first instinct had been to carry her to his own suite at the Hotel Andaluz. But then Qadim thought of what her reaction might be when she awoke in his bed, and decided it would probably be better to put her somewhere else. He was staying in a hotel, after all. The one thing it certainly did not lack was empty beds.

So he took the young woman to the room immediately below his, another suite, if not quite as luxurious. A snap of his fingers summoned fresh linens from the hotel's storerooms to put on the bed, since the old ones had been dusted with the pale gray ash that signaled some unfortunate human had met his or her demise there. Then he laid the girl down, but not before tugging off the sturdy low boots she wore, not so very different from the hiking shoes he'd appropriated.

During all this, she didn't stir, and Qadim frowned, worried that she had injured herself worse than he'd thought. He hadn't seen her head hit the pavement, and so he didn't think she had a concussion. But she was clearly unconscious, deeply so.

The reason became clear enough as he reached out to touch her shoulder and could feel the way her left arm hung at an odd angle. She must have dislocated the joint during that bad spill she'd taken. Well, he'd fixed such things in the past when his comrades in arms had been injured, and so he knew he could do the same thing for this mortal young woman. Better that she had fainted. That way, she wouldn't feel what he was about to do.

He slid the pillows out from under her so she lay flat on the bed, her arm outstretched. Pulling slowly but firmly, he could almost see the bone moving under her flesh before it slid into place. Good. The area was already bruised and swollen, but he didn't think she had broken anything.

What she needed was the joint immobilized. Luckily, the hotel had plenty of spare sheets, and within the next moment, Qadim had torn one to a more manageable size, then gently eased her arm into the makeshift sling and fastened it around her neck. Afterward, he plumped up the pillows and laid her against them before pulling up the covers to above her waist. She was still fully dressed and possibly would have been more comfortable in something looser-fitting, but he guessed she would not be pleased to awaken and find that he had tampered with her clothing.

Then he took one of the chairs from the sitting area on the other side of the room and set it down next to her bed. Perhaps she would also not appreciate him sitting there and watching her, but he did not think it a good idea to leave her unattended while she was still unconscious. It was probably the pain that had caused her swoon, true, and yet he would not forgive himself if her condition worsened while he was elsewhere.

Or perhaps it was only that he wanted to stay where he could gaze at her.

Apparently Hasan had been right, and this young woman was the human presence the air elemental had sensed. Would he have been any less implacable if he had known that his prey was so beautiful?

For she was very fair to look upon, with a glorious mane of wavy pale red hair and clear ivory skin. Her eyes were shut now, but he remembered how they had stared at him, wide with fear, before she had fainted. Those eyes had been a deep, warm green, like the finest jade, ringed with lashes several shades darker than her hair. High cheekbones, and a straight little nose, and her mouth—

Qadim had to force himself to stop there, for her full lips made him think of pleasures he guessed she would be quite unwilling to share. Still, he had to wonder who she was, and where she'd been hiding all this time. He thought she must be quite a resourceful young woman, for he hadn't heard of any other mortals who had managed to survive this long after the Dying, except for the Chosen, of course, and the band of hold-outs in Los Alamos.

Perhaps she would tell him, once she awoke.

God, her shoulder ached. That was the first thing to enter her awareness—a dull, throbbing pain in her left shoulder joint. Her eyes fluttered open, and she looked down to see that her arm was bound in a makeshift sling. The second thing she realized was that she lay in a large luxurious bed, her body supported by pillows.

And the third thing was that the djinn sat in a chair next to the bed, his dark eyes watching her with concern, and a sudden flicker of relief.

"So you are back with us," he said, his voice even more deep and resonant now that he spoke quietly rather than yelling at her to stop.

"I guess so," Madison replied, not sure what else she should say. Actually, she was mostly surprised that she was still alive. But the djinn hadn't killed her, had actually set her shoulder and put it in a sling. At least, she assumed he must have given her his version of battlefield first aid. Why, she couldn't begin to guess. She glanced down at the sling, clearly a hotel sheet that had seen better days. "Your work?"

He nodded. "You will need to take care not to move it until it has finished healing."

Right then, staying still didn't seem like much of a problem. Even shifting her weight slightly set off a low, heavy throbbing through her shoulder, and she bit her lip.

"I brought some analgesics," the djinn said, his gaze flickering toward the nightstand. Sitting there were several packets of aspirin and ibuprofen and Tylenol. He must have gotten them from the hotel's gift shop. "I wasn't sure which one you would prefer."

How did a djinn even know about over-the-counter painkillers? According to everything she'd read, the otherworldly race was immortal, or the next thing to it, and definitely not subject to mortal aches and pains. Madison decided she'd put her questions aside for later, however, and said, "The ibuprofen. I'm afraid you'll have to open it, though."

"That is not a problem." He picked up the ibuprofen packet and tore it open. His hands were strong and deeply tanned, or maybe that was his usual skin tone. After he nodded toward her uninjured arm, Madison lifted her hand and held it palm up. He tipped the tablets into her hand, then retrieved a bottle of water that had also been sitting on the nightstand.

Since she couldn't take the water from him until she'd put the pills in her mouth, she set them on her tongue and nodded at him to give her the bottle. He handed it over, and she managed to get both pills down simultaneously, although she'd always been somewhat inept at taking medication. Maybe this time around she was just eager to get that ibuprofen circulating in her system as soon as possible.

The djinn watched this entire procedure, then gave a small nod after she swallowed some more water and settled back against the pillows. "Are you hurt anywhere else?"

Was she? The pain in her shoulder had overwhelmed all the other lesser aches, but now as Madison paused to take stock, she realized that she pretty much hurt all over. Her knee was probably the worst, after her shoulder, but she was fairly certain she'd only banged it badly. Nothing felt broken, even though she knew she'd be covered in a spectacular set of bruises before all this was over with. It could have been much, much worse, however. She'd been lucky.

"I'm banged up, but I'll live," she replied. This whole situation felt completely surreal. Not only was she actually talking to one of the fearsome djinn, but she wasn't nearly as frightened as she'd thought she'd be. Maybe it was the calm way he looked at her, or just the realization that someone bent on killing her probably wouldn't have bothered to set her shoulder. She hesitated, wondering if she dared ask him the question that had been bothering her ever since she woke up. Oh, well. Nothing ventured. "But...why?"

He didn't pretend to misunderstand her. Dark eyes fixed on her face, he said, "Not all my kind are as bloodthirsty as you might have come to believe."

"The djinn, you mean."

"So you know what we are." The level, dark brows creased in a frown as he continued to watch her. "Have you had dealings with us before?"

"Not directly." She still held the bottle of water, and she lifted it and took a long drink before continuing, "I've...seen what you can do, though."

A shadow passed over his features. Up close, there was something almost breathtaking about him, about the strong bones of his face and the thick lashes that shadowed his eyes and the heavy dark hair that flowed partway down his back. No, he wasn't pretty-boy handsome, but Madison had never had much use for pretty boys. She liked faces with character and distinction.

You shouldn't be thinking about his looks at all, she thought then, although something about her inner voice lacked conviction. Maybe it was just that it felt so good to be talking to someone. Anyone. Even one of these fearsome elementals. Until that moment, she hadn't even realized how lonely she'd been, how desolate. She'd made busywork for herself so she could try to ignore how the universe seemed to have forsaken her. That same inner voice taking on a fierce note, she told herself, *He's a djinn. His people destroyed the world.*

Well, to be fair, they'd destroyed humanity. The world itself looked as if it was doing just fine.

"That is unfortunate," he said. His lips tightened for a second, and then he added, "We are not all like that."

You could have fooled me, Madison thought, but she didn't reply immediately. For whatever reason, he'd helped her, and pointing out the murderous qualities of his fellow djinn didn't seem like the best way of staying on his good side. "I guess not," she said after a pause he must have noticed.

He didn't comment, however, but only gave a small lift of his shoulders. Then he said, clearly changing the subject, "What is your name?"

"Madison. Madison Reynolds."

An expression of confusion passed over his face. "Madison? This is a woman's name? I have not heard it before."

She allowed herself a grim chuckle. "Well, it didn't used to be a girl's name. It was supposed to be a joke in an '80s romantic comedy movie, but enough people didn't get the joke that it sort of became a real name."

Now he looked even more puzzled, his brows creasing as he attempted to make some sense of what she'd just told him.

Relenting, she said, "It's okay. Don't worry about it. What's your name?"

"I am Qadim al-Syan."

The obviously Middle Eastern sound of the name surprised her somewhat, but she supposed it made some sense. The djinn had first appeared in that part of the world, or at least it was in ancient Arabia and its environs that those legends had originally surfaced. "Can I call you Qadim, or do you prefer the whole thing?"

A sudden light entered his eyes, and he almost smiled. "Qadim is fine. And is it also fine that I call you Madison?"

"Sure."

He paused then, watching her so closely that she could feel a flush rise to her cheeks. It wasn't that she detected anything leering or inappropriate in his gaze, only that she wasn't used to being subjected to that kind of scrutiny. His next question was innocuous enough, however. "Are you hungry? Should I bring you something to eat?"

Maybe it would be a good idea to eat something to cushion the ibuprofen, but Madison knew her appetite had fled for the moment. She realized then how tired she was, how much she ached all over. Crazy as it might sound, what she really wanted to do was sleep. Normally, her survival instincts would have been screaming at her not to let her guard down, even for a second, but it seemed she had done her best to convince herself that Qadim didn't mean her any harm. Otherwise, why would he have gone to the trouble of setting her shoulder and making sure she was settled in a comfortable bed?

Anyway, giving herself some time to rest was just good sense. She wouldn't be able to accomplish much of anything—including getting herself away from here, if given the opportunity—with the way she felt right now.

"I'm not really that hungry," she replied, and tried to ignore the flicker of disappointment in his eyes. "Is it all right if I just rest for a while?"

"Of course. It would be good for you to sleep, I think. I will check on you in a few hours, when it would be time for the evening meal. You can tell me then if you are ready to eat anything."

"Thank you," she said.

He nodded, then got up from his chair. The briefest of hesitations, as if he'd intended to say something else. But it seemed he thought better of it, because he only offered her another nod before he went to the door of the suite and let himself out.

For a long moment, Madison stared at the closed door, as if she wasn't quite sure that the djinn might not let himself right back in. But the door remained shut, and her own weariness was becoming too difficult to ignore. She did need to rest and let her body begin to heal itself. As to what was going to happen next, she didn't have a clue.

She figured she'd deal with that when the time came.

Madison Reynolds. Qadim let the unfamiliar syllables roll over in his mind. He'd been speaking the truth when he'd said he'd never heard that name before, but he thought it suited her. Her name was strong and yet somehow graceful, just like the woman who bore it.

He hoped he hadn't been too obvious in the way he had looked at her. His every impulse had been to drink her in, to study every angle and curve, but he knew she would have found such an inspection off-putting at best. She was injured, and weary. She needed time to become herself again.

And time as well to learn she had no reason to fear him.

Damn Hasan al-Abyad and all his murderous brethren. Qadim had seen the darkness in Madison's clear eyes, could only guess at the horrors she must have witnessed. During his demolition efforts, he'd come across streets where bloodstains had been baked right into the strange black substance humans used to pave their roads. He hadn't wanted to guess at the kind of violence that had created such a permanent marker of its aftermath...and yet Madison had seen these things for herself. He supposed he should be glad she hadn't made another attempt to flee him, even with all her injuries.

Surely that must be a good sign.

She had said she wasn't hungry, but he knew her body would require nourishment to assist it with the healing process. While she slept, he would make something delectable for her to eat. He would have to hope that she wouldn't mind if he ate his evening meal at the same time she had hers. That shouldn't be too much to ask.

The djinn had always been able to summon the components for their meals from wherever they wished, and so Qadim had no need to worry about all the food that had spoiled in the hotel's freezers and cupboards months earlier. He'd cleared all that away as soon as he'd determined the Hotel Andaluz would be his new home, then made sure everything was cleaned thoroughly. Many of his people did not care to cook, and conjured their meals already made, but Qadim had always enjoyed the process. There was something uniquely sensual about combining the ingredients to their best advantage, to experimenting and tasting and coming up with infinite variations of the same theme.

And, to be fair, he also enjoyed pouring some wine for himself to help things move along.

Because Madison was so recently injured, he wanted to make something that would be easy for her to eat and would not require any cutting. And not too heavy, either, for he wanted her to sleep easily without an over-lavish meal weighing on her stomach. A variation of an Indian dish he'd long admired would do very well, with rice and vegetables, and using chicken instead of lamb.

The ingredients he needed waited for him, either laid out on the counter or sitting in the refrigerator. While he preferred the softer, warmer glow of candlelight, he did think that electricity had its uses, especially when it came to preserving food.

As he busied himself with preparing the meal, Qadim could not prevent his thoughts from wandering upward, to the ninth floor of the hotel where Madison Reynolds slept in her borrowed bed. Just the mere image of her glorious hair spread out on the pillow was enough to send a shiver of arousal through him, but he pushed it aside. He would not deny to himself that he wanted her, but she was injured and afraid. He must be gentle and kind, and hope that she would warm to him as time passed.

Gentle and kind, he thought with a wry twist to his mouth. *I doubt there are many who would use those words to describe me.*

Certainly not Julia Innes, whom he had kidnapped to help further his sister's twisted ends. True, Qadim had ended up assisting Julia and her friends, but at the time his motivations had been anything but pure. He'd only wished to escape the Council's wrath. But, being the Council, they'd seen through him easily enough. And now he was here in Albuquerque.

Which had its own hidden treasures. He glanced upward, although even a djinn's gaze couldn't pierce through that many layers of concrete and steel to find the woman who slept nine floors above. Perhaps one day she would confide in him and tell him how she'd managed to survive more than a year all on her own, but he resolved not to prod her. If she wished to tell him, she would.

In the meantime, he had to hope that she would enjoy the dinner of chicken korma he'd prepared for her.

A delectable smell entered the room, and Madison's eyes fluttered open. For just the barest second, she had a moment of panic, since she could tell those were the last dregs of sunset peeking around the blinds, and of course the bunker where she'd been living for the past year had no windows. But then memory returned, and she remembered that she was in the Hotel Andaluz, brought here by the djinn named Qadim.

And there he was, standing by the doorway, with the incongruous companion of a room service cart next to him. "Did you sleep well?"

"I did," Madison replied, realizing with some surprise that she had. Only for a few hours, but that had been enough time for the ibuprofen to kick in and reduce the ache in her shoulder to a dull throb.

"And are you hungry now?"

"How could I not be, when you've brought up something that smells that good?"

His rather harsh features relaxed into a smile. "I am glad to hear that. This is chicken korma. Do you like Indian food?"

"Love it," she said, which was only the truth. She and Jacob used to go out for Indian food several times a month. With a slight stab of surprise, she realized that was the first time she'd thought of her ex in months. Most of her time had been spent resolutely not thinking of anyone in her past, to avoid dwelling on the dreary fact that everyone she'd known and loved was now dead. Anyway, remembering Jacob only brought on a fresh round of self-recriminations. She wouldn't go with him to Washington, and he didn't want to stay in Albuquerque. Had he died alone? In the time they'd been apart, before the Heat struck, she hadn't heard through the Facebook grapevine that he was dating anyone....

Qadim didn't appear to note her distraction, and instead wheeled the room service cart into the suite so he could set it next to her bed. Forcing herself back to the present, Madison sat up a little straighter and pushed back against the pillows. Her shoulder twinged, but not as much as it had when she'd attempted a similar maneuver only a few hours ago. That couldn't all be the ibuprofen. It felt as if the djinn had done a damn good job of resetting her shoulder.

To her surprise, she saw he'd brought up a bottle of chardonnay to go with the meal. "You're sure that's a good idea?" she asked, then worried that he might think she was asking about something besides basic drug interactions.

But he merely said, "You've only taken a low-level painkiller," as he lifted the metal cover from one of the plates. "A bit of wine should not make a difference. In fact, it will probably help."

"Muscle relaxant," she commented, and he nodded. "Precisely."

She fell silent, watching as he finished prepping the meal. Apparently, he'd already removed the cork from the wine before he came up, because he poured it right away. Not too much, only an inch and a half or so in her glass.

"You can begin with that and see how you feel," he told her.

Well, that seemed prudent enough. He'd placed the cart on her right side, so it wasn't too awkward to reach over and lift the wine glass so she could drink. The wine was cool and clean on her tongue, and she could feel the alcohol the second it hit her stomach. No big surprise, she supposed, since she hadn't had anything stronger to drink than tea since taking refuge in the shelter. Clay had wisely avoided stocking the place with anything alcoholic, and although Madison supposed she could have scooped up any of an assortment of rare and expensive wines and other liquors while she was out foraging, she'd avoided the temptation. It would have been far too easy to drink herself to death down in that bunker.

Then she realized maybe that had been rude, that she probably should have waited for Qadim to take a sip of his wine as well. "I'm sorry," she said. "That was kind of grabby of me. It's just—it's been a while."

"No need for apologies," he replied. His gaze moved from the glass she held and to her face. Only for a second, though, before he drank some of his wine. "It is quite good."

"Yes," she agreed.

"You had no wine where you've been staying?"

It seemed an innocuous enough question, but Madison couldn't help flicking a quick glance at him to see if there was any subtext she might be missing. After all, she thought it likely enough that he would want to find out where she'd been living for the past year, if only to satisfy his curiosity.

That wasn't going to happen. Okay, he'd probably already guessed that her hideout must be somewhere in the neighborhood where she'd fallen from the electric bike, but there were at least thirty houses on that street. Narrowing it down would take some time, especially since the entrance to the bomb shelter was so well hidden.

"No," she replied. "Wine isn't necessary for survival."

"I might have to disagree with you on that."

There was such a wicked glint in his eyes right then that Madison could feel her mouth curving up in a smile despite herself. "All right—it isn't necessary for subsistence."

"I suppose that much is true." He set down his glass and pushed the plate on her side of the serving cart as close to the edge as possible. "Can you reach that?"

It would be a bit of a stretch, but she thought she could manage. She wondered if she should try to sit more upright, but the pillows were supporting her shoulder nicely, and she didn't want to upset the current arrangement. So she picked up the fork and speared one of the pieces of chicken on it. "Piece of cake."

Qadim looked slightly puzzled. "Chicken," he corrected her.

Again she had to fight the urge to smile. His English was very good, but it seemed some idioms weren't in his vocabulary. "I just meant that it was simple enough."

"Ah, good." He took his own fork and scooped up some chicken and rice, then swallowed.

Madison had yet to take a bite. The food looked good and smelled even better, but what if he'd done something to it, doctored it somehow?

For what? her mind scoffed at her. *You're lying here with one usable arm. If he wanted to try something, he would have already.*

Assuming that the djinn were even interested in humans. Well, beyond killing them, that was.

So she put the piece of chicken in her mouth. Subtle spices rolled over her tongue, bringing with them another surge of memory, of sitting in that crazy Indian place out on Menaul and feeding Jacob pieces of naan in between bites of korma. Sharing food like that had gotten them both so turned on that they'd gone back to Jake's apartment and had sex right there on the living room rug because neither of them wanted to waste the time it took to get to the bedroom.

Heat flooded her cheeks, and she set down the fork and reached for her glass of chardonnay so she could take a big swallow.

"Is something wrong?" Qadim asked, giving her a curious glance. "Do you not care for the food?"

"Um, no—it's fine. More than fine, actually. It's better than anything I could have gotten in a restaurant." She didn't bother to add that the days of Indian restaurants—or any kind of restaurant at all—were long gone.

And she sure as hell wouldn't mention how that unbidden memory of her and Jake screwing like a couple of crazed rabbits on the floor had sent an unwelcome flush of heat all through her. The overall loneliness had been bad enough, but the lack of any kind of physical intimacy was even worse. If she'd known, back before the Heat swept over the world, that she wasn't ever getting laid again, she would have gone out and picked up the first promising stranger in a nightclub rather than being the good girl she'd been raised to be and waiting until the next relationship came along. Sometimes virtue was definitely not its own reward.

"I am pleased to hear that," Qadim said formally, although a certain edge to his inflection seemed to indicate he could tell she was holding something back.

She'd have to watch that. He might be a djinn, but he looked and acted human enough, and he seemed to be better at reading humans than an otherworldly creature had any right to.

Maybe it would have been better if he'd stuck to the Arabian Nights robes she'd first seen him wearing. Because right now, in that dark T-shirt and those nicely faded Levi's and work boots, he looked too damn human.

Shoving some more korma into her mouth seemed the best way to cover up the awkward pause that followed his last statement. She chewed, forcing herself to focus on the flavor. It really was very good; her earlier compliment hadn't been an empty one.

"You really made all this?" she asked, once she was done chewing.

"Yes. I like to cook."

If he'd told her he liked to put on a tutu and pirouette across the stage at the Bolshoi, she couldn't have been more startled. "Seriously?"

One eyebrow lifted. "You sound surprised."

Madison started to shrug, then stopped herself abruptly as a nasty twinge went through her damaged left shoulder. "I suppose I hadn't thought a djinn would even need to cook. You could just snap your fingers or wrinkle your nose or whatever to make the food appear."

"That is what some of my kind do," he said. "Perhaps not the nose-wrinkling, however."

"It seems as if it would be a lot easier to just blink your dinner into existence instead of making a big mess in the kitchen and taking hours."

"You don't like to cook?"

"I hate it," she said bluntly, then reached for her wine and drank some more.

Over the course of her dating life, she'd met several men who'd been immediately put off by her admission that she couldn't stand cooking. Qadim, on the other hand, appeared more curious than anything else. "Why?"

The inevitable question. She was beginning to wish she hadn't said anything at all, but something about being around another person—even if that other person happened to be a djinn—seemed to have disengaged the wall she usually put up around herself.

But he was sitting there, watching her and clearly waiting for her to reply. Maybe she should give him a glib answer in the hope that it would be enough to keep him from asking more questions.

She thought he deserved more than that, though. One might argue that she would never have gotten hurt in the first place if he hadn't pursued her, but he hadn't wished her any harm. He'd just wanted to know who she was.

And he had patched her up. She'd always owe him for that.

Another bracing swallow of chardonnay, and Madison said, "When I was ten years old, my mother got sick. Bone cancer. Very fast, very aggressive." She paused then and glanced over at the djinn, who absorbed this information with a quiet nod but didn't say anything. "You know what cancer is, right?"

"Yes," he replied. "That is, insofar as it affects humans. Djinn can be injured, but we cannot become ill. So we do not suffer from these sorts of ailments."

Must be nice, she thought. She filed away the information that djinn could be hurt for possible use at a later date. Not that she'd necessarily want to hurt Qadim, but...just in case.

"She was in and out of the hospital for treatments. They made her as sick as the cancer. My father was just trying to hold things together—he had a high-powered job and needed to stay focused—so I did what I could to help out. That included trying to feed everyone."

"Even though you were just a child?"

"Kids younger than I was have suffered a lot worse." Poverty, and starvation, abuse and neglect. At least Madison had never gone to bed hungry, had parents who loved her. Her mother's final words had been a whispered *I'm so sorry,* as if it was her fault that the cancer had risen up out of nowhere and consumed her. A few burned fingers and botched stews couldn't really compete with that.

And there was Qadim looking at her with compassion in his eyes. As if a djinn could possibly understand what she'd gone through. She didn't want him pitying her.

"That was almost seventeen years ago," she said, knowing he most likely could see right through the brittleness of her tone. "I'm over it."

His silence was eloquent, seeming to indicate he didn't believe her...but that he also wouldn't contradict her. At last he said, mouth lifting slightly at one corner, "Well, you can be reassured that I will not expect you to cook."

She offered him a tentative smile in response. With an injured shoulder and an uncertain future ahead of her, what else could she do?

CHAPTER FIVE

So much pain. It seemed that Madison Reynolds had suffered a good deal in her short life, even before the Heat had come along and swept away everything.

But Qadim could tell she didn't want to discuss the matter further, appeared sorry that it had come up at all. He let it alone, and after they had finished eating, he quietly told her that she would find any toiletries she needed in the bathroom, then left her to retire for the night. She'd looked very weary by then, her fine green eyes smudged with shadow. The day had been difficult enough for her without him bringing up unwanted memories.

She had spoken with him, though. That was something. She could have eaten in stony silence, refusing to acknowledge his conversation. Perhaps it was only that she'd been alone for so very long that any kind of interaction was its own gift, even if said interaction involved speaking with one of the race who'd been responsible for the destruction of her world.

Still, her openness was hopeful. It meant he might have a chance.

A chance for what, he wasn't sure. His body told him that was easy enough—a chance to bed her would be a wonderful thing. He could wait until she was fully healed and see what happened.

Yet....

Something told him he wanted more than that, which was foolish. He'd always been one for casual liaisons, a few weeks or nights or even years of pleasure before moving on. If he became intimate with Madison, what would that mean, precisely?

As he'd told Hasan, he had no interest in claiming a human as his Chosen. To be tied down to one woman forever? Any of his former lovers would have laughed to hear of Qadim al-Syan ever contemplating such a thing.

Also, he might have been misinterpreting what he'd seen in her face at dinner, but before the conversation had turned deadly serious, he'd seen a flush in her cheeks, had noted the way her breasts rose and fell under the shapeless T-shirt she wore. He had enough experience of women to know that some sort of arousal had moved through her, even if she'd pushed it away. Surely she must be feeling deprived after living alone for so long. What was wrong with sharing some pleasure, even if that pleasure must eventually come to its end?

Nothing at all. And once she was fully healed and capable of such things, he would see how amenable she was to the suggestion.

The next morning, Madison judged her shoulder in good enough shape that she thought she should be able to take a shower. Washing her hair one-handed would be a little tricky, but she figured she could manage. Anyway, she wanted to get cleaned up, and a quick inspection of the bathroom showed that it truly was, as Qadim had claimed, well stocked with toiletries— shampoo and soap and toothpaste and anything else she might need. There was even replacement clothing in the dresser, underwear and jeans and several T-shirts.

Nothing fancy, though, nothing frilly. Apparently the djinn wasn't going to pull the standard movie-villain maneuver of making his captive dress in something provocative so he could thoroughly ogle her before getting down to business.

But Qadim wasn't a villain. At least, Madison didn't think so. Unless he was the type of villain who liked playing the long game.

If he was, she didn't think there was too much she could do about it.

Even so, she made sure both the door to her suite and the bathroom door were securely locked. Whether that was enough to keep out a djinn, she had no idea. Probably not, but again, she was just a human female with a dislocated shoulder; her options were fairly limited at the moment.

Slipping out of the sling and then out of her T-shirt was a lengthy process, one that had her gritting her teeth in pain and wishing that she'd downed a few more ibuprofen before beginning the procedure. Once she was in the shower, though, the hot water helped to ease some of the discomfort. She wouldn't ask how there was hot running water when the entire planet's infrastructure was completely broken down. More djinn magic, she supposed, the same kind that conjured up all the correct ingredients for chicken korma and vegetables and rice. She'd brushed her teeth the night before, but she could still taste that meal, the first thing she'd had in a year that wasn't made from canned or frozen or freeze-dried ingredients. It had been sublime.

Qadim hadn't mentioned anything about breakfast, but it was early still, the sun just barely over the horizon. Normally, she didn't get up quite this early, but she'd gone to sleep at barely nine the night before. And despite the way it still ached, she could tell her shoulder had improved that much more while she rested. A few more days, and she'd probably be as good as new.

And what then? she thought as she awkwardly towel-dried her hair with one hand, then scrunched some gel into it. *Is Qadim just going to let you walk away?*

Maybe. Hopefully. And walking was all she'd be able to do, since she was pretty sure her bike was now out of commission.

She still hadn't quite figured out what Qadim wanted from her. He hadn't behaved like a man who was sexually attracted to a woman. But then, how would she even begin to guess the way a djinn might act in that situation?

Frowning, she finished getting dressed before slipping her injured arm back into its sling. The toiletries supplied hadn't included any makeup except some tinted lip balm, so Madison spread some of that over her lips. Her reflection still looked tired, but there wasn't much she could do about that. It wasn't as if she was trying to impress Qadim.

Tying her hiking boots with one hand also proved challenging, but eventually she had herself more or less together. What she should do next, she really didn't know. The djinn hadn't told her she couldn't venture forth from her room. On the other hand, maybe he'd thought she was still banged up and sore enough that she'd want to stay in bed. Other than her shoulder, though, she was doing better than she'd thought she would. The bathroom mirror had revealed some lovely bruises beginning to show up, including a spectacular blue and purple specimen on her knee, but the aches weren't nearly as bad as she'd feared they would be.

Besides, she wanted to see if he'd wrought any of the same alterations on the interior of the Hotel Andaluz as he had on the surrounding landscape.

Madison downed a couple of ibuprofen with the remainder of the bottled water before she stepped out into the hallway and shut the door behind her. At first glance, nothing much seemed to have changed. She'd never actually stayed at the hotel, but her friend Tory had gotten married here, and so Madison had been to one of the room parties thrown by the brides-maids. Here were the same mirrors, the same antique sideboards, even the same little baskets of potpourri, although it had long since dried out completely and no longer gave off even a ghost of a scent.

The sconces on the walls were dark, however. Instead, candles burned on the side tables, giving enough illumination for Madison to make her way down the corridor. When she reached the elevators, she paused. There had been electric light in her room; the candles seemed to be more an affectation than any-thing else. Even so, she didn't think it a very good idea to risk using the elevator.

The stairwell was well lit, though, and so it was easy enough for her to descend the eight flights of stairs to the lobby level. When she opened the door and stuck her head out, everything appeared to be deserted.

What did you expect? she asked herself. *Qadim's still up in his suite, probably, and it's not as if you have any friends who're going to drop in.*

And she had to pray that Qadim didn't have any friends, either, at least not the type who would come by unannounced. He seemed open and friendly enough, but she knew better than to expect all djinn to be like that. No, grim experience had taught her that they were the exact opposite of friendly.

The lobby appeared relatively unchanged, too. There were the casbahs along the wall, where you could sit with a date and have a drink and some tapas. The waterfall still flowed in one, and the bank of votives in the other flickered with restless light. Some part of her relaxed slightly, relieved that this one part of the old world had endured. She wondered if Qadim had preserved it in this state because it reminded him of the world he had come from.

Wandering past the little room that used to be the reception area, Madison came to the restaurant. Everything in here was immaculate, each table set with a small, healthy-looking succulent plant. She could almost imagine that the maître d' was about to show up and show her to a table.

But there was the view out the windows, one which should have been crowded with buildings on every side. Instead, she saw that artfully laid out desert scape, every rock and plant set exactly where it should be to create an ever-changing but harmonious vista. It was the sort of work that would have made most landscapers envious.

"Good morning," came Qadim's voice, and she turned to see him emerging from the door into the kitchen.

"Morning," she said, hoping she didn't sound too startled. "I hope it was all right for me to come down here."

"Of course, if you feel up to it."

"I do. That is, my shoulder feels much better this morning. Thank you again for setting it."

He offered her a smile. "I am glad you're so improved. I was just seeing about breakfast. Would you like to come into the kitchen?"

Most of the time she did what she could to avoid kitchens, but since he was the one doing the work…. "Sure," she replied. "Does your djinn magic include brewing up some coffee?"

"Yes. It should be about ready."

She followed him into the kitchen, which was smaller than she'd expected but spotlessly clean, with gleaming stainless-steel counters and appliances. The air was filled with the rich scent of coffee, and she sniffed appreciatively.

"If I hadn't gotten up early, would you have sent the smell of that coffee up through the ventilation system to wake me up?"

A glint entered his dark eyes. "Now, that is an idea I had not thought of. But since you seem to be an early riser, perhaps those sorts of extreme measures aren't necessary."

Madison almost protested that she wasn't always up this early, then decided to say nothing. It didn't really matter if they got used to each other's rhythms or not; in a few days she'd be healed enough to go back to the shelter, and that would be the end of it.

For some reason, that idea didn't sound nearly as appealing as she'd thought it would.

Qadim lifted the pot from the stove—no automatic coffeemakers for him, apparently—and poured a good measure of the rich brown liquid into a pair of heavy white stoneware mugs that were sitting on the counter. He handed one to her before saying, "I can get you cream or sugar if you require it."

"No, black is fine." She blew on the coffee, which was far too hot yet to drink. Some cream would have cooled it down, but she'd learned to drink her coffee black a long time ago, and coffee with cream and sugar just tasted strange to her now.

The djinn didn't bother to wait to drink his own coffee, but lifted it to his lips and sipped right away. Higher tolerance for heat or pain? That made the most sense. She didn't know if it would be rude to ask, however, and so put the question aside for the moment.

"What would you like to eat?" he said next. "I'll admit that I am not completely familiar with all your breakfast foods, but eggs are simple enough. Or perhaps I could make that thing called a Belgian waffle."

Something about the way he made the suggestion made her want to laugh. He looked completely serious, though, and so she said, her expression equally serious, "Eggs are fine. And toast, if you have it?"

"I can have anything you want."

From someone else, that kind of comment might have sounded far too suggestive. But she didn't think he was playing those kinds of games, and was merely being truthful.

"Sourdough toast, then," she said. "And some fruit. Strawberries?"

Strawberries were completely out of season. But that sort of thing shouldn't matter to a djinn.

Apparently it didn't, because he only nodded and replied, "Simple enough. You can sit on that stool over there while I prepare the food."

Where she would be safely out of the way. She didn't mind, though. Sitting off to one side was infinitely preferable to being pressed into service.

She settled herself down on the stool. For some reason, she'd expected him to snap his fingers and have all the components of the meal magically appear on the countertops, but instead he went over to the refrigerator and pulled out a bowl of eggs, a stick of butter, and another bowl of strawberries. So maybe he had conjured them, but made them appear inside the refrigerator where they could rest comfortably until he had need of them.

He went to work, breaking an alarming number of eggs into another stainless-steel bowl, whisking them, adding an exact amount of milk. Once he had that mixture going on the stovetop, he went to one of the large pantries on the other side of the room and produced a large loaf of bread, which he set down on the counter so he could cut off some slices.

Really, he was so domestic in a completely ordinary way that Madison once again had a difficult time convincing herself he really was a djinn and not just another regular survivor like she was. His robes were still MIA; today he had on a pair of jeans identical to the ones she'd first seen him wearing and another T-shirt, this one in a dark khaki green. The sleeves of that T-shirt seemed in jeopardy with every movement because of the way his muscles strained against the fabric, and Madison had to force herself to look someplace else in the kitchen so he wouldn't catch her staring. Jacob had been fit and athletic enough—he biked and ran, and the two of them would often spend their weekends hiking in the mountains around town—but he'd certainly never had muscles like Qadim's.

"So," Madison ventured, thinking she'd better do something to fill up the silence, "why the fancy xeriscape?"

"'Xeriscape'?" Qadim echoed. He frowned slightly as he took in the unfamiliar word.

"It just means landscaping for dry climates. Like what you've done outside." She made a vague gesture with one hand as she motioned toward what she thought was the front of the building.

"Ah." After dropping the bread he'd sliced into the toaster, he leaned against the counter and crossed his arms while he seemed consider her question. "This land will not support true greenery, and so I chose specimens I thought would survive here and still create a pleasing landscape."

"It is beautiful," she said, eliciting a smile from him. "So is this your plan for Albuquerque? To get rid of the buildings and have plants everywhere?"

"Eventually, yes."

That could cause problems for her. Clay's house and the bomb shelter it hid were more than a mile from downtown, and so it would probably take Qadim some time to make his way over there. Still, what in the world would she do once he'd razed that entire neighborhood and planted it with wild grasses and cactus? His demolition efforts might not do much to the shelter itself—the door that protected the bunker was supposedly rated to survive a five-megaton blast only a mile away—but once the gazebo was gone, the metal door to the bomb shelter would stick out like a sore thumb.

She decided to leave that problem aside to worry about later. Anything she said to dissuade him from expanding his planting efforts would surely lead to inquiries as to why she should care one way or another.

"How do you get the plants to grow so fast?" she asked next, since that question had been bothering her ever since she'd first laid eyes on his handiwork.

"A little djinn encouragement," he replied, the glint returning to his dark eyes. He pushed himself up from the counter and went to tend the eggs. "It is one of the gifts earth elementals share."

"Handy." Madison blew on her coffee one last time and then sipped some. By that point, it had cooled enough that she could manage a large swallow. Which she did, relishing the much-needed rush of caffeine to her nerve endings. "So what can the other djinn do?"

Qadim made rather a show of pushing the eggs around in the skillet, and Madison wondered if he was going to answer at all. Then he said, "We all have a number of skills in common, but water elementals can also cause a spring to flow up out of the ground where there was none, or make a river change its course, while air elementals can make the clouds and the wind and the weather do their bidding."

"And fire elementals?"

His face was in profile to her, but Madison could see the way he frowned. "You seem to know a good deal about us already."

"Not that much," she said quickly. "I tried to look up a few things, after—well, after it was pretty clear that the beings who were hunting the streets of Albuquerque couldn't possibly be human."

Something about his mouth tightened, but he only nodded. "Yes, I suppose that would have become obvious soon enough. Fire elementals can bring forth fire from the air and light a forge, but they can also hold back a fire before it consumes a forest."

Light and dark, yin and yang. Powers that could be used to heal...or destroy. It sounded as if the djinn might be more complex than she'd first thought, although Madison also had the impression that there was a lot more going on here than Qadim had told her. Now that she'd begun to get past her initial fear of him, she wanted to ask more questions. Why had his people destroyed humanity? What were their plans for the now-empty planet?

And maybe the most pressing, and also the most frightening to her.

Why am I still alive when everyone else is dead?

"It's ready," Qadim said, breaking into her thoughts. "I have already set a table in the dining area. Go and sit down, and I will bring out our breakfasts."

She almost protested and offered to help, then realized she wouldn't be of much use to him with her arm in a sling. So she slid off the stool and took her coffee with her one good hand, saying, "All right."

He'd chosen a table by one of the windows. Madison sat down, trying to ignore the pang that went through her as she remembered the last time she'd eaten here. It was right after Jake had been offered the teaching position in Bellingham. They hadn't fought, but the tension was already thick between them. He'd wanted her to come with him to Washington, saying she could just as easily find work at the college there.

Part of her had really wanted to go, to try living someplace green and damp and with the ocean nearby. But she knew she'd never leave her father alone in Albuquerque. True, by then she wasn't living at home anymore. Still, she'd been only ten minutes away from the house where she'd grown up. And she was the only family her father had in New Mexico. Everyone else was either in California or in Illinois, thousands of miles away. Even more than ten years later, her father still mourned the loss of his wife. If Madison left, too, he wouldn't have anyone.

She didn't want to reflect on the irony of her staying, just to have him leave her when the Heat took over the world.

Qadim approached the table then, hands laden with plates of food. Somehow he also managed to keep a grip on his coffee cup with two of the fingers of his left hand while he lowered the plates to the tabletop.

"Sorry I couldn't help more," Madison told him as he took the seat across the table from her.

"It is fine. The important thing is for you to be careful of your arm. There is no point in you hurting it again, just to help me do something I can manage very well on my own."

Any other apologies would have been belaboring the point, and so she just nodded and picked up her fork. One bite was enough to tell her these were probably the best eggs she'd ever had—light and fluffy, and with exactly the right amount of salt. Judging by the dinner she'd eaten last night and the food set before her now, she was going to be extremely well fed during the time she was here. Good thing she'd dropped around fifteen pounds over the last year, between spending a lot of time in the home gym Clay had set up in the shelter, and not being all that interested in the nourishing but bland food with which the shelter had been stocked.

She helped herself to some more eggs, then set down her fork. Across the table from her, Qadim had been similarly occupied with eating the main part of the meal before it got cold. He seemed to sense that she wanted to say something, though, because he also put down his fork and gazed at her expectantly.

"Why?" Madison couldn't seem to get out more than that one word.

The djinn didn't ask her to explain herself, however. He reached for his mug but then paused, as if he knew he had only meant to drink the coffee as a way of delaying his reply. "That is...rather a difficult topic for breakfast discussion, don't you think?"

"I don't know," she said. "Is it?"

Again he hesitated. "I want you to know that I had no part in what happened, save perhaps by inaction. I suppose there are some who would say I was complicit because I did nothing, but I would still argue that is not the same as actively seeking the destruction of your kind."

Her stomach churned, but she ignored it and instead reached for her toast, thinking that might help to calm things down. She'd asked, after all. So she would listen to what he had to say, no matter how much it might hurt.

Qadim seemed to be waiting for some sort of response, though, and so she said quietly, "Just tell me what happened. *Why* it happened."

At least he didn't blink, watched her with a steady gaze, dark eyes sorrowful. This close, she could see the thickness of his lashes, the way their shadow made his eyes seem almost black, as if there was no real difference between iris and pupil.

"That is a tale with its beginnings back at the very creation of your people. The djinn were the first race created by God, but he cast them aside when he created Man and gave this world over to your race as their own. The djinn were banished elsewhere, to a place we think of as the otherworld, when we refused to acknowledge the superiority of God's new creation."

Was he really talking about God as if He actually existed and had done all these things? Madison couldn't detect any hint of irony in Qadim's tone, so apparently he meant for her to believe what he was telling her.

Since she didn't quite trust herself to speak, she only nodded.

"We resented mankind but could do nothing to change our situation. As the millennia wore on, we became more dissatisfied with our lot. The otherworld is not like this world—we djinn can survive there, but it is a harsh place. A faction began to grow among the djinn, one that called for the destruction of mankind so we could take back the world that had once been ours."

A few sips of coffee helped to steady Madison somewhat. Fingers wrapped around the mug she held, she said, "So...somehow you cooked up the disease that killed everyone?"

"Some of the djinn did, yes. And then they set it loose upon the world."

"And none of you did anything to stop it."

A curious expression flitted across Qadim's features and then was gone. Madison couldn't say exactly what it was, however. Regret? Annoyance? Anger?

Maybe a little of all three.

"There were those who made their disagreement with the decision known. And so another decision was made, so that the protesters would be able to save one each of the Immune, and—"

"Wait," she broke in, heart beginning to beat a little faster with terrible hope, "you mean there are more people like me out there? People who survived the Heat?"

"There were," he allowed, then stopped.

"What do you mean, 'were'?"

"They were hunted down, just as you saw people hunted down and killed here in Albuquerque."

Even the warmth of the coffee mug she held couldn't dispel the chill in her fingers. "So I'm the only one left?"

"Not precisely." This time he did drink some of his coffee, then set the mug back down. "As I was trying to tell you, those among the djinn who protested mankind's destruction were allowed to save one person from among the Immune. These humans are called Chosen. They dwell now with their djinn."

Qadim didn't say anything beyond that, but Madison got the feeling that the relationship between those dissenting djinn and their Chosen must be closer than merely protector and protected. She wished she could ask for more details, but she worried that Qadim might think she was inquiring about human and djinn relations because of a particular personal interest in him, and that was the last impression she wanted to give.

"So how do you get to be Chosen?"

This time his gaze lingered a little too long on her face. He seemed to realize he was staring, and returned his attention to the plate before him. "As I said, you must be Immune. All the Chosen were twenty-five of your years old or younger, mainly between twenty-two and twenty-five, I think."

Well, that explains it, Madison thought, not sure whether she should be irritated or relieved. *A handsome djinn didn't come sailing along to my rescue because I was too old.*

"Why so young?"

"Djinn are nearly immortal. Our appearance does not reflect our true age. A human who is Chosen also becomes ageless. So it makes sense that the djinn would want their Chosen to be at the peak of their appearance."

"Because we humans really start to go downhill at twenty-six."

He looked up then, frowning. "You are offended."

Well, yes, she was. But since Qadim clearly hadn't been the one to determine who was good "Chosen" material and who wasn't, Madison didn't think there was much point in being angry with him. "But you didn't want to 'choose' anyone?"

"At the time, I did not think it was the correct path for me to take."

A good non-answer if she'd ever heard one. But she also realized that it really wasn't her place to be asking him those sorts of questions. She barely knew him. He'd saved her, but she still didn't really know why. Maybe he was bored with planting cactus and manzanita and thought a human project might be an interesting change of pace.

Deciding it was better to move on to something a little less personal, she said, "Then the only surviving humans are Chosen?" *Except me, that is....*

"There is a small community in Los Alamos of survivors who are not Chosen," he replied.

"Really? Why haven't they been hunted down?"

"One of the scientists there created a device that repels djinn and robs them of their powers. This is what protects the Immune who live there."

Qadim delivered this astonishing news as if it was of no real import, but again Madison experienced the sharp shock of unlooked-for hope. A community of real people, not djinn. True, Los Alamos was almost a hundred miles from Albuquerque, and she had absolutely no idea how she would get there if there were still djinn roaming the world, looking for the last survivors. But to be around people again....

She realized Qadim was watching her closely. To cover up her distraction and make it seem as if Los Alamos wasn't that big a deal, she picked up a strawberry and bit off the end. The fruit was sweet and lush, and she wondered where in the world the djinn had found it. "How does that even work?"

"I have no idea. I've only suffered the effects of the device once, and that was enough for me." Mouth grim, he picked up his fork and stabbed a piece of egg with it.

So Qadim had been in Los Alamos, or at least close enough to feel the effects of such a thing? Judging by his current expression, he didn't look as if he'd enjoyed the experience very much. Were the effects of the device physically painful?

Again, Madison thought she'd better not ask. "But it's djinn everywhere else except Los Alamos?"

"As far as I know, yes. The Chosen live with their djinn in communities that have been designated for them. There is one in Santa Fe."

Well, that seemed fitting. The perfect djinn and their presumably perfect partners should be living in New Mexico's most beautiful town. She wondered if the Southern California djinn and their partners were holed up in Beverly Hills. Or maybe Malibu was more their speed.

"And you're in Albuquerque because...."

"It was granted to me. The whole of the city, up to that place you called Bernalillo, and then to the east as far as the mountain pass, and west to the hills there."

Granted by whom, Madison didn't know, but she figured there must be some sort of djinn government or something along those lines. Someone in authority who'd made the decision. But why Albuquerque? It really wasn't that much of a gem, not when you considered the whole world was up for grabs. Maybe those people in power didn't like Qadim very much, for whatever reason.

"Well, I think you've improved it a good deal," she commented, and something about the tight set of his jaw appeared to relax somewhat.

"I'm pleased you think so," he said.

And she suddenly wondered if she'd made a mistake in complimenting him. But she couldn't take back the words now. She offered him a small smile, then returned to the remnants of her meal. All the while, though, her thoughts were churning.

Los Alamos. A community of people like her.

Somehow, she'd have to find a way to get there.

CHAPTER SIX

SOMETHING HAD SET HER OFF. QADIM COULD TELL that Madison was preoccupied, and after they'd finished eating breakfast, she told him her arm had begun to ache again, and that she thought she'd better lie down for a while. He hadn't protested, simply because her excuse was plausible enough.

So he merely said that he would see her up to her room, then took her uninjured hand so he could transport her up to the ninth floor where her suite was located. It wouldn't do to have her climb all those stairs; the movement would jostle her damaged shoulder far too much.

Madison's stared at him in astonishment as they reappeared in front of the door to her room. "How...?"

"It is how we travel," he said. "I would have brought you down in the same way, but you had already left your room. I thought this would be easier for you. Walking up all those steps could have jarred your shoulder."

"I suppose you have a point." She stopped and looked all around them, as if she still wasn't quite certain of her surroundings. "Thank you for breakfast, Qadim."

"You are very welcome. What would you like for your midday meal?"

"Oh, I—" Seeming a little flustered, she shook her head. He tried not to stare at the way those rose gold curls bounced against her shoulders and then fell down her back. "Breakfast was so big, I'm not sure I'd want lunch, especially since I might end up sleeping right through it. Can we just skip ahead to dinner?"

"Of course."

She offered him a quick smile and went inside, then closed the door behind her with a soft *snick* of the lock. For a moment, he lingered outside, but he knew he could not stand there forever. She would emerge when she was ready. And, as she had said, she did need to get her rest.

So he went downstairs and cleared away their breakfast dishes. Not using his djinn powers, but carrying the plates and mugs into the kitchen so he could set them in the sink. Eventually he would snap his fingers and send them, sparkling clean, into their respective cupboards. For now, though, he left them all behind so he could stand in the front entrance of the hotel and gaze at his handiwork.

It was a fine day, the sun out, a brisk breeze blowing through the grasses and trees he had planted, light glinting as their leaves glistened in the wind. Qadim breathed in deeply, hoping the fresh air might help to clear his thoughts, but no matter what he did, he could only think of Madison lying upstairs in bed. Would she be asleep already, lulled into slumber by the meal she'd eaten and her body's own need for rest? Or would she be lying awake, thinking of everything he had told her?

Perhaps it had been a mistake to mention Los Alamos. He'd seen the way she'd grown quiet and thoughtful afterward, although she'd done her best to hide her reaction. It was only natural that she would yearn to be with others of her own kind. After all, she had just spent more than a year alone.

But she was not alone now. She had company. His company. Should that not be enough?

Then he wanted to shake his head at himself. Through the millennia, many djinn women had been glad enough to spend time with him, but their pleasure in his company should not have given him such an inflated sense of his own attractions that he believed they could outweigh the lure of a chance to be among one's own people.

Perhaps he could change that. Perhaps he could show her that she would do very well to be with him. And then when he had tired of her, he could take her to Los Alamos himself—or at least as near as he could without being affected by one of Miles Odekirk's infernal devices. Madison should be able to traverse that last half mile without too much trouble.

He saw no reason why he would not tire of her at some point, since that had been the eventual outcome in all of his previous liaisons. Anyway, it was better that they should enjoy one another for a time and then part ways before things grew sour, or he became bored.

Of course, that particular scenario was predicated on the belief that she would eventually succumb to him, and she certainly had not yet shown any signs of doing so. But she was not healed, and had suffered one shock after another. Time was the one thing djinn had plenty of, and so Qadim was prepared to give her whatever she required.

Assuming that Hasan al-Abyad did not make another unannounced visit. He would surely detect Madison's presence, and things could get nasty. Or perhaps not. Qadim thought he might be able to convince the other djinn to let her alone for as long as she was in Qadim's keeping. A few hints that Hasan could do as he pleased with her as soon as Qadim was finished should be enough to get the air elemental to retreat for the moment. Hasan didn't have to know that Qadim planned to see Madison safely to Los Alamos once their relationship had run its course.

Yes, that sounded like quite a good plan. While she was here, though, Qadim knew he could not go forth and continue with the demolition of Albuquerque's man-made features. The landscaping would have to wait, because he did not think she would be safe here if he left her alone.

Not that it mattered all that much. He had plunged into his transformation of the city because he had had nothing else to occupy his time. Now, though, he had something far more distracting to fill his days.

He moved out onto the sidewalk that remained and gazed upward, toward the floor where she now slept. Soon enough she would wake, and he'd begin his pursuit of her in earnest.

Sleep was the farthest thing from Madison's mind. After she'd locked the door to her room, she'd made sure all the blinds were firmly shut so no one—not even Qadim—would be able to see inside. Yes, certain things he'd said made it sound as if he was the only one of his kind remaining in the city, but what if those rampaging djinn she'd seen months before were still at large in Albuquerque, trying to sniff her out? Best to be safe, even if she had the completely unfounded impression that Qadim would do his best to protect her.

Right then she wished more than anything that she was back in the shelter so she could access the excellent map library Clay had gathered there, the really detailed topographical maps hikers used, along with super-accurate USGS charts. Then she could try to plot a course from Albuquerque to Los Alamos, see if there was some way she could take side roads and routes hidden in canyons and creek beds and manage to avoid any djinn interference.

But she was more than a mile away from the shelter, so that idea was out. For now, she'd have to rely on her own somewhat hazy memories of Los Alamos as she began to formulate a plan. In a few days, Qadim would let her go, and then—

What makes you think he's going to let you go?

The thought popped into her mind so vivid and clear that she knew she couldn't ignore it. She wished she could, but she'd never been one to avoid unpleasant facts, and she wasn't about to start doing so now.

Yes, Qadim had been friendly. Maybe too friendly. No, he hadn't seemed interested enough in humans to save one by making her his Chosen, but now that he'd had a human female basically dropped in his lap, it was entirely possible that he'd decided it might be a good idea to amuse himself with her for a while. He was probably waiting for her arm to heal itself. A one-handed lover could be somewhat limiting.

Oh, come on, she thought then, *do you really think you're that irresistible? Why have you when he could be with a djinn woman instead?* She'd never seen a djinn female, but if they were anything like their men, then they were all probably extremely attractive as well.

That all sounded very sensible. But....

Coming to terms with one's own beauty was always problematic. Madison had never paid all that much attention to her own looks, except for wishing on numerous occasions that she'd inherited her father's nice straight hair instead of this curly mass that only did what it wanted to and seemed to laugh at any actual attempts at styling it. However, when strangers—both male and female—started approaching her when she was at the mall, handing her business cards that advertised various modeling agencies, she'd begun to realize there must be something appealing or at least interesting about her looks. She'd never called any of those phone numbers, partly because she wasn't that interested and partly because she knew her father wouldn't approve. Still, she'd always carried in the back of her head the strange notion that someone, somewhere thought she was attractive enough to be a model.

And then there had been that creepy T.A. during her sophomore year of college, the one who told her she looked like something out of a Botticelli painting and who kept wanting to sketch her. She'd said no repeatedly, but he wouldn't leave her alone, and eventually she'd gone to the head of the department and made a complaint. The T.A. was removed from her class soon afterward, and she felt guilty about the situation... but not too guilty. After all, she'd given him plenty of chances to tone it down, and he hadn't.

But even with all that, she still didn't see anything entrancing enough about herself to make her think Qadim was anything like that long-ago T.A.—well, nothing except the way she'd caught him staring at her on several occasions. She wasn't a complete imbecile; she knew what that spark of interest in men's eyes generally meant.

Even if the man in question happened to be a djinn.

All right, so maybe Qadim was contemplating getting a little human booty. Maybe the best thing to do would be to act as if her arm was still hurting even after it was actually healed. Then all she'd have to do was wait until he wasn't paying attention—maybe while he was in the middle of making dinner—and then she could make a break for it.

Framed that way, her plan seemed a little cruel. He hadn't done anything to her. He hadn't even said anything suggestive. He'd only looked at her a few times in a way that made her uncomfortable. She could be misinterpreting everything, including his very obvious kindness to her.

Damn it.

She sat down at the table by the window and used her good hand to separate the blinds slightly so she could peek outside. This room faced north and west, so she could pretend that she was able to see all the way to Los Alamos, even though she knew in reality it was too far away for her to glimpse anything of that mountain town. From this angle, she couldn't even see all the way to the edge of Qadim's "grant."

What she could see was the evidence of his work all around—the strangely altered skyline, the open grassland with its careful groupings of trees and bushes and rocks at regular intervals. All seemed quiet, though; it didn't appear as if he was working on his project today.

He's sticking close by because he doesn't want to leave you alone here, she thought.

Unfortunately, that idea seemed too plausible for her to even bother denying it.

Dinner on the rooftop bar, he thought. It might be rather cold for Madison, but the space had been equipped with large portable heaters. Qadim didn't have any trouble getting them started, as they were still filled with propane, waiting for guests who would never come.

The notion saddened him for some reason, and he pushed the thought away. This space would have one very important guest tonight.

He wished she had something more becoming to wear, however. The clothing he'd placed in her room was functional and nearly identical to the pieces she'd been wearing when he found her, but it wasn't exactly suitable for a romantic evening. He thought then of the shimmering golden outfit he'd had Julia Innes wear when she'd been his captive, and let out a breath. She'd looked like a goddess.

But gold wouldn't suit Madison. No, she needed something more delicate—a soft green, or a pale blush color. Would she even wear something he provided?

Only one way to find out, he supposed.

He'd left her alone all afternoon so she could get her rest. That had given him time to decide what to make, how to decorate the rooftop space. The water fountain at the edge of the roof, with its blue lights and line of flames along the angular obelisk that dominated the water feature, couldn't be improved. While poking around the hotel, he'd found lengths of filmy cloth he guessed must have been used to decorate the ceilings, and he hung some of that in swags from pillar to pillar, softening the angular lines of the walls that surrounded the area. No need for a crowd of tables when it would only be the two of them; he placed one round table and two chairs in an intimate corner, then covered the table with a dark red cloth.

Truly, for an artifact made by human hands and not djinn, the place was very lovely. It would be lovelier still with Madison sitting there.

He conjured an ensemble identical to one that a woman of his people would have worn—a long fitted tunic with a low-cut neckline, filmy, blousy trousers, jeweled sandals. In the end he'd decided on a soft rose color, thinking it would do very well in the warm light cast by the flames that topped the water feature. Now all he had to do was see whether she would wear the outfit.

And what he would do if she happened to refuse.

After a while, Madison had lain down and dozed for a few hours. There wasn't much else for her to do, and even though she was normally the active type, the energy her healing shoulder required seemed to tire her out more quickly than she was used to.

A soft knock at the door woke her, and she sat up in bed, heart pounding, until she realized it had to be Qadim. Even if the worst had happened and one of his more bloodthirsty brethren had appeared at the Hotel Andaluz, she doubted that sort of djinn would knock politely and wait for her to answer the door.

She swung her legs over the side of the bed and got up. As she moved, she realized the low-grade ache in her shoulder was nearly gone. So maybe all the naps really were helping.

When she opened the door, she saw Qadim waiting outside, something filmy in a soft blush color draped over his left arm. "Did I wake you?"

"No," she said. "That is, I was just dozing." Her gaze moved to the bundle of fabric he held, then back to his face.

He looked impassive enough, so there wasn't much for her to see there. "It is a fine evening, and so I thought we might dine in the rooftop bar. I brought this for you." He extended his arm, and so Madison didn't have much choice but to take the silky bundle of fabric he offered her.

As she awkwardly draped it over her own arm, she realized it was some kind of clothing, although at the moment she couldn't tell much about its shape. All the same, she had to fight to keep herself from smiling wryly. Yes, he'd waited a whole day, but now here he was, asking her—more or less—to wear something he'd brought her.

"So this is a formal dinner?"

His shoulders lifted slightly. "Let us say that it is a lovely spot, one that deserves something more than a T-shirt and jeans."

Madison couldn't help giving him a raised eyebrow, since he was wearing basically the same thing, although at the moment she was minus her shoes, while he had on a pair of scarred motorcycle boots.

"I will change as well," he said, apparently not embarrassed at all by her unspoken question.

"All right," she said. If he was going to play along, then it would seem rude of her to refuse to wear the outfit he'd brought. While she couldn't see any details, there seemed to be enough fabric involved that she didn't have to worry about squeezing herself into a micro-mini or something. "What time?"

"Seven o'clock. On the roof," he added, as if he'd thought she'd forgotten.

Her suite actually had a functioning clock radio, and it matched the time on the watch she always wore now. Back before the world had collapsed, she'd relied on her phone to tell her the time, but cellular networks were now a thing of the past. The shelter had been equipped with an atomic clock, and so she set her watch by that. Anyway, Qadim had given her about an hour to get ready, which seemed like overkill, but she'd go with it.

"I'll see you then," she said, and he smiled.

"Thank you, Madison."

He turned and strode off down the hall, and she shut the door, feeling slightly mystified. There had been something almost diffident in his manner, as if he hadn't been entirely sure whether she would agree to come to dinner. But what real choice did she have? She had no reason to decline, except a bunch of vague misgivings that didn't add up to much of anything.

Pushing back a sigh, she went over to the rumpled bed and used her one good arm to lay out the garments Qadim had brought for her. They seemed similar in appearance to a style of clothing she'd seen women from India wear, with the long, fitted tunic and full-cut trousers. The fabric was a lightweight silk, the body of the tunic lined, although the sleeves and the pants were semi-sheer. Around the neckline was delicate embroidery in shades of pink and dusty mauve, accented with coppery metallic threads and dull-cut stones. Rose quartz, maybe.

The ensemble was really quite stunning, as were the little jeweled sandals that had been rolled up inside the bundle. Although she didn't particularly want to try to impress Qadim, Madison wished then she had a little more makeup to play with than the tinted lip balm that had been included with the rest of her toiletries. The outfit that lay before her seemed to deserve more than something so minimal.

Since she couldn't really do anything about the lack of cosmetics, she thought it was best to get dressed and see what she could manage with her limited resources. Slipping out of the sling didn't hurt nearly as much as it had previously, a very good sign. If she continued to mend this quickly, she'd probably be able to go back home the very next day.

If Qadim allowed it...a very big if.

Madison put that thought aside for the moment. If she played her cards right tonight, then maybe he'd be feeling mellow enough that he'd agree to let her go. Or not. So much depended on his expectations, and she still didn't know for sure what those might be.

It did hurt a little to pull off her T-shirt and replace it with the snug-fitting tunic, but not so much that she did anything but wince slightly as she used a couple of one-handed tugs to get the tunic to lie where it was supposed to. And...damn.

The fit was perfect. She had no idea how Qadim had managed that, but she supposed djinn had all kinds of esoteric powers, including—apparently—the ability to just look at a person and know what size she was supposed to wear. Well, scratch that—the fit was almost perfect. If she'd been trying the tunic on at a store, she would have taken it off and hung it right back up again, because she'd never been the type to wear anything that low-cut. Not that she was in danger of spilling out or anything, but the scooped neckline showed off far more of the curve of her breasts than she was comfortable with.

She kind of doubted that had been an accident.

With a sigh, she climbed out of her jeans and into the filmy trousers that matched the tunic. At least they were loose-fitting, but she had a feeling Qadim wasn't going to be looking at her legs.

There wasn't much she could do with her hair except finger-comb it and then splash some water on her hand and use it to scrunch her unruly curls into something a little less frizzy. At least the lip balm added some color to her mouth, and she used a trick a friend from college had taught her by taking some of that same lip balm and rubbing it on her fingertips, then using it to smudge a little color high up on her cheekbones.

The combination of these makeshift techniques worked out better than she'd hoped, and a far more polished version of herself than she'd expected stared back at her from the mirror. Her simple hoop earrings didn't really go with the outfit, but Qadim hadn't provided any jewelry, so they'd have to do.

It seemed a shame to have to put the sling back on over all this splendor. However, Madison's arm was beginning to ache again, and she didn't want to tip her hand and let the djinn know that she was healing far more quickly than expected. So she slipped the sling over her head and tucked her arm back into it, then stepped into the little jeweled sandals he'd provided.

The sight of her bare toes made her want to sigh all over again. She'd gotten her last pedicure of the season just before the Heat had struck Albuquerque, and ever since then she kept her toenails short but hadn't bothered with them otherwise. What was the use in painting her toes when she went around in hiking boots all the time?

Don't worry about it, she told herself. *With this neckline, I doubt Qadim is going to be looking at your feet, either.*

That thought wasn't particularly reassuring. What if he did try something? There was no way in the world she could fight him off. Not even when she had the use of both arms, and certainly not with one of them currently bound up in a sling.

It wouldn't come to that. He might be trying for some kind of seduction—Madison had been to the hotel's rooftop bar before, and so she knew that it was a very romantic setting—but he just didn't seem the type to force her. He could have done that anytime during the past twenty-four hours.

She went and picked up her watch. Five minutes to seven. Close enough. So after checking her appearance one last time in the bathroom mirror, she went to the door to her suite and let herself out.

Candles flickered on the side tables in the hallway, but they'd been there the day before. It wasn't as if Qadim had left a trail of rose petals down the corridor or something. Once again she went to the stairwell and headed downstairs, only this time she exited onto the mezzanine and followed the signs that guided her to the rooftop bar. She passed a room that had once been used as a reception area, then came to a door.

Madison opened that door and walked out into fairyland.

All right, maybe more like an enchanted kingdom. Flames danced along the top of the fountain at the far side of the roof, and pale cloth had been swagged from pillar to pillar to give the feeling of a canopy overhead, even though the louvered roof was currently open to the sky. Several tall propane heaters glowed cherry-red, and votives in glass containers flickered along every surface.

Movement in the shadows at the far side of the rooftop bar caught her eye, and then she had to hold in a gasp as Qadim stepped forward. He'd gone back to his djinn attire, only this time the dark open robe he wore glinted with embroidery in gold and silver. That open robe didn't do much to hide the heavy muscles of his chest, or the sculpted outlines of his stomach.

Well, *damn.*

This might be harder than she'd thought. And then she realized he was holding two glasses of wine, one of which he extended to her.

"Madison," he said. "You are looking very beautiful."

So was he, but no way in hell did she have the courage to return the compliment. "Thank you," she managed to say as she gratefully took the glass of wine from him with her one good hand. "This is all pretty amazing."

"You like it?"

"It's gorgeous." At least that was nothing more than the truth. She sipped some of the wine—a shiraz, she thought—and added, "I've been to this bar a couple of times, but it certainly never looked like this."

"I did add a few touches." With his free hand, he gestured toward a table tucked into one corner. It was darker back there, but more votives glowed from the tabletop, and from someplace—possibly the hotel's store of wedding supplies—he'd found a set of large wrought-iron candle stands and placed a thick pillar candle on each one. They all helped to cast their own warm light, even though they flickered a good bit in the brisk evening breeze that blew over the rooftop.

Madison went where he'd indicated and began to sit down, only to have Qadim hurry over so he could pull out a chair for her. She startled, but then let herself sink down onto the seat, wondering if that was also something standard in djinn society, or whether he'd somehow learned that little act of courtesy from humans.

He went around to the other side of the table and sat as well. In the uncertain light of dusk, with the candles flickering all around him, his features seemed even more saturnine, his eyes set deep in shadow.

Not sure what she should do, Madison picked up her glass of wine and took another swallow. There. That

She wasn't sure why that thought should make her feel a little sad.

"Hasan did mention a good number of trees."

Another shiver went over her, and Madison began to wonder if she'd been premature in telling Qadim that she was comfortable up here in the night air. "Hasan? So he was one of the djinn I saw?"

"I'm afraid so." Qadim snapped his fingers, and in the next instant a serving cart laden with all sorts of delectable-smelling dishes appeared beside them.

She'd seen him use his powers in small, subtle ways before this, but it was all she could do to keep herself from jumping out of her seat at that apparition. Convenient, she supposed, because this way Qadim wouldn't have to leave her to go fetch the food, but still....

"Let us not talk of Hasan," he continued. "For I wanted this to be a good dinner for you, and I would not wish to spoil your appetite."

"You're right," Madison said. "As you said, he won't bother us."

A nod, but she caught the flicker of unease in his expression before he turned so he could start dishing up their food. She barely held back a shiver as she remembered the manic delight in that other djinn's eyes as he cheerfully slaughtered Albuquerque's few remaining survivors.

And she wondered just how confident Qadim truly was in his belief that this Hasan would actually stay away.

CHAPTER SEVEN

QADIM WISHED THAT THEY HAD AVOIDED THE SUB-
ject of Hasan. Madison seemed to accept his explanation that the other djinn would stay far away from them,
but...would he?

Do not think of that, Qadim admonished himself.
Think of the woman before you.

For truly, she was an astonishing sight. Even in the
oddly sexless clothing she seemed to prefer, he had seen
that she was beautiful, but now, outfitted in something
which enhanced her form rather than hid it, he could
see how lovely she truly was. Very slender, yes, almost to
the point of thinness, but her breasts were still rounded
enough for all that, and her waist tapered in a way that
made him ache to slip his arms around her. The soft rosy
hue of the silk ensemble he'd provided for her lent some

color to the clear pallor of her fine skin, and once again he had to resist the urge to reach out and touch her hair, to feel the soft springiness of it against his fingers.

And he might be flattering himself, but he'd noted the expression of shocked admiration in her eyes when she saw him in the dress of his people, rather than the human garments he'd lately adopted because of their practical nature. Her expression had quickly shifted to one of pleasant neutrality, but he couldn't forget what he'd seen. Perhaps she was not quite as indifferent as she wanted him to think.

Which of course pleased him greatly. He knew that at any time he could have cast the djinn glamour on her to make her think that she desired him, but he did not wish to do so. That particular subterfuge had not worked very well on Julia Innes, true. Even so, he had no reason to think the glamour would not be effective on Madison Reynolds, although she certainly seemed as strong-minded as Julia, perhaps ever more so. He had no true frame of reference, for all his former partners had been djinn, and more than willing. Something kept him from attempting the experiment, though. She should want him because she truly did want him, and not because he had used his djinn powers to convince her otherwise.

Now she sat quietly, eating the ragout of venison he had prepared—another dish where everything had already been cut into bite-sized chunks, and so she wouldn't need to use her injured arm. Once or twice he'd seen her move it without wincing, which seemed to indicate that she was healing quickly, but he still thought she would require a few more days to recover her full range of motion.

"Would you like some more rice?" he asked politely.

"Yes, please." He dished it up for her, and she offered him a smile. It looked somewhat more relaxed than the one she'd given him earlier, but perhaps that was only because of the wine and the food. Then she said, "This is amazing. Where do you get all the ingredients?"

"I gather them to me as I need them," he replied. That seemed to be the simplest way to explain how he was able to draw items from all over the world to create their meals. Sooner or later those stocks would begin to be depleted, he supposed, and the djinn would have to lend their talents to agriculture and animal husbandry, but for now there existed enough abundance that he could call to him the things he required.

Her eyes were full of questions, but she seemed to understand that he didn't want to go into more detail than what he'd already provided. "Do you work from recipes, or do you just make it up as you go?"

"It depends. I have had this ragout many times before, and so I could re-create it from memory. But if you wished for me to make one of your New Mexico dishes—"

"Blue corn chicken enchiladas with Christmas chile," she broke in, an impish light in her eyes. Or perhaps that was only a reflection from the candlelight.

She might as well have been speaking a different language. "Precisely. I have no idea what that is. Something you make at your holidays?"

That question made her actually chuckle. "Not exactly. 'Christmas' just means you're asking for both green and red chile on top of your food. That's all."

"What is chile, precisely?"

Madison shot him a look of mock-horror. "You're living in Albuquerque and you don't know what chile is? It's a sauce made from chile peppers. There are red and green varieties, and they range in heat level from mildly interesting to nuclear explosion."

None of this was making much sense. Yes, his people had some spicy dishes, but what Madison had just described seemed very different. "And a nuclear explosion is good?"

"In this sense, yes. I mean, some people take a lot of pride in how much hot food they can eat. That is, could eat," she amended, the light in her eyes dying out abruptly.

He knew she must be thinking of all the people who had died from the Heat, and wished he'd been able to guide the conversation in such a way that the topic could have been avoided altogether. That wasn't possible, but he still wanted to do what he could to take her mind off the subject. "And you liked nuclear chile?"

"No, I was always somewhere in the middle." She reached for her wine glass and took a larger gulp than she'd probably intended.

Qadim obligingly poured some more into her glass. He didn't wish for her to become truly intoxicated, but on the other hand, if she was just a little elevated, she might be more open to...whatever might come next.

"Perhaps if I attempt to make something with chile, you can assist me?" he asked then.

"Well, I don't know how much help I would be at making it from scratch," Madison replied. "We always just bought ours at the store. But I suppose I could do some taste testing for you."

"That would be very helpful." Indeed, he had a sudden vision of her perched on one of the stools in the kitchen, licking chile sauce—whatever that was, precisely—from a wooden spoon. The image made his groin tighten, and he reached for his own wine, glad of the dimly lit corner where they sat and the baggy nature of his trousers.

"It's a plan, then." She smiled, apparently distracted from the topic of the Heat's victims, and Qadim found himself relaxing as well. Surely she wouldn't be talking about helping him in the kitchen if she planned to leave any time soon.

Would he allow her to leave? That was a question he'd wrestled with himself ever since he'd brought her back here. He didn't want to make her his prisoner, of course, but he also didn't want her to leave, if for no other reason than he thought she'd be safer here with him.

No, that was a specious argument, for she'd been able to survive without his help for more than a year. It was only that he wanted so very much for her to stay, at least until a time when they both decided that it was time to move on.

So yes...he would allow her to leave...as long as it suited his own purposes.

Damn it, Madison, what the hell were you thinking? You might as well have said you were going to move in with him and start picking out glasses from the Pottery Barn catalogue or something.

She settled back in her chair, wishing there was some way to put a little more distance between herself and the djinn. There wasn't, though, not without making herself very obvious.

That comment about taste testing the chile had come out of nowhere. She'd been babbling, letting the wine do the talking for her, probably because talking about people's tastes in chile had made her think about how her father could eat anything slathered in sauce so hot he might as well have been consuming ignited rocket fuel. And how Jake had been just the opposite, and she used to tease him unmercifully about what a wimp he was and how he needed to turn in his New Mexico card.

Well, she supposed in a way he had. Turned it in so he could move to Washington.

But she didn't want Qadim to know how those memories had brought a sting of tears to her eyes, so she'd quickly taken another of swallow of wine and let it warm her and help her to forget.

No, she'd never forget. Not really. It would be easier if she could.

Now the djinn was removing their dinner plates and setting down small ramekins filled with a dark chocolate-y substance topped with raspberries and whipped cream. She raised an eyebrow, and he said, "Chocolate mousse. It was a delicacy, wasn't it?"

"You could say that." At this point, nothing he might do in the culinary department would really surprise her. For all she knew, he'd spend all night studying cookbooks about New Mexico cuisine and would surprise her the next day with enchiladas and sopapillas and calabacitas, followed up by dulce de leche cake.

Anyway, chocolate mousse sounded amazing. The shelter had a cache of organic, high-cacao-content chocolate bars because of their health benefits, and Madison had allowed herself a small piece several times a week. But a few bites of dense, dark chocolate wasn't the same as chocolate mousse with whipped cream and raspberries on top.

A single bite was enough to tell her that she'd never had anything this good in a restaurant. If only the ramekin wasn't so small....

She ate every bite, then wished she was alone so she could lick the bowl. God knows how Qadim would have reacted to that sort of display, so somehow she managed to restrain herself.

"Good?" he asked, once she was done and had set her spoon crossways on top of the ramekin.

"Better than good. Amazing."

"That was what I wanted to hear."

They were both quiet then, gazing at each other across the table. Madison found herself studying his features, finding nuances like the high bridge of his strong nose, or the cleft in his chin, mostly hidden by the neatly trimmed beard he wore. It was probably just the wine talking, but once again she realized she was asking herself if it would truly be such a bad thing for things to take a turn for the physical. And it sure didn't help that her body was telling her no, it wouldn't be a bad thing at all. She'd tried to take care of herself as best she could, thanks to a few helpful items looted from adult stores in town, but using a collection of carefully designed toys wasn't the same as being with a man, feeling his hands on you, feeling him in you....

She put her good hand on the tabletop and pushed herself upward. "I—I'm starting to feel a little tired.

This has been a wonderful dinner, Qadim, but I think I need to go to bed."

The second the words were out of her mouth, she wanted to curse herself. Why the hell had she been stupid enough to use the word "bed"?

He didn't react, though, except to say, "Of course, Madison. Let me take you to your room."

Somehow, that sounded like a very dangerous suggestion. "Oh, you don't need to do that—"

"It would be churlish of me to leave you to fend for yourself when I can make the process so much easier." He rose from his seat and came toward her, then took her by her good arm.

She managed to keep herself from flinching. Not that it felt bad to have his arm around hers—actually, it felt good, just as it felt good to have the heat of his body helping to protect her from the night wind as they left their sheltered little corner and went toward the stairwell. But it shouldn't feel good. He was a djinn, not some random survivor she'd met here in the ruins of Albuquerque. If he'd been human, then maybe....

One of those jarring blinks, and then they were standing outside the door to her suite. Next to her, Qadim seemed calm and imperturbable. He certainly didn't appear affected by their proximity. Once again she told herself that she'd been seeing things that weren't there, manufacturing a tension between them that really didn't exist. All he'd done was guide her to her door, and now he would leave her to her lonely bed. Anything else was just a crazy fantasy she'd concocted in her mind.

No need of key cards anymore; the door swung open as soon as she rested her fingers on the handle. She turned back toward Qadim to find him standing much closer than she'd expected—so close, in fact, that the hem of his robe brushed against the toes of her right foot.

That whisper of silk against her bare foot made her shiver, even though it was much warmer in here than it had been on the rooftop.

"You did take a chill," he said, his voice a soft rumble.

At once she shook her head. "No—no, it's just—"

"Just what?"

Madison forced herself to look up at him. Those dark eyes seemed so very close. And his mouth—why hadn't she noticed the sensual curve to his lower lip before?

"I'm just tired," she said. She knew she needed to get herself inside before she did something spectacularly stupid. Kissing him wouldn't solve anything, would only create a whole host of new problems. The thrill of need that she'd felt just then as she gazed at Qadim—that was only the wine talking. Wine, and loneliness. But if she managed to get away from here, run to Los Alamos, maybe she could meet someone who was just as lonely as she. A nice human guy, not someone who belonged to a race that had done its best to wipe humanity right off the map.

"You're not cold?" Qadim asked. Something in his voice seemed to intimate that he knew all too well how to warm her up.

"No, I'm fine. Thank you for dinner." She pushed on the door handle and made herself put one foot in front of the other. Another step or two, and then she would be safely inside and could shut the door behind her. Only, would she really be safe? Qadim could blast that door right out of existence if he wanted to.

He didn't, however. He remained where he was, a certain sadness entering his deep, dark eyes. "You're most welcome. Sleep well, Madison."

Before she could say anything else, he'd turned and was walking down the hallway toward the stairwell for some reason, even though he could have simply performed another one of those blinks to get him to his own room. A mad impulse went over her to call out to him, to tell him to come back, but she pressed her lips tightly together and shut the door before she could do anything so stupid. Once it was closed, she leaned her forehead against the hard surface and wondered if she'd really made the right choice—or whether she was being a stubborn fool.

Qadim went down to the bar and poured himself a glass of late-harvest malbec. A large one.

He'd been so certain of her. The way her lips had parted, a certain flush to her cheeks—those were signs of desire, of need. And then she had coolly thanked him for dinner and shut the door behind her.

Perhaps he had been foolish in allowing his scruples to prevent him from using the djinn glamour. He sensed that she required only the slightest push, only the smallest bit of persuasion, to bring her to him. But no, he'd vowed that he would do no such thing, that he would wait for her to be ready. He wanted her on her own terms, and not because he had forced her into any kind of intimacy.

Even so, his body ached with need for her. He'd been so very sure that this evening would end with her in his bed. Or him in her bed. Either way would have been just fine.

He tossed back a large swallow of malbec, entirely disregarding the delicacy of the vintage he was drinking, a rarity that should have been savored in small, measured sips. Was Madison in bed already, or was she as wakeful as he, wondering if she had made the right decision?

"No, you did not, Madison," he said aloud, and poured himself more of the wine. Perhaps the Council had thought they were punishing him by giving him Albuquerque as his territory, but he doubted they would have considered it such a hardship if they'd realized the quality of the wines to be had here.

It was not easy for a djinn to become drunk, as their systems were far more hardy than those of humans, but the thing could still be accomplished if one possessed a steady will and a large wine cellar.

Several more large swallows later, he felt the jangling in his nerves begin to quiet somewhat. Patience, he told himself. After all, he and Madison had only spent a few days together. She needed time to get used to the idea of being with him, to understand that there wasn't anything terribly strange about the two of them becoming intimate. There had been many human/djinn liaisons throughout history, some consensual, some...not. But she didn't know that. Somehow she'd managed to retrieve some information about the djinn, but Qadim had the impression that her sources had not covered that particular ground.

So...a few more days together, a few more meals, more shared wine.... He was fairly certain the situation would require little more than that, and she would be his. She was already very close. All it would require was a small nudge.

Thus heartened, he poured himself more of the malbec. One thing he knew for sure about Madison Reynolds.

She would be well worth the wait.

Madison stared up at the bits of bright sunlight reflecting on the ceiling, then over at the clock radio. Seven twenty-five.

She'd slept the whole night through without interruption. Why that had surprised her, she wasn't quite sure. Qadim really didn't seem the type to sneak up on an unsuspecting woman.

Now was the moment of truth.

She sat up in bed, then slipped the sling over her head and dropped it on top of the bedspread. Jaw clenched in anticipation of the expected pain, she slowly lifted her left arm and extended it so it was parallel to the ground.

A slight twinge, but nothing she couldn't handle.

Next, she moved her arm forward and then swiveled it so her palm faced the ceiling. Again, she could feel a small ache in her shoulder, but it wasn't significant. She clenched her fist several times, tightening the muscles all up and down her arm. Some pain, just not enough to stop her from doing anything she needed to.

All right, time for the real test.

Madison placed both hands flat against the bed and pushed against them, putting all her weight on them so she could swing her legs over the side of the bed and stand up. That hurt more, but she was able to do it. Her left arm didn't buckle, seemed perfectly capable of supporting her.

Well, that seemed to clinch it. She might still have some healing to do, true. That didn't mean she wasn't capable of moving around more or less normally. Which meant....

There was no need for her to stay here. She could go back to the shelter, gather the necessary items, and strike out for Los Alamos and—possibly—the world's only remaining community of humans. Qadim might be upset, but after some time had passed, she was sure he'd understand why she should be among her own kind. That would leave him free to focus on being with a djinn woman. Why he wasn't already attached to someone, she didn't know, but that was for him to sort out.

First of all, though, she needed to figure out how to get safely away.

She showered and got dressed in her jeans and a fresh T-shirt, then put the sling back on even though she'd determined she really didn't need it. Through all these preparations, she resolutely ignored the beautiful blush-colored outfit Qadim had brought for her. That was for special occasions, no matter how good she might have felt in it, and it certainly wouldn't do her any good where she was going. But she did put the colored balm on her lips and her cheeks, and did her best to tame her wild locks into something resembling orderly curls. She needed to make the djinn think that she was softening toward him, and that all she needed was a little extra time to come to terms with the idea of a possible relationship with him.

A little pang went through her at that thought. She hated the idea of misleading anyone. And the sad truth was, she'd felt how her body had reacted to him the night before. If she didn't get out of here soon, she might lose any self-control she still possessed. Part of her wanted to be with him, wanted to know what it would feel like to have his mouth on hers, those strong arms, heavy with muscle, wrapped around her, holding her close.

Even now, the mental image was enough to make her flush with heat, then shiver. This would have been a lot easier if he hadn't been so damn hot.

Courage, she told herself. All right, the odds of finding anyone equally smoking hot in Los Alamos were probably slim to nonexistent, but she couldn't let that little detail shake her resolve. He was a djinn, and she was human. They weren't supposed to be together.

She took in a deep gulp of air and then let herself out of her room and headed for the stairwell. It was now getting close to nine, and so she thought she'd once again go down to the kitchen in the hope that Qadim would be there, preparing breakfast.

But the kitchen was empty when she got there, although she found evidence of his handiwork in the form of a large quiche with a couple of slices already removed, and a clean plate sitting next to it. Next to the plate was a piece of hotel stationery with the words "help yourself" written on it in thick black marker. The writing was in all caps, squared off and as neat as an architect's notations. The note surprised her, although she supposed that if Qadim could speak English as well as he could, then it wasn't that great a leap to being able to write in that language, too.

A pot of coffee sat on the stove, so she poured herself a mug and went back to the quiche and cut herself a large wedge. She wouldn't ask where in the world a djinn had managed to learn how to make quiche— if he could figure out venison ragout and chocolate mousse, then quiche lorraine was probably a piece of cake, so to speak.

Madison ate quiche and drank coffee, and wondered where Qadim had gotten to. Maybe it was foolish for her to be sitting here and quietly consuming breakfast when this might be her one and only chance to make a getaway, but something kept her rooted in place. The problem was, she didn't know where the djinn had gone. The last thing she wanted was for him to reappear suddenly while she was trying to make a break for it. Better to stay put until he returned, then get a better idea of what he planned to do with the rest of his day.

Also, staying here and finishing her breakfast would show that she didn't plan to go anywhere, and that could only increase his trust in her. A misplaced trust, true, but she hoped that eventually he would understand why she'd felt she had to leave.

She was just pouring herself a second cup of coffee when he reappeared. Since he'd abandoned his robes and was back in Levi's and a dark green T-shirt—and because that T-shirt was already stained with dirt and sweat—Madison guessed that he'd been out tending to his "garden."

"Good morning," he greeted her. If he was annoyed with the way things had gone the night before, his current expression showed no indication of it. He looked a little tired, but content enough. "I see you found breakfast."

"I did, and it was wonderful, as usual." She lifted her mug in salute. "I even left you a little coffee."

"Thank you, but I've already had mine. I came here for some cold water."

"It looks like you've been busy."

He waited to reply until he had fetched some water from the big industrial refrigerator and poured it into a glass. Again Madison wondered how he managed to keep power going in the hotel when the rest of the town was completely dead, but she decided this probably wasn't the best time to ask. "I wanted to check on how things were doing. I think I may have come up with a way to divert more water to this area."

"I thought you were an earth elemental, not a water elemental."

"I am." Qadim tilted his head so he could drain the contents of his glass in one long swallow. That seemed to be quite the thirst he'd worked up. "But, even though I cannot have water come at my bidding,

I can guide what's already there. The infrastructure exists to bring water to this place—it only needs a little re-engineering."

"And you can do that?" Madison asked, impressed despite herself.

"I believe so, yes." He gave her a quick glance. "How are you feeling today?"

"Good," she said. That seemed safe enough. "Better, I think. The arm still hurts, but I can tell I only need a day or two more in this sling."

"That is good news." He went back to the fridge and poured himself another glass of water. "Do you mind if I leave you here for a little while? I have things to do that require me to go to the river, but I have already done some reconnaissance, and I could find no sign of Hasan or any other djinn. You should be safe here."

"No, I don't mind," Madison replied, praying that she sounded calm and unconcerned. "I just noticed that library room off the lobby. I can go into one of those little grotto things and read and put my feet up. I'll be fine."

Qadim appeared relieved by her answer, because he nodded, some of the tension going out of his shoulders. After drinking some more water, he set his glass down on the counter and said, "I won't need to be gone for long. Possibly an hour, if even that."

Better and better. In an hour, she could get back to the shelter, even if she had to walk the whole way. "Do what you need to do, Qadim. I'll just rest and take it easy. And if this Hasan person does show up, I'll tell him to go hunt you up by the river."

The djinn's face clouded. "I would not make light of it. If he does return for some reason—" He stopped himself short, and gave the smallest shake of his head, as if telling himself not to borrow trouble. "But he will not. He is far from here, and has lands of his own to manage. And when I return, we can decide what to do for dinner."

"Sounds great." Was that too chirpy? She didn't want to seem as if she was happy that he planned to leave her alone...but of course she was thrilled by the opportunity he was giving her.

"An hour, then." This time, he didn't bother to leave the room before he dematerialized, or whatever it was that djinn did. He merely disappeared with a strange popping noise, as if air had rushed in to fill the vacuum he'd just created.

Madison let out a breath, then waited. There was always the possibility that he might have forgotten something and would come back for it. But a minute passed, and then another, and the hotel remained empty and quiet around her. All right. There wasn't anything up in her borrowed room that she needed, so she could head out the front door and keep going.

Time to run.

CHAPTER EIGHT

THE RIVER FLOWED SERENELY BEFORE HIM, SOME of the trees on its banks beginning to show bright hues of yellow and orange. He'd been studying the flora of this land, and so he knew the names of a few of them. Cottonwood, and sycamore, and acacia and manzanita and mesquite. Down here, the landscape was quite lush, a contrast to the sere desert that surrounded the city on all sides.

In his planting efforts, he'd made sure to use native trees and shrubs, specimens that could rely on the region's meager rainfall to stay alive. But he enjoyed the fountain in the rooftop bar, and thought it would be pleasant to have a stream meander past the hotel, perhaps spill in a cascade to a pool below. To do that, he would need to divert some of the river's water. Not so much that the alteration would affect it adversely, but just enough to provide some welcome moisture in the place he had decided to call home.

A water elemental could have called the water there, and it would have dug a new path to follow that command, but Qadim would have to dig that new, narrow tributary himself. Nothing that would be too terribly taxing, although having it traverse the mile or so that separated the location where he stood now from the Hotel Andaluz would most likely take him at least a day, possibly more. At the moment, he was only attempting to determine the best spot to have the water branch off and travel to the east, rather than heading due south as it did now.

As he walked up and down the banks, testing the soil, eyeing the rise and fall of the land, he couldn't prevent his thoughts from returning to Madison. She'd seemed calm and quiet this morning, but he'd noted a certain tension about her.

And why does that surprise you? he asked himself as he squatted down to take a handful of sandy loam in his hand. *No doubt she was sitting there and wondering if you were going to mention dinner, or whether you possibly might try to pick up where you left things the evening before.*

He wished it could be that easy. But if she would not fall into his arms when she was flushed with wine and so obviously ready to let him kiss her, then he did not think she would be amenable to any advances made during the cold light of day.

With a sigh, he straightened and brushed the soil from his hands. The wind had picked up, and clouds were moving in from the west. He didn't think it would rain, but the day, which had begun bright and cheerful, began to grow steadily darker, a fitting match to his mood. Over the years, he had grown accustomed to the contrariness of djinn women—his sister providing a prime example of their willful behavior—but for some reason he had not thought that human females would be the same. Madison, however, seemed determined to do precisely the opposite of what he wished. Yes, she was pleasant and good company, and yet she didn't seem to have the common sense to know what was best for her.

A cloud passed over the sun. The sudden darkness made him think of Hasan, and Qadim frowned. He had reassured Madison that the air elemental would stay away, but now Qadim was not so certain. The mere thought of what might happen to her if Hasan should appear suddenly made Qadim's blood run cold. He should have brought Madison with him here to the river, rather than leaving her there alone at the hotel.

His concentration was already in tatters, and so he decided he had done enough for now. He would return and make sure she was all right, and then decide whether he would come back here with her, or put off any improvements to the river until tomorrow. After all, the Rio Grande wasn't going anywhere.

That settled, he closed his eyes and envisioned the lobby of the Hotel Andaluz, the high coffered ceilings, the wrought-iron railing that ran around the perimeter of the mezzanine. In the next instant, he stood in the center of the space, then glanced to the side, thinking he would see Madison seated in one of the casbahs with the book she had mentioned.

But she wasn't there, not in the alcove with its small waterfall, nor the one with its wall of votive candles. He hurried over to the restaurant and on back into its kitchen, but she was nowhere to be found in either of those rooms. His heart began to speed up, but he told himself to remain calm.

For it is just as likely that she has gone up to her room to lie down, he thought. *She did say that she was feeling better, but not all the way better. Perhaps sitting and reading in the lobby was not as comfortable as she thought it might be.*

That made sense. He blinked himself up to the hallway on the ninth floor, then went to the door of her suite and knocked.

Nothing.

"Madison?" he called out, and waited for the reassurance of her reply.

But she did not answer. Frowning, he knocked again. "Madison!"

Silence.

He touched the door's handle and pushed it open. A quick glance told him she was not on the bed—it was neatly made, the pillows plumped and pushed up against the headboard—and neither was she sitting at the table by the window.

The bathroom door was ajar. Qadim knew she would be quite angry with him for interrupting her in such a private place, but he had to know. He pushed the door open further, only to see that the bathroom was just as empty as the rest of her suite.

Where had she gone? His heart seemed to skip a beat as he considered the very real possibility that Hasan might have discovered her. There was no evidence of any kind of a struggle here, but that meant very little. The air elemental could have captured her and blinked away in the next instant so he could toy with her elsewhere, perhaps back on his lands in Chama.

Cold sweat breaking out on his forehead, Qadim forced himself to leave the suite and go back downstairs. Perhaps Madison had gone into one of the meeting spaces, or the small office that had once served as the reception area for the hotel. After all, he had not made a very exhaustive search of the ground floor.

But he could not find her in any of those places, either. When he paused outside the casbah where he'd thought to find her reading, however, he saw what he had overlooked previously—a small piece of the hotel's cream-colored stationery. Written on it were two words in graceful handwriting he didn't recognize but which had to be Madison's.

I'm sorry.

Hasan had not taken her. She'd run away.

Rage flamed through him, and he had to resist the urge to release that anger in a shockwave he knew would damage the hotel. He drew in a breath, then another, willing himself to remain calm. Perhaps, for all his restraint, he'd still intimidated her, had made her think that he would end up forcing her somehow, even though he could recall nothing he had said or done which would have given her that impression. He had to remind himself that she'd been alone and frightened for more than a year, that she'd had no contact with another living being until their paths had crossed a few days ago. That didn't excuse her rudeness, but at least he began to understand it.

Very well, she'd gone. But where?

Back to where she'd been hiding all that time before he found her. He'd caught up with her before she'd gone to ground last time, and so he didn't know the specific house that had been hers, but he could recall that street of modest-appearing dwellings all too well.

In the next instant he had materialized there— and none too soon, for he heard the slam of a door somewhere up ahead and to the right. Jaw tight, he ran in that direction, toward a two-story house with a large mesquite tree growing in its front yard and not much else.

The front door was unlocked. He threw it open and stalked inside. "Madison!"

No answer. Not that he'd really expected one. He paused in the foyer, noting the plain furniture and lack of decoration, and how the few items there appeared to be thickly covered in dust. From what he'd seen of Madison, she seemed to be a neat and tidy person, and he doubted she would have allowed herself to live in these conditions.

From the backyard, he heard a metallic clang. Forgetting the disorder he'd just seen around him, he hurried through the house and out the sliding glass door in the back, breaking its mechanism in his haste to see what had made that hollow clanging sound. The backyard was nearly covered in rosebushes, and at the center of those rosebushes was an incongruous gazebo, its white paint beginning to fade from the merciless desert sun.

Some kind of strange scrabbling noise was coming from beneath the gazebo. As he stared at it, he noticed that there was an opening in the latticework at its base. Had Madison gone *under* there?

Qadim couldn't see any sign of her, and so it seemed that indeed was where she'd gone to ground.

There was no way he would suffer the indignity of attempting to fold his nearly two meters of height into such a confined space, and so he raised a hand and sent a shockwave forward that caused the flimsy structure to splinter outward in all directions, raining debris on the roses and knocking a flurry of loose petals to the ground.

Only...there was no Madison hiding beneath the gazebo. Instead, Qadim saw a round metal door set into the very earth itself.

If that indeed was where she had secreted herself for all those months, no wonder that Hasan or any of his brethren had been unable to find her. Qadim went to the door and pulled on the strange round handle, but it wouldn't budge.

He didn't bother to call her name this time. He knew she wouldn't respond, but would wait down there to see if he would give up and go away.

Unfortunately for her, he was not the type to surrender easily.

The door was metal, and metal was of the earth. Which meant he could order it to do as he wished.

Once again he wrapped his fingers on the handle, only this time he sent forth the command to its very component atoms, telling them that they must obey his will. And at once the handle began to turn, and in the next moment he was able to lift the door and see inside.

A drop of about a meter and a half, and a smoothly planed dirt floor that sloped downward. Qadim lowered himself into the opening, then stooped so he could close the door behind him. He realized now that the gazebo had been placed there to provide protective camouflage. The wooden structure was gone, but he saw no reason to advertise the presence of the door it had concealed, just in case any unfriendly eyes might be looking down from above.

He had to walk three or four meters before the floor had sloped enough for him to be able to stand upright. All along this strange little corridor were metal lockers that he assumed must be storage compartments of some sort. At the end of the hallway was another door, this one set into the rock itself. It, too, had one of those strange circular handles, but again he was able to command the metal to do as he asked, and it opened inward. Now he stood in another hall, albeit a much shorter one. In the background he could hear an odd humming noise, although he couldn't tell precisely where it originated. And then there was yet another door, although this one had a normal-looking doorknob on it, as if it had been decided that if a person had gotten this far inside, he was meant to be there.

So far he had seen no sign of Madison. She must have retained enough presence of mind to keep locking the doors behind her in the hope that they would be a sufficient deterrent to prevent him from pursuing her. Clearly, she still didn't understand much about how his powers worked.

When he opened that final door and stepped through, it was as if he'd walked back into a suite at the Andaluz, or at least into a very well-appointed home. To one side was a large piece of furniture with hooks to hold coats or hats; a puffy-looking jacket hung there, along with a knitted cap. On the other wall was quite a fine painting of the Rio Grande gorge at sunset. Yes, he supposed that if one were to live underground, then having a number of landscapes hanging on the walls might be a good way to pretend that they were actually windows, that the person hiding there wasn't living like a mole.

The foyer area continued into a hallway, and opening off that hallway were various rooms, all well-furnished and spotlessly clean. In one bedroom, he saw an easel and a half-completed painting of the Sandia Mountains resting on it. So Madison was an artist? She'd never mentioned that.

Because you never asked her, he thought then. *You never asked her anything about her life before.*

He would have to remedy that lack.

"Madison!" he called out, taking care to keep his tone as gentle as he could. "I know you're here. Please come out."

Still more silence, but a listening one. She had to be in here somewhere.

He kept moving forward, peering into the rooms on either side as he went. All of them were empty. In the last one on the left, though, he saw something that gave him pause—a sketchbook lying open on the low table in front of the couch.

The charcoal sketch in that book was of him.

The sight was so surprising that he felt himself compelled to move forward and pick up the sketchpad. The picture was a quick study, but in a few lines she had captured the hawkishness of his profile, the way the wind had caught his hair and blown it away from his face.

Seeing the sketch heartened him. For one thing, he thought Madison had made him more handsome in the picture than he was in reality. For another, surely she wouldn't have sat down to draw him at all if she hadn't found something compelling about him. Her fear had caused her to run away, true, but that didn't mean some sort of attraction didn't exist within her, even if she was doing her best to push it away.

Well, he would have to figure out a way to make her understand that she had nothing to fear from him.

He set down the sketchbook and continued down the corridor. Not that he had much farther to go; beyond the room where he had found the sketch was only the kitchen, which was also empty. The hallway ended there.

Flummoxed, he stood in the middle of the kitchen for a moment, surveying the space. It was small but well laid out, with stainless steel appliances and a concrete floor. In the wall opposite was a door, one Qadim assumed must lead to the pantry.

He really didn't think Madison had squeezed herself in there with the canned soup and boxes and bags of dry goods, but he told himself he must look, since she seemed to have disappeared otherwise. When he opened the door, though, he could only stand there with his mouth slightly agape, staring at the world he had just uncovered.

That was no pantry. It was not even a storeroom. Storehouse, more like, for racks of food and other supplies seemed to stretch in every direction. How long could all this sustain one person? Years, it seemed. Possibly longer. So with all this at hand, why had Madison ever felt the need to come above ground?

Curiosity, or boredom, or perhaps a mixture of the two. Qadim didn't know how long he could live without seeing the sky or feeling the wind in his hair, even if that sky was only the livid, ever-shifting heaven of the otherworld. Yes, this place could have sustained Madison for a long time, but only if she could manage to survive the feeling of being buried alive.

Somewhere up ahead he heard a faint noise, as if something on one of the shelves had been bumped into. The lighting down here was poor enough,

consisting of a few widely spaced fluorescent fixtures—
to save energy, he supposed—so he could understand
how Madison might have misjudged where she stood.

But that misstep was all he needed. He headed in
that direction, moving slowly and deliberately now that
his quarry was almost in sight. And there she was—
backed up against the cinderblock of the far wall, face
pale and frantic in the semi-gloom.

"So," he said. "I've finally managed to find you."

CHAPTER NINE

He couldn't be here. How was he here? She'd locked all the doors behind her, and those doors had been rated to withstand near-miss tactical nukes and a variety of other nasty weaponry. Clay Michaels had always said that absolutely nothing could get through those bomb shelter doors.

Obviously, Clay Michaels hadn't thought about making them djinn-proof.

Because Qadim stood there, only a few feet away from her. His dark eyes glittered dangerously in the uncertain light, and he took a step forward. Madison wished there was someplace she could run to, but her back was up against the wall, and she knew she was trapped.

"And here I thought I was being such a good host," he went on. His gaze shifted to her left arm, now free of the sling, which she'd discarded as soon as she left the Hotel Andaluz. "Ah, and apparently you are more healed than you wanted to let on. I see."

Her throat was so horribly dry, but she managed to force out his name. "Qadim—"

He stepped forward again. Now only a foot separated them. "I am curious to hear your explanation. Or should I more accurately say your excuse?"

"I—" God, it had all made so much sense in her head. Now, though, seeing his very real anger, she wasn't sure what to say. She swallowed, then continued, "I—I was feeling better, and I knew if I told you I thought it was best that I should go, then you might try to stop me."

"And why would I do that?"

Because I could tell you wanted me. No, she could never say that. It would be putting things far too much out in the open. She still wasn't sure how she felt about the tension that had grown between them. Her common sense had told her she needed to get out, even though her emotions revealed a very different story. He was glaring at her, obviously expecting her to say something. "I—when you told me about Los Alamos, I knew that was where I needed to go."

Madison could tell that her reply surprised him. The heavy eyebrows lifted, then pulled together as he frowned. "Why would you want to go to Los Alamos?"

"Because you said there was an entire community of regular people like me living there. Why else?"

Something in his expression softened. "My dear, the last thing which could be said about you is that you're a regular person."

A small shudder went through Madison. The casual use of the endearment surprised her, because Qadim had never spoken to her in such a way before. He had been pleasant, but also polite. It was only now that she'd begun to get a better read of the emotions that had been roiling under the surface. Of course, it also didn't help that he was standing so close. Once again she thought of how good he smelled, like warm earth and dry grass.

"A regular person who isn't djinn or Chosen," she said, glad that her voice sounded far steadier than she felt. "So doesn't that mean Los Alamos is the best—maybe the only—place for me?"

He didn't reply right away. Instead, he stood there and watched her for a moment, as if weighing the best thing for him to say next. Another step, and then he was almost upon her. If he'd still been wearing his robes, they would surely have been brushing against her jeans. "I don't want you to go to Los Alamos."

Of course he didn't. And actually, with him that close to her, Madison could feel her body telling her that it didn't want to go to Los Alamos, either. It could have been the flush of her journey here, when she'd jog-walked the whole way, constantly looking over her shoulder, that made her so warm.

Somehow she didn't think so.

And it seemed that Qadim could sense her response as well, because he placed one hand on the wall next to her and leaned in, so close she could feel the heat of his breath on her cheek. Every nerve ending in her body seemed to tingle.

His voice was a low rumble. "Do you really want to go to Los Alamos?"

She swallowed. *God, say something,* she commanded herself, and yet the words wouldn't come. Why did he have to be so physically overwhelming, so overpowering that she couldn't respond like a rational human being? She'd never had a man affect her like this before.

Because she knew she didn't want to go to Los Alamos. The plan that had seemed so clear to her only a few hours ago now sounded like a fool's errand. Why would she want to go to a place where she didn't know anyone when she could stay here in Albuquerque with Qadim?

His voice pressed on her again. "Do you?"

Still the words seemed to stick in her throat. She couldn't say anything, could only stare helplessly up at him.

At her continued silence, a flicker of triumph showed in his dark eyes, and he bent even further, was so close that his mouth nearly touched hers. Forcing her to meet his stare, he said softly, "Do you want me to stop?"

He was going to kiss her. She knew that was what he had planned, and yet she also knew she wouldn't do anything to prevent him from doing so. He must have seen the uncertainty in her expression, or else he wouldn't have challenged her to see if she truly would ask him to stop.

But she wouldn't. She couldn't. Maybe that was crazy, but the world hadn't been sane for a very long time.

A corner of his mouth twitched. Was that the beginning of a smile? Madison couldn't tell, because in the next instant that mouth was pressed against hers, his lips hard and strong and insistent, and she couldn't do anything except open her mouth to his, feel his tongue touch hers as need exploded all through her body. His arms went around her—or maybe hers went around him—and in the next instant she was all but grinding herself against him, wanting to feel every inch of his hard, magnificent body clasped against hers.

She was drowning, disappearing into him. The whole world had become the feel of his arms around her and the taste of his mouth and the warm scent of his skin. But it was all right if she fell, because she knew he would hold her up.

Her legs were shaky, and dimly she could tell her shoulder had begun to throb again, but none of that mattered. All that mattered was that Qadim was kissing her, and all of her worries and concerns had melted away as if they'd never been. How could it be wrong when no other kiss had ever felt this right?

At last he did break the kiss, but gently, and he still held her close. "You didn't tell me to stop."

"No." She attempted to chuckle, but it came out sounding shaky and something close to a sob, and so she went on quickly, "I decided I didn't want to."

"Ah." He touched her shoulder, his palm warm through the thin fabric of her T-shirt. "Did I hurt you?"

She shook her head. "It's a little sore, but it's all right."

With a gentleness that surprised her, he bent and laid his lips against her shoulder. "I'll try to remember to be careful." He straightened, and when he met her gaze, it was with a new glint in his eyes. "Although it seems you've healed far more quickly than you let on."

"I—I'm sorry about that."

"I will forgive you this time. But don't lie to me again, Madison."

His mouth was almost smiling, but the stern tone of his voice told her that she'd upset him. She went and leaned her head against his shoulder. "I won't. It was cruel of me. I was just—I guess I just didn't know what

I should do. This thing—this attraction—it scared me. I had to reconcile what I knew of the djinn with the little I knew about you, and I guess none of it made sense."

"I fear I can't fault you for that too much." His hand moved over her hair, and something about the gentleness of the gesture made her want to weep. Maybe it was only that she'd gone so very long without the comfort of another person's touch, or the sound of their voice. "But now perhaps you can show me more of this astonishing home of yours, and how you ever came to be here."

She led him out of the storeroom, explaining as they went that the home above them and the shelter where she'd been living for the past year had belonged to the man her father worked for, a man who apparently thought of Madison and her family as his own, since he was alone in the world. This man had worked with weapons, had known of the dangers that lurked in the human world, and so he had built this structure, a project that had taken him many years.

"Of course, I don't think he really had djinn in mind when he designed it," Madison said, then led Qadim into the family room. Her gaze fell on the sketchbook, and she quickly lifted it from the coffee table and shut it.

"I fear I already saw that," Qadim told her, amused by the flush of embarrassment in her fair skin.

"Oh." She put the sketchbook back down. "I suppose it's just that it had been so long since I'd seen anyone that I wanted to commit you to memory. It was just a quick little doodle."

"I'd say it was far more than a doodle. You are a very talented artist, Madison."

A lift of her shoulders. Clearly, she was just as discomfited by compliments on her art as she was by praise for her appearance.

"And I would have known that," he continued, "if I had but thought to ask. I apologize for that."

"'Apologize'?" she repeated, looking surprised. "Why would you apologize for not asking me about what I did for a living? That was all in the past."

"Perhaps," he said, then reached out a hand. She took it, and let him pull her down to sit next to him on the sofa. There, that was better. For they did need to talk. The tour of the shelter could wait a little while. "Although I might say that if you worked at something you did not love, then it would be in the past. But the painting I saw on the easel in one of the other rooms seems to tell me differently."

"Oh, well." Her shoulders lifted, and he noted the way her mouth tightened, as if the movement had pained her. So yes, she was doing much, much better, but she was not all the way back to normal yet. He would have to remember that, and perhaps be gentler than the fire currently surging in his veins wished him to be. "I had to do something to fill up the time." Then she straightened, and her chin went up slightly. "But you're right. I do love to paint. That's mine, too." She nodded toward a piece on the opposite wall, done in heavy brushstrokes in shades of purple and gray and deep earth tones.

"It is quite exceptional," he said honestly. In all truth, he had never been one to study art, as human artistic expression was something his sister had been rather obsessed with. The djinn had artisans, but not artists. Some had postulated that there was something about the limited lives of humans which made them strive for the ineffable, to reach for something they could never have, whereas the djinn were content to create pieces that were beautiful and functional, and nothing more than that.

"You're going to give me a swelled head if you keep saying things like that."

"'Swelled head'?"

Madison chuckled. "Modern American idiom. All it means is you're going to puff up my vanity."

"I'm not sure vanity is involved when the person in question is truly gifted."

"There you go again."

The only proper response was to pull her to him and kiss her again. Her mouth opened to his right away, eager and warm and tasting better than anything he could have ever imagined. He had dreamed of what it would be like to hold her in his arms, but the reality was so much better than his dreams.

And what he wanted even more was to push her down into the sofa cushions and claim all of her, taste all of her—and yet he knew she was not quite ready for that. Soon, he thought, but for now he would have to content himself with the sweetness of her lips.

When they parted, her breaths came quickly, and once again her cheeks were flushed. "So are all djinn such good kissers, or is that just a particular talent of yours?"

"As to that," he replied, attempting to sound casual, "you would have to ask some of the Chosen for their opinions on their lovers' kisses. Although some of them might be biased, if they were influenced by djinn glamour in order to be more...pliable."

"Djinn glamour?" Madison asked, a frown creasing the smooth skin of her forehead. She didn't exactly pull away, but Qadim could sense a stiffening of her posture that hadn't been there a few seconds earlier.

He probably should not have said anything. But he had told Madison there would be no more lies between them, and that promise should apply to him as well. At any rate, in this particular matter, he had nothing to hide. "The djinn possess the ability to make humans susceptible to their charms, for lack of a better term.

A human will think that she—or he—is madly in love with the djinn, and will become intimate with them. This is where your legends of the incubus and the succubus arose. But those were not demons who had laid down with humans, but djinn who found it amusing to trick mortals into becoming intimate with them."

Some of the color left her cheeks, but she appeared calm enough as she asked, "So it was like mind control?"

"A crude way of putting it, but something like that, yes."

A dawning fear showed in her eyes, and this time she did draw away from him. "Did you—did you do that to me just now?"

"No," he said at once, although she didn't look particularly reassured by his adamant response. "To be honest, I considered it early on, but then I realized that I did not want a counterfeit of desire. I wanted you to want me because that was your wish, and not something I imposed on you."

"But—"

He leaned toward her and pressed the softest of kisses against her cheek. Her eyes shut, dark russet lashes startling against her pale skin, but Qadim could not tell for sure whether that was because she enjoyed the caress...or because she didn't want to look at him in that moment.

"Dearest, I am telling you the truth because that is nothing more than you deserve. You fled from me, but I could see that you were conflicted. But if you had tried to stop me back there"—he inclined his head in the direction of the storeroom—"then I would have stopped. It would have pained me greatly, but I have never been the sort of man to force a woman. I had no need to."

"Popular with the ladies?" she teased, although he could see the flicker of disappointment in her eyes.

"Again, I will not lie to you. We djinn live long lives, and I have spent time with a number of women. But you are the only person in my life right now."

Madison was silent, and Qadim feared she might ask him for an exact number of his former lovers. Women could be odd about such things. He hoped she would not ask the question, for truly he had lost count centuries ago.

"How long?" she said then.

"'How long'?" he repeated, not sure what she was asking.

"How long do you live?"

"Many of your lifetimes."

Again she went quiet. He wanted to reach over and touch her, give her some sort of reassurance, but he sensed now was not the time. This was all new to her, and she needed to absorb the information in her own way.

And what if she asks why you have not made her your Chosen, if you desire her so much? he thought then. He had no real answer for that. For he did desire her, but he had never found any woman so entrancing that he could stomach the thought of spending eternity with her. One of his former lovers had remarked acidly that just because his own sister was such a calculating harpy, he should not think all women were the same. Perhaps Reveka had been right, but it was not a risk he'd ever wished to take.

"And is it rude to ask how old a djinn is?"

"Not rude, precisely," he replied. "But sometimes it is a question we cannot answer, for as the centuries flash by, it becomes more and more difficult to keep track. But I think I can safely say that I am some years older than you."

She didn't smile. "And you don't think it's strange to be attracted to someone who might as well be a child to a djinn?"

"Oh, you are most certainly not a child." Her expression remained solemn, and so he did reach out to take her hands in his. "Humans and djinn are different, true, but I know you are an adult woman, capable of making your own decisions. And capable of many other things, I would hope."

This time the corners of her mouth did twitch faintly. "Oh, I'm capable." Her fingers tightened on his. "I suppose I'm just trying to figure out how this would even work."

"Why make it so difficult for yourself?" he asked. He used their interlaced fingers to pull her nearer to him. "I want you...and it seems that you want me... and so I don't see what the trouble is." Because they were so close, it was easy enough to place his mouth on hers again, to kiss her and feel once again the way she responded to him.

When they pulled apart, her breathing had sped up, and a warm flush had spread over her cheekbones. "Well, when you put it that way—"

"I do."

"Okay." To his disappointment, she let go of his hands and rose from the couch. "Let me show you the rest of the place."

Because he could tell she needed to put some distance between them, he didn't argue, but got up so he could follow her out into the corridor and down to the other rooms. He had already seen the family room— which also served as a sort of media space, where she would watch the television or listen to music—but there was also a dining chamber with a long table that could seat as many as eight or ten people, several other bedrooms, bath chambers and rooms that seemed to function only as storage areas.

"I want to know how you got through all those airlocks," Madison said as she led him out of the main living area and into the hallway where he'd first entered the shelter.

"Airlocks?"

"These," she replied, and pointed toward one of the heavy metal doors with the strange round handles.

"Ah. So how is an airlock different from a door?"

"These were made to seal against all kinds of chemical, biological, and nuclear contaminants. Of course, even they probably weren't much protection against the Heat."

"Was...anyone down in the shelter when the sickness struck?" Qadim generally did not consider himself squeamish, but he didn't much like the thought of Madison living down here while trapped with the remains of one of her associates.

"Oh, no," she said at once, repressing an obvious shudder. "My—my father passed away in his own house a ways from here, and I honestly don't know what happened to Clay, the man who built this shelter. There was no sign of the dust in his home. I think he must have been at the labs when it happened." She stopped there, her expression sad and faraway, and Qadim found himself wishing he had not asked the question. "Anyway," she went on, in a brisk tone that he didn't quite believe, "you didn't answer me about how you were able to open those doors."

"I am an earth elemental," he said. "Metal comes from the earth, and so it obeys my command. All I had to do was tell the doors to open for me, and they did."

"Well, damn. If I'd known you were able to do that, I would have—" Madison broke off there and shook her head.

"You would have what?"

She offered him a rueful smile. "I probably wouldn't have run in the first place. No place to go."

"It was not my desire to make you feel trapped."

"I don't. I'm not." This time she went to him and wrapped her arms around her waist, then laid her head against his chest. At once he put his arms around her as well, breathing in the sweet scent of her hair and reveling in the sensation of her breasts pressed to his stomach. In fact, he could feel himself stiffening, and he willed the arousal away. This was not the time. She continued, "You gave me the choice. I could have said no. But then I realized I really didn't want to say no. I wanted this."

How could he debate the subject with her any further? As she'd just told him, she wanted this. She'd had to fight to acknowledge that truth within herself, but it seemed she had abandoned that fight...at least for now.

Madison pulled away and looked up at him. "Let me make you dinner to apologize for running off like an idiot."

"You are not an idiot." He arched an eyebrow at her. "Besides, I seem to recall you telling me that you hate cooking."

"I do," she said frankly. "I figured that would be my form of groveling."

"I don't need you to grovel." She appeared unconvinced, so he wrapped an arm around her waist and pulled her toward him. "Why don't we both make it together? Perhaps that way you'll decide you don't hate cooking quite so much."

"Sounds like a plan." Then she shot him a quizzical look. "Here, or at the hotel?"

"The kitchen there is much bigger."

"True. Can I pack a few things to bring with me?"

Qadim thought he liked the sound of that very much. If she wanted to bring some of her belongings with her back to the Hotel Andaluz, then that must mean she planned to be with him for some time.

For how long, he didn't know. But he figured he'd let the universe decide what to do about that.

CHAPTER TEN

Qadim didn't comment when she put her things in the same room where she'd been staying previously. Oh, they both knew where this was going to end up—with her in his bed—but she didn't see any reason to force the issue. It could be tonight, or two days from now. No, scratch that. Madison knew she didn't have the willpower to last that long, not after the way they'd kissed. She'd felt his arousal as he held her, and she could tell Qadim didn't want to wait much longer, either.

But they should be able to hold out until after dinner. Maybe.

She went to join him in the kitchen after she'd hung up the clothes she'd brought and put the extra toiletries in the bathroom. He had a cookbook propped up on a stand and was reading it with the sort of intensity that usually was reserved for people trying to follow a bomb-defusing diagram.

"Everything all right?" she asked, then went on her tiptoes so she could kiss his cheek. Back in the day she would have said she didn't care much for beards, but something about the feel of his short, crisp hair against her lips sent a little shiver through her. And at least it was a short, neatly trimmed beard. She couldn't stand those bristly faux-lumberjack things guys had started sporting the last few years.

Well, she could say one good thing about the Heat. At least it had gotten rid of the hipsters.

"It is fine," Qadim replied, still glaring down at the cookbook. "I wanted to give you a New Mexico meal, but this may be more involved than I thought."

"You don't have to," Madison told him. "I'm fine with some steaks and baked potatoes. Something easy. Anyway, I'm supposed to be helping you, remember?"

"No, I would like to try this cuisine," he replied. "And I did not really expect you to assist me, except to help clarify a few things. But I will admit that trying to analyze these recipes is somewhat like learning a new language."

"Well, your English is excellent. So I'm sure you can manage this without a problem."

"Hmm."

But despite his apparent concern, once he got to work, Qadim seemed far more on top of the situation than Madison knew she would have been if she'd attempted to prepare the same foods. Before she could even blink, he had red chile sauce simmering on the stove and was flame-broiling some chicken for the enchilada filling. Then back over to the counter to chop up summer squash and onions for calabacitas, the side dish Madison had been craving for months, since she didn't have the fixings at the shelter to make anything remotely similar. There had been frozen vegetables in the kitchen at the shelter, but not squash. And then Qadim began working on the rice, and the black beans, which he must have used some djinn magic to coax along, because otherwise they should have been soaking for hours before they ever went into the pot.

The combination of those wonderful smells made her mouth begin to water. Clay had made sure the shelter was stocked with food items that were nourishing and which could also last a long while, but he hadn't been worried about preserving his home state's cuisine. Madison hadn't breathed in the wonderful aroma of warm red chile sauce for over a year, and likewise the more delicate scent of the green rice that Qadim had just begun to toss together, with its coating of cilantro and parsley and peppers.

And sopapillas, and flan for dessert—

"How on earth do you think I'm going to be able to eat all this?" she asked as Qadim began assembling the enchiladas.

"You must have worked up something of an appetite when you ran all the way back to the shelter," he said slyly, and she gave him a sour look.

"Not as much as you might think," she replied. "Are we eating here, or on the roof?"

"It is too cold for the roof today, I think. I have a table prepared for us out in the dining room."

Madison nodded. A sudden thought came to her, and she asked, "How long before it's all ready?"

"Perhaps ten minutes. Why?"

"Oh, just something. Do you mind if I go upstairs for a little bit?"

He looked slightly puzzled, but only said, "No, of course not."

She kissed him on the cheek again and headed for the stairwell. One thing was for sure—between climbing all these stairs and that hasty trip she'd made to the shelter earlier in the day, she wouldn't have to worry about how many calories she might consume during the extravagant dinner Qadim was making.

Because he'd gone to so much effort, Madison wanted to go to some effort, too.

She hadn't brought any "nice" clothes with her to the shelter, since she hadn't thought the world she was headed into would require heels or dresses. But she had taken a few pieces of jewelry, and Qadim had already provided something more beautiful than any dress she'd worn in her previous life.

The blush-colored outfit was still hanging in the closet where she'd left it, and so she stripped out of her jeans and T-shirt, and pulled on the silky garments. They slid, smooth and sensual, over her skin, making her wonder what it would feel like to have Qadim remove them, to have those big, strong hands of his move over her body, reach down to cup her breasts....

She bit her lip as the warmth of arousal awoke between her legs. This was crazy, getting herself so worked up. But God, it had been a long time.

And she'd never been with anyone like Qadim. True, he was a djinn, and so that made him beyond the pale right there, but there was more to his differences than merely his otherworldly heritage. She'd always been drawn to people who were unusual-looking rather than conventionally attractive—Jacob had always seemed to her like the love child of Adrian Brody and Ichabod Crane—and while Qadim could also be said to be more interesting in appearance than truly handsome, there was something about him that evoked a bad-boy biker vibe. Maybe it was the hair, or maybe it was the beard.

She could only imagine what her straitlaced father's reaction would have been back in the day if she'd brought home someone who looked like Qadim. Pure horror, probably.

The thought sent a little pang of sadness through her. Tom Reynolds would never get to meet Qadim al-Syan, for good or ill. Most of the time Madison had managed to ignore the enormity of her loss—of the world's loss—but every once in a while it sneaked up from behind her and brought everything rushing back.

Don't think about that, she told herself. *Your lovely djinn is down there making a meal fit for a king, so don't screw it up by getting all maudlin.*

She took a breath, then went into the bathroom to complete the sprucing-up process. Among the items she'd brought with her was the wide-toothed comb that helped to keep her hair from looking like a bramble bush. A few cosmetics—blush and mascara and her favorite rosy-colored lip tint. She put on the makeup, but sparingly, just enough to wake up her complexion and make her look a bit more polished.

And then finally the silver filigree dangling earrings that had once belonged to her mother, and the antique locket that had come down from much farther back—it had been her paternal great-grandmother's, bought in New York for her by her fiancé. The locket was engraved white gold set with tiny single-cut diamonds and rubies, and it was Madison's most treasured possession, especially because of what was inside: a tiny reproduction of her parents' wedding picture, the two of them looking young and happy, Sarah Reynolds with the same curly hair as her daughter, although it had been light brown instead of pale red. The red hair had come from Madison's father.

She closed the locket and hung it around her neck, then gave her appearance one last quick inspection. Yes, she looked far better than she had when she'd woken up this morning, and even better than last night, since then she didn't have the makeup to help things along.

Would Qadim like it?

Back down the stairs, and then on into the restaurant, where she could smell all the various aromas of the New Mexican feast he'd prepared for her drifting on the air. The table he'd set up was off in one corner, intimate and safe; candles flickered all around.

Qadim was just setting down the bowl with the calabacitas in it as she approached. The light in his eyes as he took in her outfit and her overall appearance told her everything she needed to know.

"You are a glorious creature, you know that?" he asked, then went to her so he could take her hands in his and pull her close.

"No, I didn't know that," she replied. "But if that's what you think, I'm okay with it."

"It's not just what I think. It's the truth." He kissed her, but softly, as if he was also aware of how close to the edge they both were, how they needed to be careful for the moment. Then he pulled away and cast a rueful glance down at himself, at the stained T-shirt and jeans he wore. "I fear I am not quite as splendid as you. But I can remedy a small portion of that lack." A wave of his hand, and the shabby clothing was gone, replaced by the open djinn robe and billowy pants, these in a deep steel gray bordered in black.

Madison swallowed. Sure, Qadim looked amazing in jeans and a T-shirt—how could he not, with those fabulous arms of his—but there was something about the djinn garb that made him smolderingly hot. Of course, a lot of that could have something to do with the way the robe bared his broad chest and showed off the hard muscles of his stomach.

Suddenly, that warm, throbbing sensation was back between her legs.

"Dinner looks amazing," she said quickly, hoping that if she focused on the here and now, she could force her body to behave itself.

"Thank you. I suppose we should see if it tastes as good as it looks."

He pulled out a chair for her, and she sat down, again wondering if that was a human custom he'd borrowed, or whether djinn men always showed that same courtesy toward their women. Because he spoke English so well, and did seem to understand something of modern American culture, it was sometimes difficult for Madison to know for sure.

After she was settled, he seated himself in the chair to her left. A bottle of wine sat on the table, already opened. So it could air, she supposed. Qadim lifted the bottle and poured some of the dark wine within into her glass, then filled his halfway as well.

"This is one thing we djinn and humans have in common," he said as he raised his glass. "For we also make some kind of pledge when first we drink, if there is something we wish to celebrate."

"And is there?" Madison asked, although she thought she knew how he would answer.

His gaze lingered on her lips, and she felt blood rise to her cheeks. Would she ever stop reacting to him like this? It was as if, once she'd acknowledged to herself that she wanted him, her body wouldn't stop reminding her that it needed more than merely shared glances and a few kisses.

"Oh, I think so," he replied.

Trying not to look away from him, she lifted her glass so they could clink the two of them together.

"To...explorations," he said as their wine glasses just barely kissed.

Oh, dear God. She knew she wanted to explore every inch of his perfect body. "To explorations," she echoed, then drank quickly in an attempt to ignore the tide of heat that had begun to wash through her. At this rate, she was never going to make it through dinner.

The wine was good. A local vintage, she noticed as she read the label, from Casa Rondeña Winery. Had Qadim found it in the hotel's cellars, or had he done more exploring around Albuquerque than she'd thought? Casa Rondeña was located at the north end of town, up in Rio Rancho, actually, and so while it was within the borders of the djinn's "grant," it was still a good ways from the hotel and the center of town.

Qadim seemed impressed, too, because he nodded and took another sip from his glass before he set it down and turned his attention to the various dishes and serving bowls on the tabletop. "If I may?" he asked, then gestured toward Madison's empty plate.

"Thank you," she responded, handing it to him so he could load it up with enchiladas and rice and beans and calabacitas. The finishing touch was a sopapilla placed carefully between the rice and the calabacitas so it wouldn't get too soggy. He'd even set out a bottle of honey on the table so the sopapilla could be eaten in the traditional way.

Clearly, djinn were fast learners, or Qadim was some sort of savant when it came to all things kitchen-oriented.

She waited while he filled his own plate, then took another sip of wine before plowing into the enchilada. Maybe it was only that she had sex on the brain, but that combination of blue corn tortillas and grilled chicken and cheese and red chile was positively orgasmic.

"This is insanely good," she told Qadim once she'd finished chewing.

An almost boyish look of pleasure passed over his face. "It is?"

"God, yes. If the world were a different place, I'd be telling you to open a restaurant."

His smile faded slightly. "Unfortunately, the world is as it is. But at least I have you here with me."

He was so oddly romantic. Madison had seen that quality in him the previous evening, when he'd turned the rooftop bar into a veritable fairyland. She'd never been with someone like that before; Jacob had been smart and funny and sensitive in his way, but he'd never think to swag a roof with filmy fabric, or place candles on every available flat surface. Qadim, on the other hand, seemed to pay attention to those small details, to all the elements that went into making an evening memorable.

"I'm glad I'm here with you," she said softly, and the djinn's dark, dark eyes took on a warm glow.

"No more running?"

"No. Well, not unless it's toward you."

He set down his fork and reached under the table so he could lay his hand briefly on her leg. Not suggestively—he touched her down near her knee, no higher than that—and yet the sensation of his fingers against the thin fabric sent that fluttering heat all through her body once more. If he could do that to her with just the smallest of gestures....

Taking a sip of wine seemed to be the safest thing to do. The deep, dark liquid flowed down her throat, but all it did was wake an answering warmth in her stomach. At this rate, she'd never make it all the way through dinner.

Qadim withdrew his hand and went back to eating as if nothing untoward had happened. That seemed like a good idea, so for a few moments they ate in silence as Madison sampled the green rice and the black beans and the calabacitas, all of which were just as amazing as the enchilada. Focusing on the food did help to quench some of the unwelcome heat the djinn's touch had awakened, although Madison knew the meal was only a stopgap, and that eventually one of them would do or say something to awaken the inferno.

Better to bring up a topic that had nothing to do with either of them. Qadim shouldn't be too annoyed by her asking about Los Alamos, since she'd flat out told him a few hours earlier that she would never go there. After washing down some more enchilada with another sip of wine, she said, "You mentioned that someone had created a djinn-repelling device. Was he one of the scientists from Los Alamos, or was he another refugee who ended up there?"

That question elicited a lift of the eyebrow, but to her relief, Madison couldn't see any real annoyance in Qadim's expression. More like resignation, as if he'd expected her to ask about Los Alamos again even though she'd sworn she had no interest in going there.

"I'm just curious," she added, and he let out a breath.

"I believe he was one of the scientists at the laboratory there. But I don't know much more than that."

"But you were close enough to feel the effects of the device?"

"He built several. One of them ended up in Santa Fe, in the possession of a woman called Julia Innes."

Something in the way he said her name made warning bells go off in Madison's mind. There had been just a small pause, accompanied by a certain softening of Qadim's expression.

"Who was she?" *God, I hope that didn't sound too desperate....*

"One of the survivors from Los Alamos. She was in charge there for a while, but now she is Zahrias al-Harith's Chosen and lives with him in Santa Fe.

Madison had to take a few seconds to process that statement. From the way Qadim had spoken before, he'd made it sound as if the djinn had been with their Chosen almost since the Heat wiped out most of the population. But this last revelation seemed to indicate that this Julia had become Zahrias'—whoever he was—Chosen fairly recently.

Which meant...what? That even if you'd been skipped over in the beginning, there might be some hope for you if you met the right djinn?

She didn't want to acknowledge the hope that blossomed in her at the thought. That seemed to be pushing things way too soon. A few days spent together and a few exchanged kisses were really not enough basis for planning an eternity together. According to Qadim, that was what being Chosen meant—that you'd spend the rest of an unending life with that one djinn, in exchange for which you'd be given everlasting youth and health.

On the surface, that sounded like a pretty good deal. But what if you decided after you'd spent some time with your djinn that he snored or hogged the covers or didn't laugh at your jokes, or any of the hundred niggling little things that might not seem like such a big deal at the beginning of a relationship but which would be magnified a thousandfold if you had to tolerate them for all eternity? Then it wouldn't be such a great deal, would it?

She stole a quick glance at Qadim, who was calmly breaking off a piece of sopapilla and then putting honey on top. His expression was almost blank, so she couldn't read much from his face. Did he even realize that he'd just dropped a bombshell on her?

Apparently not.

Time to leave that little matter aside for now. Maybe at some point she'd get the nerve to ask more questions, but in the meantime Madison thought it was probably better to focus on something else. "So who's in charge in Los Alamos now?"

"I have no idea." Qadim set down his half-eaten sopapilla and sent her a quizzical look. "Madison, I don't wish to force the issue, but I believe you told me earlier that you had no interest in Los Alamos."

"No interest in going to live there." Which was true enough, so she gave him what she hoped was a reassuring smile before she continued, "I suppose I'm just curious about a place where people have managed to survive—humans, I mean, and not djinn or Chosen. How many of them are there?"

"Again, I have no idea. Several hundred?" He shrugged and broke off another piece of sopapilla, but he didn't eat it. "Possibly a thousand? They were mainly refugees from here in Albuquerque and from Santa Fe, perhaps some from the towns to the north of there. It would have been difficult to travel farther than that without running afoul of the djinn who were hunting them."

A shudder went through her, and Madison took another swallow of wine. Yes, she could see how that would have been hard. Downright impossible, really. She had to applaud anyone who'd been able to make it to the sanctuary of that mountain town. "The refugees here must have had someone pretty skilled leading them for them to get all that way without being caught."

Qadim's mouth twisted. "I suppose you could say he was skilled. He was also a rapist and a murderer."

Madison's fingers tightened on the stem of her wine glass. Not sure she'd heard him correctly, she asked, "Excuse me?"

"Richard Margolis, the man who took the refugees from here in Albuquerque up to Los Alamos. Let us just say that the apocalypse did not agree with him."

"How did you even know him, if he was based in Los Alamos?"

"A long story. For a time, I found him useful, or rather, he managed to accomplish a few tasks that were set before him. After that, though, he proved to be too dangerous, and had to be disposed of."

Had Qadim just said what she thought he'd said? Madison wasn't sure whether she should sip some wine to steady her nerves, or whether the alcohol might curdle in her suddenly knotted stomach. "'Disposed of'?"

For a long moment, Qadim said nothing. He set the remnants of the sopapilla he held down on his plate, then picked up his own glass of wine so he could take a long drink. At last he spoke. "He was dangerous. So I killed him."

Cold washed over her. She could only sit there, staring at Qadim as he calmly swallowed some more wine, as if he hadn't just told her that he'd once murdered a human being. Or did the djinn even think of it as murder? Maybe to them, killing an annoying human was no different from swatting a fly.

No, she couldn't believe that. She was human, and Qadim had held her, kissed her, told her she was beautiful. He'd brought her here and tended to her dislocated shoulder. How could anyone do all those things and still look on a human being as no better than an insect?

"We said there would be no more lies between us," he went on. His voice was quiet but firm. He obviously could tell that he had shocked her, but it seemed he wouldn't attempt to deny what he'd done. "Captain Margolis might have been a good man before the Dying changed his world, but somehow I doubt it. At any rate, he was responsible for the death of innocents, and for assaulting a woman. His is not a death that should be mourned."

The world had changed. Madison knew that. There were no more courts and judges and lawyers, no orderly processes for dealing with someone who crossed over the line. But to know that Qadim had killed someone, even if he thought he was carrying out his own form of frontier justice....

"What about the djinn who are murderers?" she asked then, and Qadim tensed.

"What do you mean?"

"There are djinn who are responsible for killing millions—no, *billions* of innocent people. Will they ever face any kind of justice?"

"That is different."

"Different how?"

"Madison—"

She couldn't look at him directly. She wasn't sure if that was because she couldn't bear to see him, now that he'd revealed he had blood on his hands, or because she was afraid if she met his eyes, she'd soften, find some way to rationalize what he'd done.

In the next instant, he had set down his wine glass and was kneeling on the carpeted floor next to her. His hands went to hers, and he tugged on them so she had no choice but to shift on her chair so she was more or less facing him.

"My dear," he said, his tone quiet but intense. The impulse she'd had to pull her fingers from his grasp died suddenly. His dark eyes were latched on hers, imploring. "I have already told you that I had no part in unleashing that vile disease. Neither did I participate in the hunt for survivors that took place after the Heat had done its work. What I did to Margolis—it was necessary, like putting down a mad dog. Would you have thought it better if he lived to continue violating women, or killing those who had done nothing wrong, save to oppose him?"

Those words made sense. Too much sense, really. "No," she said at last. "I understand why you did what you did. I just wish the djinn I watched massacre people in the streets of Albuquerque could face their own justice."

Qadim rose to his feet, bringing her with him. Suddenly, his arms were around her, and she felt his warm, heavy hand stroking her hair. "I know," he murmured. "I know. There are others who feel the same way. But we are in the minority, I fear. All I can do is make sure that you are safe. And I will."

There was such a fierceness to his tone that she had to look up at him. His mouth was set, almost angry, but she could also see the glow in his eyes as he stared down at her. That glow awakened the heat in her body, and her mouth parted.

That was all the invitation he apparently needed. Before she could even pull in another breath, his lips had caught hers, and they were locked together, their kiss almost despairing, as if they both understood that they needed this connection to make any sense of their world.

Then his arms were around her, and he was lifting her as if she weighed nothing, sweeping her off the floor just before the restaurant disappeared around them. Less than the blink of an eye, and he was laying her down on a large bed in a room she'd never seen before but knew must be the penthouse suite Qadim had been occupying. In one corner, a kiva-style fireplace flickered with light, logs burning happily away in the hearth.

But that was the only impression she was able to get, because then Qadim's mouth fastened on hers again, his hands moving over her body. She had it easier than he did, because his open robe allowed her to reach beneath it to touch his bare flesh, to feel those hard muscles under her fingertips.

Something else was hard, too. His arousal was plain enough through the lightweight trousers he wore. She moved one hand downward to touch him, and he let out a hissing gasp of breath, right before he grasped the neckline of the fitted tunic she wore and tore it away.

Madison made a sound of protest—not because she wanted him to stop, but because she hated to see something so lovely ruined.

"Don't worry," he whispered in her ear. "I can get you another one just like it. But it was in the way."

And he bent so he could brush his lips over her breast, take her nipple into his mouth. Any further objections faded away at once, and she reached up to wrap her arms around the back of his neck, to hold him close. The heat between her legs flared again, pulsing with need.

Had he sensed it? She couldn't know for sure, but a second later his fingers caught at the drawstring for her pants and yanked it loose, then grabbed her underwear and the trousers at the same time and pulled them down. Now she was completely naked in front of him, but she didn't care. All she wanted was for him to be as revealed to her as she was to him.

She grasped his robe and drew it off, tossing it to land on one of the suite's side chairs. His pants also had a drawstring, and she pulled it so they came free. Getting them off him was more difficult, since she had to ease them down past his erection. And God, he was huge. Yes, he was a big man, more than six and a half feet tall, but....

Qadim didn't give her a chance to inspect his proportions any more closely, because he moved from suckling her breast to kissing his way down her stomach, moving lower and lower.

He wasn't...?

Oh, yes, he was. She gasped, then moaned as his tongue touched her, as he explored her with his mouth. Yes, of course she'd done this before, but this was the first time when it felt as if a man was actually making love to her with his tongue, rather than performing an act he knew he must do in order to be fair to his partner. Qadim wasn't being fair...he was just hungry.

And God, the sensation of his long hair falling against her, brushing the sensitive flesh at the inside of her thighs. Already the orgasm was building, warm pulses of pleasure throbbing in her very core. She wasn't sure why she should be surprised by that; it had been a very long time.

Then the climax burst through her, and she cried out, hoarse animal sounds that might have embarrassed her once, except she knew Qadim didn't care, that he reveled in the way he'd made her feel, because he didn't stop right away, kept caressing her with his tongue until another, smaller tremor went through her. And then he was kissing her belly again, moving up to her breast, his mouth closing on her once again. She sighed, eyes shutting as the afterglow swept over her. But no, she wanted her eyes open. She wanted to see him.

He was there, his dark, hungry gaze fixed on her face, staring at her as if he'd never seen her before.

"I want," she began, her voice a hoarse whisper.

"What do you want, darling?"

"I want you in me."

A low growl escaped his throat, and then he gave her a slow, lascivious smile. "If you wish."

He was pressed against her. She reached down and took him in her hand, feeling the heavy heat of his shaft, the way her fingers couldn't even close around him. Maybe at some other time she would have worried about taking him into her, but she knew right then that it didn't matter, that everything would be just fine.

A slight shift in their positions, and then he was pushing in, filling her. She gasped again, reveling in the sensation of him going ever deeper, joining their bodies with an inevitability that made her almost want to weep. Had it ever been this good—the magnificent weight of his body pressed against her, the slow rocking motion that seemed to light up a new set of nerve endings with every thrust?

His hair brushed against her face, smelling of clove and cinnamon. Madison inhaled, wanting to breathe him in, to take him into every pore, every part of her. Their eyes met, and she saw a naked wonder in his. Why? He was no inexperienced boy. He obviously knew what he was doing. And yet—

His movements sped up, and all thought fled. The world became this fire-lit room, the heat of his body against hers, the throbbing need in every cell of her body. She was about to come again.

He must have felt it, too, because he moved with her, his fingers tangled in her hair, his skin warm and damp. And then a convulsive thrust, as she locked her legs around him and drew him in just that much deeper, needing just that much more before another cry forced itself from her throat, all the loneliness and the hurt and the want bursting from her in that moment of climax.

His arms were around her. He held her as she came, as she shuddered and came apart in his embrace. He said her name, the deep rumble of his voice bringing her back to herself.

"Madison."

She clung to him, wanting to remain locked together like this forever. Because once she let go, she'd have to face what she'd just done.

He was a djinn. What that meant, she still didn't know.

CHAPTER ELEVEN

THEY LAY THERE FOR A LONG WHILE. AT LAST, though, Madison murmured, "I need to get cleaned up," and slipped off the bed, then went into the bathroom and shut the door.

Qadim watched her go, and made no protest. He sensed that she needed some time to be alone with her thoughts. Indeed, he thought he could use some time himself.

He rolled over onto his back and stared up at the ceiling, bathed in the flickering light from the fire in the hearth. It had not been so very long for him—his last liaison had been a few months ago, over the summer— and yet it seemed to him in that moment that he'd been waiting years, or decades...or centuries...for a woman who could satisfy him the way being with Madison had.

Perhaps it was merely that she was a mortal, and not djinn. In appearance, the two races were not so very different, but her reactions, the sweet taste of her—those were all Madison, and Madison alone. Djinn women tended to be accomplished lovers, true. How could they not be, with so many years of practice? But they had none of Madison's fire, her pure need.

She came out of the bathroom then, face glowing and slightly damp. It appeared she'd splashed some water on her skin. But she hadn't taken the robe that hung from the hook on the door, and neither had she wrapped a towel around herself. She strode toward the bed, proudly naked, and a wave of arousal washed over him, hot and hungry and needful. It didn't matter that they'd climaxed together less than a quarter-hour before. He wanted her all over again.

"Come here," he growled, and a slow smile spread over her full lips.

"What, that wasn't enough to satisfy you?"

"Was it enough to satisfy you?"

Her smile widened. "I thought it was, but...."

Without finishing the sentence, she slipped under the covers and pressed her naked body up against his. He didn't know for sure what inner battles she'd fought during those few moments she'd spent in the bathroom, but clearly she did not seem to have any problems with continuing to explore their intimacy.

His hands moved down to cup her breasts, so heavy and full and soft, even though the rest of her body was almost too slender. Before Madison, he would have said he preferred his women more rounded, but he loved every inch of her form, including her long, lean legs and the very subtle curve of her hips.

And that hair. It brushed against him, warm and tantalizing, every fine strand seeming to awaken a new nerve ending. A soft moan sounded low in her throat as he took her nipple into his mouth and suckled, even as he reached down to touch the delicious wetness between her legs. Yes, she was so very ready.

He wanted to see all of her as they joined again. Without giving her any warning, he took her by the slender waist and lifted her so she could settle down on top of him. She gasped, and then her eyes shut in obvious pleasure as he filled her and they began to move together, finding their rhythm once again. Qadim reached up to caress her breasts, and her head tilted backward, those long, luscious curls brushing against his thighs.

By God, it took all his effort to keep himself from climaxing then and there. But he pulled in a breath, knowing that he wanted this to continue for as long as possible, for him to feel her tight and warm around him, to slip his fingers over the sweet buds of her breasts and listen as her moans grew louder and louder. He'd always enjoyed women who were vocal, and clearly

Madison had no problem with letting him know how much she enjoyed his touch.

But her breathing began to accelerate, and he saw a glow of perspiration on her forehead, and he knew it wouldn't be much longer now. Good; he could have held off a little longer, but he wanted that release as well, wanted to spill inside her and listen to her cry out in pleasure.

Which she did as she fell forward, her hair brushing against his face. She gave quick, panting gasps, her entire body trembling around him. Just a second or two later, he let the orgasm rush through him, dark and shuddering and so very, very good.

He put his arms around her and held her while she lay against his chest, her breathing still rapid, her heart pounding against him. Then, very gently, he kissed her on the temple and breathed in the sweet scent that clung to her heavy hair.

At last she pushed herself off him and collapsed on her back. For a long moment, she didn't say anything, only breathed in and out, clearly trying to gather herself. Eventually she rolled over onto her side so she could look at him. Obliging her, he moved as well so they were face to face.

Some kind of worry flickered in her eyes, and he immediately reached out to brush a stray strand of hair away from her lovely, lovely face. "My dear, what is it?"

"Can djinn and humans—I mean, do I have to worry about getting pregnant? It's been a long time since I was last on the pill."

He didn't know precisely what this "pill" was but guessed it must be some kind of contraceptive. Since humans couldn't control their reproductive cycles internally, they had no choice but to resort to external means to prevent pregnancy. "Djinn and humans can reproduce," he began, then continued before that trace of fear in her eyes could flare into anything worse, "but only if they choose to do so."

"If they choose—" She stopped there, gold-flecked green eyes narrowing. "What do you mean?"

"I mean that a djinn has to consciously decide that he or she wants to be fertile for a pregnancy to occur. I certainly would not make such a decision without you agreeing to it, and so these two times we were intimate, I made sure that I would not be fathering any children."

The worry in her face disappeared, to be replaced by a certain amusement. "So you were shooting blanks?"

He wasn't sure if he understood the idiom. "Shooting...what?"

A flash of a grin, and she moved forward so she could kiss him on the cheek. "Just an expression. So I really don't have to worry about getting pregnant, no matter how many times we have sex?"

"No, there is no need to worry." Qadim stopped there, wondering if he should be offended by her very obvious relief. Not that he wanted to have children any time in the near future—he'd certainly avoided fatherhood so far, had ended several relationships because the women involved did wish to begin families—but he didn't know if he quite liked Madison being so overjoyed by the prospect of *not* bearing his children.

"Good." Then she gave a very small shake of her head before reaching out to run a hand over his hair. "That's not an insult, Qadim. I'm sure we'd make very pretty babies together. But things are complicated enough right now that it's probably a good idea to avoid the whole reproduction thing for a while."

He had to agree with that. After all, he had no real plans for any of this to be permanent. Right now everything was new and fresh and wonderful, but in his experience, that state of affairs never lasted. Still, he wanted to enjoy it while he could, and the prospects for doing so seemed infinitely better without bringing the messiness of children and pregnancy into the equation.

"Very sensible," he said then, since she was obviously waiting for a reply. "In the meantime, how about some dessert?"

"Dessert?"

"I made that thing your people referred to as 'flan.' I have never had it before, but the components promised something delicious."

"It is." Madison paused then, an expression of dismay going over her face. "But oh—we left all that lovely food out. We need to go downstairs and pack it all up and put it in the refrigerator."

"No need," he told her, somewhat amused by her concern over wasting the remainder of their dinner. "It has already been packaged and put away. So I suppose in the next day or so I will be able to experience that human custom known as 'eating leftovers.'"

She flashed him another smile and then snuggled closer, laying her head on his chest. For the moment, he was sated, and so he could simply enjoy the feeling of her warm, soft hair against his skin and the exquisite brush of her breasts on his stomach. "That's good. And dessert sounds lovely, but...." She yawned. "Is the flan in the refrigerator, too?"

"It is."

"Then let's save that for tomorrow. I don't want to move."

"You don't have to," he replied softly, because he could tell from a slight shift in her breathing that she was so very close to falling asleep. He wanted her to go to sleep in his arms, wanted to hold her forever like this.

The problem was, nothing lasted forever. Not even for a djinn.

Madison couldn't recall when she'd fallen asleep, but clearly that second round had knocked her out, because she didn't wake up until sunlight was peeking through the gaps in the curtains that hid the tall windows on the other side of the room. Next to her, Qadim seemed to still be sleeping, eyes shut and his chest rising and falling with regular, deep breaths.

So djinn did sleep. She'd wondered about that, wondered if he would just pretend to be asleep so as not to make things seem too strange to her, but clearly the djinn weren't so different from humans in that respect. As for herself, well, it had been a long day, and having a heavy meal and several spectacular rounds of sex just guaranteed that she would pretty much pass out.

It seemed that Qadim wasn't too worried about the time of day, since the clock on the nightstand said it was three twenty-two, and she doubted they'd slept that long. Her mouth felt gummy, though, and she needed to use the bathroom. Moving as quietly as she could, she slipped out from under the covers and went into the bath, then took care of business and stopped to rinse her mouth out. Before leaving the bathroom, she took the robe off the hook behind the door and slipped it on. As she approached the bed, Qadim's eyes flickered open.

"I didn't mean to wake you—" she began, but he only shook his head.

"No, it was time for me to be awake. Usually I'm up before the sun."

"Did I wear you out?"

He shot her a look from under his eyelashes, the kind of glance that sent the blood, pulsing and warm, between her legs. But his tone was mild enough as he replied, "Hardly. Although now that we're both awake, perhaps it would be wise to have some sort of breakfast in order to replenish our...reserves."

"You're probably right." Would she have been up for round three? Her body seemed to be saying yes. Then again, some coffee would be good. And some of Qadim's amazing scrambled eggs. Neither of them was going anywhere, so why not have a leisurely breakfast and see what happened from there?

He watched her as she reclaimed her panties from where they'd been lying discarded on the floor. The lovely blush-colored silk outfit was also on the floor next to the bed, and she couldn't help making a sound of dismay as she lifted it and saw that the tunic appeared to be shredded beyond repair.

"I told you not to worry about that," he said, then pushed himself to an upright position in the bed, although the sheets and duvet covered everything below the waist.

"I know. But it's still sad to see something so beautiful get ruined."

His expression softened. "Bring it here."

Mystified, she leaned across the bed so she could hand the tunic to him. Luckily, the trousers seemed to have survived unscathed, so after Qadim had taken the tunic from her, she bent to retrieve the pants and drape them over a nearby chair.

The djinn moved a hand over the tunic and then shook it out. Madison's eyes widened. The neckline had been ripped, and most of the buttons down the front torn out. Now, however, the garment appeared good as new, with no sign of the damage Qadim had inflicted on it the night before.

"How...?"

He smiled, then extended the tunic toward her. She took it from him with fingers that shook slightly. "We djinn have our elemental powers, the ones that allow us to control earth and air, fire and water. But we also possess other powers, the sorts of things that allow us to keep the electricity going, or the water flowing—or to make sure the leftovers from a dinner make it safely into a refrigerator."

"And to repair clothing, apparently."

"Precisely."

"Well, that's handy." Madison wasn't sure if being flip was exactly the right response, but she needed a few seconds to absorb that information. Clearly, she had a lot to learn about the djinn.

"It can be helpful, true." Qadim pushed aside the bedclothes and got up.

Good lord, but that man had an amazing body. Madison tried her best not to stare at his sculpted backside, at the long, hard muscles of his thighs, but it was difficult. Never in her life had she been this close to a man built like that. But then he bent and retrieved his own discarded clothing, slipping on first the trousers, and then the loose robe.

Show's over, she told herself, fighting back a pang of disappointment. In the past, she'd never been the type to obsess over a man's appearance, but it was awfully hard with Qadim. He was so eminently stare-able.

"Are you ready to go downstairs?" he asked her, and she nodded.

"But can we go down the old-fashioned way?" she replied. "All that blinking in and out can be a little disconcerting."

He smiled. "If you would prefer it, of course."

So they went out of the suite and down the stairs—all nine flights of them. Once or twice, Qadim gave her a sidelong glance, as if to see whether she was still enjoying doing this the "old-fashioned way," but Madison didn't say anything. After all, they were going down, not up. Anyway, she used to hike and run and bike all the time. A few flight of stairs was no big deal.

And with the way Qadim seemed prepared to feed her, she knew she'd better keep herself active or she'd start to spread out like an amoeba.

The restaurant was spotless when they entered, with absolutely no sign of their feast from the night before. Yes, Qadim had said he'd taken care of everything, but somewhere in the back of her mind, she hadn't been completely convinced. However, there wasn't a single crumb left on the tabletop, and when she went to the refrigerator to take a peek, she saw that all the uneaten food really was carefully packaged in plastic containers, ready for the next go-'round.

"You look surprised," Qadim said as she shut the refrigerator door.

"I do?" Madison shrugged. "As I mentioned before, this is all going to take a little getting used to. But it's okay. I'll get it figured out eventually."

In response, he came over and kissed her, proving another important point about djinn—they didn't seem to get morning breath. He tasted warm and just the slightest bit sweet, and she knew if he kept kissing her like this, she was going to make him take her right there on the counter.

His gaze slid over to the shining metal surface, as if he'd somehow read her thoughts. With a quirk at the corner of his mouth, he said, "It does appear to be about the right height."

For a normal-sized human, maybe not. For a six-foot-six specimen like Qadim....

She didn't say anything. She didn't have to. In the next instant, he'd lifted her to the counter and was untying the sash on the robe. His hands closed over her bare breasts, and she shut her eyes in ecstasy. Yes, she'd always been sensitive, but there was something about the djinn's merest touch that made her feel as if he was about to send her over the brink at any second.

Turnabout was fair play, though. She pulled at the drawstring of his trousers, then slid them over his already impressive erection. As if by its own volition, her hand went to grasp him, to move slowly up and down as she felt the silky softness of his skin, a shocking contrast to the iron-hard flesh beneath. He made a growling sound far back in his throat, black lashes sweeping down as he shut his eyes for a moment. Then those dark eyes opened again, and Madison thought she could see a reddish, lustful flame in their depths.

His fingers slipped into her, skillful. She was already wet, but his touch only made her that much wetter, moans coming from her throat as he caressed her. But she didn't forget herself enough to neglect him; her hand still slid up and down his shaft, wanting to bring him to the edge—just not over it.

It wasn't very long before he let out a sigh, then took her hand away. And in the next second, he was grasping her by the hips and pulling her toward him.

He slid into her, and she wrapped her legs around his waist to pull him in further, the angle at which he filled her almost unbearably erotic.

God, I'm letting a djinn fuck me on a kitchen countertop, she thought, but after that she couldn't really focus on anything except the sensation of his cock driving in and out of her, the way he leaned close so his long hair slipped over her shoulders, still covered by the borrowed bathrobe she wore. Underneath her hands, which she had planted flat to keep herself semi-upright, she could feel the cool steel of the counter, such a contrast to the heat of Qadim's body.

This time the orgasm was so intense that she screamed out loud, the sound echoing off the walls. Good thing there wasn't anyone around to hear except Qadim, and, judging by the feral grin he wore, he didn't seem to mind a bit. Just a second or two later, he let loose as well, a groan escaping his lips as he spent himself in her. Then he bent and kissed her breasts, first the left and next the right, all while she was doing her best to remain propped up instead of falling over right where she was.

Very slowly, he drew away, and Madison tried to pull her robe closed—with limited success, since she was sitting on part of it and it really didn't want to budge.

Qadim took mercy on her and lifted her from the counter. "You looked rather stuck."

Well, she supposed she could have jumped down. But that would have jarred a few things loose. As it was.... She went over to where a paper towel dispenser was fastened to the wall and gathered a bunch, then wiped up as best she could before pulling her underwear back on.

Behind her, Qadim said, his tone carefully neutral, "Perhaps it is time for some coffee."

"That's a great idea."

No messing around with a coffee pot this time— in the next instant, he held two white mugs, both of which were filled with some amazing-smelling Italian roast. He extended one to her, and she took it gratefully. At the same time, though, she lifted an eyebrow at his open robe, at the way everything was on display.

"You going to put that away anytime soon?"

"I wasn't sure if you still had need of it."

Madison gave him a jaundiced look, then blew on her coffee. She heard Qadim chuckle, and a faint clink as he put his mug down so he could climb back into his pants.

"Better?" he asked as she turned around.

"I'm not sure 'better' is the right word," she replied. "But definitely less distracting."

He grinned, a flash of white teeth against the darkness of his beard. Then he retrieved his coffee and took a sip while she blew on her coffee a few more times.

"So, what's on the docket for today?" she said. "More xeriscaping?"

"Actually, my plan was to create a spur off your Rio Grande so we might have a creek running past the hotel. I thought it would be pleasant to have water flowing here—and it will help to encourage some of the larger trees."

By now, maybe she should have been more used to the casual way in which he announced that he planned to do seemingly impossible things. "Just like that, huh?"

His expression grew puzzled. "How else would I do it? Yesterday I went and inspected the river due west of here to see if my plan was feasible. There are no real impediments, as far as I can see. It will take even me some time to create the channel, but after that...." He shrugged and drank some more coffee.

"Where do you plan for this water to go, though? That is, I thought most streams and rivers had to empty into another body of water." Since her own coffee seemed cool enough now to drink, she took a sip, then added, "Anyway, I thought you were an earth elemental. Can you really make a new river?"

"I am an earth elemental," he said calmly. "And that will stand me in good stead as I create a new channel for the water to flow through. But I will not be summoning the water, or creating it from nothing. As for where it will go, I thought a pond or small lake over

there would complement the park area I left standing."
He gestured with his free hand in the general direction
of the location where the convention center had once
stood.

"Oh." Madison had to admit to herself that she
didn't know much about rivers and streams, or their
general characteristics, since bodies of water of any size
were something of a rarity in New Mexico. But Qadim
sounded confident in his ability to take on the project, and it did sound as if it would be lovely to have a
stream flowing past. She'd always found the sound of
running water to be soothing, had had one of those
tabletop fountains in her studio so she could listen to
it as she worked. The djinn was watching her, clearly
waiting to see what else she had to say. And she liked
that. She liked that he wanted to hear her input.

"Well," she said. "I guess we'd better have breakfast.
Then we can get to work."

CHAPTER TWELVE

FOR SOME REASON, QADIM HAD NOT EXPECTED Madison to take such an interest in his work. He knew many women of the djinn who would have laughed at him for trying to make an oasis out of such a desert. But Madison didn't think it laughable. She thought it a challenge.

True, she was an artist, and as such probably wanted to surround herself with things of beauty, to create symmetry and grace where there had been none. Back in her jeans and T-shirt, she went with him to the river and watched as he made one last survey before he began the real work.

The earth would obey his command, and so he told it to part, to create a channel approximately four arm's lengths across and about half as deep. At once the sandy soil flowed out of the way, and the waters of the Rio Grande rushed in, following them as they walked ever eastward and the deep furrow in the ground grew longer and longer.

"How does the water not rush past where you're working?" Madison asked.

"Because it knows not to," he said simply.

Her brow puckered at that reply, but she didn't say anything. After only a few days together, she'd already begun to understand that some elements of djinn magic were almost impossible to explain. They simply *were*.

The two of them walked along, the wild October wind catching at both their hair, his a blur of dark brown, Madison's a shimmer of pale copper. And before them the ground continued to open up to receive the Rio Grande's waters. They were making good time. He had feared that this task might require several days, but it seemed he would be done before the sun set.

They were quiet after that initial exchange, but Qadim did not mind. He needed to concentrate on what he was doing, and Madison seemed to sense that. But he realized something else as they made their slow and steady progress toward the hotel.

He was content.

True, some measure of that contentment could be attributed to the way his body had been sated by the woman who walked along next to him. Her appetite surprised him, but he certainly wouldn't change anything about that. Indeed, it was refreshing to find someone who was so responsive. That the woman who was such a close match to his needs had turned out to be human was perhaps the strangest part of the entire situation, but Qadim thought he could learn to accept that.

But his had always been a restless spirit, never entirely satisfied with anything he had. No doubt that restlessness was another reason why he never lingered with any one woman for too long. And though he told himself that the scant few days he'd been with Madison was certainly not a long enough span of time to change him, he did find himself rather astonished that he should find himself so at peace. As one of his former lovers had once sourly remarked, he was not an easy man, in any sense of the word.

When he and Madison came closer to the hotel, he had the new stream veer slightly to the south so it would skirt the edges of the small park-like area with the red rocks and trees, the only human-made thing still standing in the downtown area except the Hotel Andaluz. And there it waited while he moved the earth to create a pond nearly fifty meters across and twice as long. That earth he set aside for later use, and as soon as it was gone, the water rushed into its new home, filling the cavity he had opened in the ground.

As the sun began to dip to the west, it painted the surface of that new lake with gold and amber. The wind ruffled the water, and off to one side, the cottonwoods and mesquite trees he had planted shimmered in the warm light as well.

"It's beautiful," Madison said. She had stood next to him in silence as he worked, and now she slipped her hand into his. He liked the feel of it, the touch of her warm, slender fingers. They seemed to fit perfectly around his own fingers. "You know, as we walked, I was thinking."

"About?" he asked, hoping she would not bring up Los Alamos again. Yes, she'd retired the subject the night before, but he couldn't get rid of the idea that the town, with its population of human survivors, still held some sort of unhealthy allure for her.

"What you've done so far is amazing," she said. "But I just remembered how Clay had stocked the servers back at the bomb shelter with all sorts of horticultural information, a lot of it about native plants and the sorts of crops that can be sustainably farmed in this part of the world. I know you're not from around here"—she flashed him a quick grin, one so irresistible that he was forced to smile back at her in response—"and so I thought maybe I could go back to the shelter and see what I could dig up that would help. It's beautiful, but it probably would help to start growing some actual crops. Not now," she added quickly. "Winter is just around the corner, and it can get kind of brutal in northern New Mexico, although Albuquerque usually doesn't get hit too hard. In the spring, though...."

Her words trailed off then, and Qadim thought that the flush in her cheeks wasn't entirely from the wind. Perhaps she thought she might be presumptuous in assuming that the two of them would still be together when springtime came.

Perhaps she was presuming things, but at the moment, he had to hope that she was correct in her assumption. All things came to an end; he knew that much. And yet he did not want to think about what it might be like for her to be gone, for him to never see her again.

When it happens, it happens, he told himself. *It could be sometime in the spring, or a year from now. I will worry about it when the time comes.*

"That is a very good idea," he said gravely, and was gratified by the way she seemed to relax slightly. "If we gather that knowledge now, then when spring comes around again, we will be prepared. But," he added when it looked as if she was about to speak, "you can go to gather that information tomorrow. The sun is setting now, and I think we have put in enough work for one day."

"You mean you've put in enough work," she remarked with a small quirk of her lips. "Mostly I watched."

"It went easier, having you there."

That comment made her smile, so he led her into the hotel, where the fountains still flowed, and the large fixtures overhead still sent forth the illumination necessary to light up the lobby, even though the power companies that had once supplied their electricity were long gone.

"Why don't we eat in here tonight?" Madison said, pointing to the one casbah with the wall fountain of glimmering translucent tile. "It might be fun. Intimate."

Qadim thought he liked the sound of that. His labors had wearied him somewhat, but not enough that he wouldn't be able to rise to the occasion, so to speak. A meal of small plates, tasty morsels as they served in Spain. He thought that would do very well.

"Yes, but let us change for dinner." A glance down at the human attire he wore told him that he had gotten somewhat grubby during his exertions, and while Madison had fared better, he still would prefer that she wear something more elegant. He would have to make sure she had a few surprises waiting for her when she went upstairs to get out of the T-shirt and faded jeans she was wearing.

"So formal," she teased, but he could tell she really didn't mind all that much. "Should I go now, or do you need me to help you? It seems as if cooking on top of all the work you did today might be pushing it a little."

"No, I will be fine," he said. He didn't bother to add that he planned to use his powers to create the entire meal, something he normally did not do. But he was rather weary, and since they really hadn't eaten anything since breakfast, it would be far easier and faster for him to magic up their meal.

Her expression told him she was somewhat dubious, but she didn't argue any further, and instead went on her tiptoes to give him a kiss on the cheek before she headed off for the stairs.

The sensation of her lips pressing against him seemed to linger on his skin long after she had disappeared. Qadim thought he could get used to this.

And that, he thought, was exactly the problem.

Madison went up to her suite, since that was where all her personal items were still stored. The opportunity really hadn't come up for her to ask whether she should take her things into Qadim's penthouse suite. Maybe that was presuming too much. Yes, they'd been intimate, and yes, they were more or less spending every waking moment together, and yet that might still not be enough reason for him to make their cohabitation a bit more formal.

Just as well, she told herself. She'd always been used to having her own space. Jacob had made hints about moving in together, but they hadn't progressed beyond the talking stage before he got the offer to go to Bellingham, and that was the end of that.

Well, at least Qadim had repaired her blush-toned tunic and pants, so she'd have something to wear. When she opened the closet, though, her eyes widened in shock. Instead of that one dressy outfit and a few shirts, she saw a veritable rainbow of clothes, silks shimmering with metallic embroidery and beadwork, each one more exquisite than the next. And on the floor of the closet were shoes to match, some little beaded flats, some jeweled sandals.

Qadim, of course. Apparently he'd wanted to give her a little variety in her dress-up wardrobe. It still shocked her, the way he could just pull things out of thin air for her, but in this instance, she was all too happy that he possessed those djinn powers.

She rummaged through the rack of clothes, trying to decide which outfit she should wear first, and then finally decided on a white tunic decorated in teal and gold beadwork, the yoke composed of heavily embroidered flowers in glass beads and metallic threads. The teal up near her face brought out the green in her eyes and seemed to make her red hair appear a little deeper and richer in tone than it usually was, and she smiled at her reflection after she applied some lip gloss and mascara. She didn't look anything like the windblown woman who'd walked into the room a half hour earlier.

The clothing wasn't the only surprise he'd left her, though. Just as she was about to head out the door, Madison noticed a large wooden box sitting on top of the dresser. Curious, she went closer and raised the lid.

Inside was a veritable king's ransom of jewelry— heavy, intricate pieces in both silver and gold, picked out with precious stones in shades of green and red and blue and purple. She was no expert, but she recognized emerald and ruby, sapphire and amethyst, and many more. A pair of dangling earrings in gold set with opals seemed the perfect complement to her outfit, so she took out the plain silver hoops she wore and put in the gold earrings. There was a ring that seemed to match, and then a set of gold bangles that had a definite Bollywood vibe.

All put together, the ensemble was quite impressive, and she tossed her head a little, feeling the earrings brush against her neck. Normally, she would never have worn anything so extravagant, and the effect made her feel a little wicked.

She'd have to see what Qadim thought.

Her jeweled sandals slapped against the metal stairs as she hurried back down to the ground floor. As she came out into the main section of the lobby, she paused and looked up in awe. Qadim had taken the same fabric he'd used to decorate the rooftop bar a few days earlier, and this time had draped it from one side of the mezzanine to the other. Underneath, a number of wrought-iron candelabras glowed with numerous pillar candles. All of the casbahs, however, were dark—except one. The little alcove with the water feature on one wall had more candles gleaming on every side, and on the table in the center was a number of small plates, each with a different but equally delicious-looking item placed on it.

And there was Qadim, standing outside the entrance to the casbah, obviously waiting for her. Madison's breath caught at the sight of him, because instead of his usual somber robes, he had on garments in dark wine-colored silk. Wide bands of gold covered both his wrists. The effect was not feminine, though—really, the exact opposite. With his heavy dark hair falling down his back, he had a sort of barbaric splendor, and Madison could feel her heart begin to beat faster at just the sight of him.

"You are stunning," he said, coming forward so he could get a better look at her.

"So are you," she replied. "I like the new outfit. And mine, too," she added hastily. "That's some wardrobe you conjured for me."

"You needed more clothing that would suit your beauty. While I understand the need for the utilitarian nature of some of your things, there is no reason why you can't have something more elegant for the times you are here in the hotel."

True, there really wasn't a reason why she shouldn't get dressed up while she was here. She wouldn't wear these things while she was out with Qadim, helping him with his reconstruction of Albuquerque. That just didn't make sense. But she liked the idea of making their dinners together something of an event, one that required clothing far more formal than her usual attire. Back in the day, people had dressed for dinner. It would be fun to reinstitute that custom.

"Well, they're beautiful," she said. "And the jewelry, too. I don't think I've ever seen anything this impressive outside a museum, or maybe some of those really high-end stores up in Santa Fe on the plaza."

His expression darkened ever so slightly when she mentioned Santa Fe, but then his face cleared. "I am glad you like everything. But now...are you hungry?"

"Famished," she said honestly.

"Then let us sit down."

Madison followed him into the casbah, where she took a seat next to him. A bottle of white wine sat chilling in one of those ceramic coolers, and Qadim pulled it out and then poured some for each of them. She was a little surprised by that choice, simply because they hadn't shared anything besides red wine so far, except during their first dinner, but it did seem to work well with the lighter fare he'd set out for them tonight. There was a board with cheese and fruit, and bacon-wrapped dates, and all sorts of other delicious morsels—a kind of patty of stacked potatoes and cheese, and broiled chicken on skewers, and a bowl of sliced mushrooms and peppers bathed in olive oil, with bread for dipping.

A few of the items she recognized from the times she'd had tapas, but others she'd never tried before. Once again, she wondered how Qadim had managed to put all this together. Their other meals he'd basically cooked the old-fashioned way, and yet she couldn't figure out how he'd done so on this go-'round. There simply hadn't been enough time.

"You want to let me in on your secret?" she inquired as she picked up a small slice of toasted sourdough bread and spooned some of the mushroom/pepper mixture on top.

"I am a djinn," he replied, a glint in his dark eyes. "Is there any other secret besides that?"

"Well, no, I suppose. It's just that I actually saw you cooking the other meals, but...."

He lifted his wine glass and sipped before replying, "Yes, I did use my powers to prepare this one. I hope that does not make it any less appetizing."

She had to think about that revelation for a second. Then she realized it really didn't matter one way or another. After all, she was fairly certain that he'd coaxed a few things along while putting together all their meals, even if he'd done most of the work himself. "No, it's all wonderful," she said. "In a way, that makes me feel better, because then I know you didn't wear yourself out trying to get all this ready."

"No, I most certainly did not wear myself out." His gaze lingered on her mouth, and a welcome warmth stole over her, the one that told her it didn't matter that they'd already had sex multiple times in the last twenty-four hours. Her body still craved more.

"Well, that's good to hear."

He slanted her a sidelong look but didn't say anything, and instead popped one of the bacon-wrapped dates into his mouth. They ate in silence for a few moments, both of them content to concentrate on the varied flavors of the food before them. In the background, the sound of the waterfall, and, a little farther away, the fountain in the center of the lobby, both combined to soothe away the quiet. For the first time, Madison realized that Qadim never put on any music during their meals. She wasn't sure why this was the first time she'd noticed that lack, except maybe she'd had so many other things to focus on that it really hadn't entered her mind.

Back at the bomb shelter, she'd had music on all the time. Anything to fill the silence, to make her feel that she wasn't so alone. Clay had compiled an eclectic library—everything from Mozart to Daft Punk—and she'd loaded the favorites she'd had on her phone as well. The playlist varied from day to day, but the only times she wasn't playing some kind of music were those occasions when she'd watch one of the numerous movies or TV shows he'd stockpiled on the shelter's servers.

She hadn't really missed any of it. Madison supposed that had a good deal to do with the man sitting next to her.

"Do djinn play music?" she asked then.

He shifted so he could face her a little better. Expression thoughtful, he said, "Yes, but again, I would classify those of us who play and create music more as artisans than artists. They are not striving for anything more than to create something soothing or lovely that can be played in the background. They do not think of it as art." An eyebrow went up as he appeared to contemplate her expression. "Would you like some music?"

"It's not really necessary," Madison replied. "But I always listened to a lot of it."

"Music is easy enough to supply. They had a system in place for that here." His eyes shut briefly, as if he was concentrating on something. In the next instant, the sounds of Spanish classical guitar began to flow from speakers hidden around the lobby.

"Thank you," she said. "I suppose I didn't realize how much I missed it."

"Then we shall always have music, if it pleases you. Is what is playing now acceptable? It's what was set up on the hotel's system, but I can get something else if you like."

"No, it's lovely," she said honestly. After all, what better in a setting like this than the impassioned sounds of a lone guitarist playing Rodrigo's *Concierto de Aranjuez*?

"I find it pleasant as well," Qadim said. "I will admit that I rather feared you would choose something cacophonous, as that seemed to be what was popular with your people lately."

You kids get off my damn lawn! Madison thought with some amusement, but she didn't say anything. She doubted Qadim would get the reference, and really, it was probably expecting a lot to think that a being who'd been around for thousands of years would appreciate modern pop rock or hip-hop.

Actually, she couldn't stand hip-hop, either, so she and Qadim had something in common there.

"Well, I liked to get down with the best of them," she remarked, "but generally not while I'm eating dinner." His brows drew together in a frown, and she chuckled. "Dancing. Do djinn dance?"

"Oh, yes. Our own dances, but we have learned some of yours as well. Do you know how to tango?"

Only horizontally, she thought, but then shook her head. "No, I never learned how to do any kind of ballroom dancing. Jacob and I tried salsa a few times, but unfortunately we were both a couple of gringos with left feet."

"Jacob?"

There was no ignoring the edge to Qadim's voice. Jealousy. And how foolish was that, when almost every other human male on the face of the planet had been dead for more than a year?

"Ex-boyfriend," she said casually as she reached over to pick up her wine glass from the low table. "We split up long before the Heat came to Albuquerque. He'd been living in Washington State for almost a year."

"Ah." Qadim did seem to relax then. He selected a piece of sliced cheese from the wooden board and laid it on top of a piece of bread, but he didn't eat it right away. Instead he asked, "And there was no one else?"

"No." The line of questioning might have sounded odd, but Madison thought she understood the reasoning behind it. He wanted to make sure she wasn't still mourning a lover lost to the Heat. "I saw a few people here and there, but nothing really clicked. And I was busy with my work."

"Your art."

"Yes. I'd gotten a couple of lucrative commissions and was really focused on that. I always thought there would be more time. Time," she repeated, a trace of bitterness entering her voice. Why, she wasn't really sure, except that when you were twenty-six years old and doing better than you'd ever hoped you might, you got the idea that you were invincible. That there would always be another chance just down the road.

Qadim didn't miss the sharpness of her tone. Frowning slightly, he put down his bread and cheese and moved closer to her. "I wish...." He paused, as if sorting through his thoughts, attempting to make sense of what he was thinking. "No, I will not lie and say I wish things had been different for you. Because if they had, then we would not be sitting here like this, and I can think of nothing I want more than you."

There was a whole host of things wrong with his statement. Intellectually, Madison understood that, knew their present happiness was certainly no fair trade for all the lives that had been lost. But she also knew no one—not even a djinn—could change the past. Things were what they were, and so she could be glad that, crazy as it all was, she had somehow ended up with Qadim, a man who seemed to cherish her in a way no one else ever had.

She didn't know what he saw right then, looking at her. But his eyes filled with a certain warmth, and he plucked the wine glass from her hand, then set it down on the table. In the next moment, his mouth was on hers, sweet and sharp with the sauvignon blanc they'd been drinking, but hot in a way that nicely chilled wine had never been.

Oh, yes, that mouth, those kisses—they could make her forget. They could push aside the world she'd lost, the voices and faces that still haunted her thoughts.

When she was in Qadim's arms, she didn't need to think about anything else.

CHAPTER THIRTEEN

THE NEXT DAY, MADISON WENT BACK TO THE BOMB shelter so she could gather information to aid Qadim in his planting projects. He'd wanted to come along, but she pointed out that there was no real reason for him to do so.

"You'll get bored out of your mind, sitting there and watching me dig things up on the computer," she told him. "And you still have work of your own that you wanted to get on with."

He grinned at her. "I very much doubt that I would get bored by looking at you."

"I'm serious, Qadim."

"So am I."

"Anyway," she began, because she knew if she let him, he'd tease her right back into bed. As tempting as that might be, they couldn't spend every waking moment having sex.

Well, all right, maybe they could, but that really wasn't very practical as a long-term survival strategy.

"You have work to do, and I have work to do," she continued, hoping she sounded severe enough to convince him. "And it's perfectly safe for me to go around Albuquerque. That one djinn—"

"Hasan," Qadim supplied, mouth tightening slightly.

"Yes, Hasan. He's obviously made himself scarce, and it looks like all the other djinn have, too." She paused and added, "Have *you* seen any of them lately?"

"No," he was forced to admit. "Even in the otherworld, we tended to keep to our own palaces. Now that we each have our lands here, I believe that we will be even more inclined to stay in one place."

She smiled. "You see? They're all of getting settled into their own territories. So there's really no reason for you to be hovering over me all the time."

"Is that what you think I do? Hover?"

"No. That's not what I meant." They'd been in the kitchen, cleaning up after breakfast. She set down the coffee mug she'd just rinsed out and went over to him, putting her arms around his waist. Damn, that felt so good. Making love with him was spectacular, but there was something to be said for the quieter pleasures of merely holding him, feeling the strength of his body pressed against hers. It could simply be that it had been so long since she'd had any physical contact with anyone, but she thought there was something more to it than that. "I appreciate you being worried, but at this point, I really don't think there's any reason. And I'll be careful. I got around Albuquerque for a year without being caught, remember?"

He didn't reply at first, only put his arms around her and held her tight. She felt his lips brush against the top of her head, just before he said, "Yes, I know that. And I never intended to imply that you did not know how to take care of yourself."

"Well, then." She pulled away so she could look up at him. His expression was unsmiling, his dark eyes worried. "It'll be fine. And I'll only go for a couple of hours."

"Very well. I don't like it, but—very well."

She kissed him and offered a smile, but he still looked somber. And a few minutes later, she headed out on foot for the shelter, since her electric bicycle was now permanently out of commission. She wished she had it with her now, but a walk would do her good. If she had time, maybe she'd take another look at the bike, which she'd dragged inside Clay's old house before coming back to stay here at the hotel with Qadim. Even though it might be damaged beyond repair, she hadn't wanted to leave it just lying in the street. It had served her well for months, and it seemed disloyal to abandon it like a piece of junk.

The weather was fine but windy, the air penetrating the T-shirt she wore. She'd need to pick up some warmer clothes when she was at the shelter. Qadim had given her a wardrobe fit for a princess, but that wouldn't do her much good when winter came and she had to venture outside.

It was a little scary to walk alone through the open fields near the hotel. She knew Qadim was probably keeping watch until she reached the shelter of the buildings he'd yet to tear down, but she couldn't help glancing upward from time to time, making sure that Hasan or one of his buddies wasn't up there somewhere, ready to swoop down and grab her.

However, the sky remained blue and empty, and she reached the concrete ribbon of I-25 without incident. Once she was hidden under its bulk, she paused and took a breath. So much for protesting to Qadim that there was nothing to be worried about. Obviously, she was worried, or she wouldn't have kept checking to make sure she was alone.

The rest of the journey was better, just because she fell into her old habits, scuttling from alley to alley, flattening herself in the shadows of buildings when no alleyway was to be had. When she turned down the street where Clay Michaels' house was located, she let out a little sigh of relief, then sprinted the rest of the way, since there was no real shelter to be had there.

And none in the backyard, either, thanks to the way Qadim had blown up the gazebo in a fit of pique. The metal door seemed painfully obvious now, glaring in the bright October sun. Well, there wasn't anything she could do about it, except get in there and shut it behind her as quickly as she could.

Which she did, slipping inside and closing the hatch, then spinning the wheel so the locks would slide into place. She did the same thing at the next airlock, and then she was at the main entrance, where she entered the key code and went inside.

Even though she'd only been away for a few days, the place felt unused, abandoned. Luckily, she wasn't the type to leave a mess behind her before she went out, and so the kitchen was tidy, the bed made. But the shelter still seemed oddly forlorn.

Well, she couldn't worry about that right now. The shelter had served its purpose, keeping her alive until she could find a better place to go. True, she probably would never have guessed that her next sanctuary would be the Hotel Andaluz, but neither would she have thought she could end up with one of the hated djinn. She didn't hate Qadim—far from it. In fact, she—

No, she needed to stop there. She'd allow herself to say she cared for him, cared about him as well, but their relationship certainly hadn't progressed far enough for her to admit anything else.

Anyway, she wasn't here to analyze her feelings for Qadim al-Syan. She was here to get some intel.

Her laptop was still sitting in the bedroom where she'd left it plugged in. She gathered it up and went into Clay's office, where the interface for the server was located. Because she'd already inventoried everything in his desk, she knew it contained a number of blank thumb drives. She'd put the information she needed on as many of the drives as was necessary. Then she planned to bring all the drives and her laptop with her back to the hotel. At that point, she and Qadim could sit down and go over the information she'd gathered, see what was there that might be useful.

Even though she knew this room almost as well as she knew her own, the lack of any sort of personal items in the office still bothered her. Yes, she'd always understood that Clay was apparently alone in the world, and yet it seemed strange that there wasn't one photo of his parents, or of anyone else, either. The walls had been hung with high-end photographs, mainly of the northern part of the state, up around Santa Fe and Taos. They were beautiful, but the space still didn't have any more personality than a high-end hotel suite.

She didn't have time to worry about that now. Clay had taken his secrets to the grave with him, and Madison knew she should just be grateful that he'd created this shelter and felt enough of a connection with her family that he'd allowed her to use it. Without the shelter, she would have been dead months ago.

The terminal was only sleeping, not completely shut off, so once she wiggled the mouse and typed in the password, she was in. A few more clicks of the mouse had her navigating to the section of the database that held all the agricultural and horticultural information. She already knew that Clay had basically dumped the knowledge bases of several universities into the system. Where he'd gotten all that information, she had no idea. For now, she could only be grateful that it hadn't been lost along with so many other artifacts of the world before the Heat.

She drilled down further, finding the items either specific to New Mexico itself or to arid, high-desert climates. Even so, the information she needed would probably take up at least four or five of the thumb drives.

After starting the first transfer, Madison got up and went into her bedroom—although she really didn't think of it as "hers" any longer—and got the overnight bag down from the top shelf in the closet. Some more underwear, more bras, and then a couple of long-sleeved T-shirts and sweaters, followed by a few extra pairs of socks. Yes, she supposed she could have scavenged all that from Albuquerque's abandoned stores, but these things were hers, and she wanted them with her.

When she was done, she headed back to Clay's office, ejected the first thumb drive, and then inserted the second one and started all over again. This time she went to the family room to collect the sketchpad she'd left lying there. The drawing of Qadim stared up at her, and she gently ran a thumb down one side of the paper. Yes, she'd gotten fairly close to what she would consider a faithful representation, but what she hadn't been able to capture was the gleam in his eyes, or the wicked curl at the corner of his mouth. To be fair, she'd done this from memory, and from a glimpse caught from many yards away, but she still thought he deserved a better portrait. Maybe he'd let her paint him. He deserved to be done in oils instead of this rough charcoal.

Which meant she'd have to transport a ton of supplies to the hotel. *Not today,* she told herself. Painting a portrait was a frivolity, nothing that had to happen anytime soon. But maybe if the idea appealed to Qadim, she could have him come here and "blink" everything she needed back over to one of the empty rooms at the Andaluz. It would definitely be a lot easier than having to carry everything on foot, now that the bike was pretty much out of commission.

She took the sketchbook into the bedroom and slid it on top of the overnight bag. After that, it was back to the office and another thumb drive. Rinse and repeat.

The silence in the shelter unnerved her. She'd switched off the sound system before she'd left on her last trip into town, and hadn't yet turned it on when she came back in. Of course not; she'd been hurrying to get away from Qadim. In retrospect, that seemed like the most ridiculous idea ever. But back then, she hadn't known what he would come to mean to her.

Actually, she still wasn't sure exactly what he meant to her. She only knew that she couldn't imagine being without him.

The fourth and final thumb drive was full. All in all, the entire process had only taken about forty minutes, which was better than she'd hoped. Right then, she decided against inspecting the bike. She wouldn't need it any time soon, after all. And it was fine where it was, leaning against the wall in the entryway of Clay's house. With that project postponed, she'd be back at the hotel in the next half hour. Qadim might be out, continuing with his project to remove all of Albuquerque's ugly man-made artifacts, but she'd have her laptop and could start sifting through the data. That way, when he returned, they could begin analyzing the information and then decide what else they might want to add to the plants and trees he was setting out all over the newly cleared land.

She stuck all the thumb drives in the side pocket of her overnight bag, then set her laptop on top of the clothing inside before she zipped the whole thing up. The sketchbook wouldn't fit, but she could slide that on top of the bag. The handles should hold it in place well enough as she walked. After all, she wasn't planning to run or climb. Just a nice sedate walk back to the Andaluz, and then she could unpack everything and wait for Qadim.

Force of habit made her seal up all the airlocks behind her as she left the shelter. They really needed to do something about that exposed door, though. The rosebushes didn't do much to hide it. Maybe she could have Qadim plant a large shady tree where the gazebo had once been.

But why? she asked herself. *It's not as if you're going to be living here ever again. Who cares if it's visible?*

Good question. She supposed she found the idea disrespectful somehow, as if she was dishonoring all the hard work Clay had put into constructing the bomb shelter by leaving it so open to anyone who might pass by.

Besides, she really had no idea what was going to happen with her and Qadim in the long term. Everything was sunshine and roses right now because they were still firmly in the honeymoon phase of things, but she wasn't so naive as to think that state of affairs could last indefinitely. And once they decided this whole human/djinn thing wasn't really working for them, what then?

Well, they'd go their separate ways, she thought with a pang she really didn't want to acknowledge. If she analyzed her feelings too closely, she could get herself in trouble. But she knew she needed to be sensible about this. What kind of future could a djinn and a human who wasn't Chosen have, after all?

Maybe she could convince him to take her as close to Los Alamos as possible without actually being affected by the devices—whatever they really were—that protected the town from djinn incursions. She should be able to make it the rest of the way, and then... what? They'd take her in, no doubt; she had a feeling they would welcome some new blood, especially since they probably wouldn't have seen any other survivors for a while now. Of course, the flip side of that situation was probably that everyone was already paired off, since they would have all been sharing the town for an entire year. She'd be on the outside, that was for sure.

And man, are you borrowing trouble, she scolded herself as she headed out of the side yard and down the street. As before, it was empty and quiet, the weeds and the rust and the wind slowly whittling away at the artifacts man had left behind. *You and Qadim are doing just fine. More than fine. It's not so crazy to think that he might still want to make you his Chosen, if you give him enough time to warm up to the idea.*

What that would be like, she wasn't really sure. Certainly she'd never thought she might one day be immortal, forever preserved at the peak of her youth. Or maybe not quite her peak, according to the djinn. She still wanted to shake her head at them only wanting to take humans who were somewhere between the ages of twenty-one and twenty-five.

Anyway, if the past few days had been any indication, then maybe spending eternity with Qadim wouldn't be so bad.

She rounded the corner that brought her out of the housing development where Clay's home was located and began moving down the sidewalk, going as quickly as the burden she carried would allow her. This had always been her least favorite part of the journey, since there really wasn't anywhere to hide. Once she was in the more commercial areas off University Boulevard, she'd feel a lot better.

A shadow passed overhead, and she startled until she realized it was only a large raven, sailing along on the wind, black wings outstretched. It circled lazily, clearly enjoying the updrafts created by the warmth of the asphalt road next to her.

When Madison looked back down, however, she knew she was about to pay the price for her momentary distraction. Standing there on the sidewalk in front of her was the handsome, cruel-faced djinn she'd seen tear several of her fellow survivors to shreds. His deep blue robes shimmered in the breeze, almost the same color as the narrowed eyes that were now fixed on her.

Her heart skittered, jumped. She knew escape was impossible, but it was the only thing which sprang to her mind in that endless, terrible moment.

Run.

She dropped the overnight bag and bolted, headed between two shabby mobile homes. Where she thought she was going, she had no idea. She only knew that if she stayed where she was, she'd surely die.

His laughter followed her, rich and mocking. As she emerged into a backyard cluttered with a rusted-out swing set and an impressive collection of old tires, the djinn descended from the sky and stood in front of her, arms crossed and a smirk on his sculpted mouth.

"Going somewhere, Madison Reynolds?"

CHAPTER FOURTEEN

QADIM GLANCED UP AT THE SUN AND FROWNED. Madison had sworn to him that her errand shouldn't take her more than an hour or an hour and a half at the very most, and yet he knew more time than that had passed. He'd been hard at work, planting trees so they might form a pleasant border to the pond he'd created the day before, and so had lost some sense of how long it had been since she left. But the sun was telling him now that at least two hours had gone by, probably more.

Scowling, he turned back toward the hotel. Perhaps she had returned, but had gone straight there rather than disturb him at his work. He would have preferred that she check in with him. Better that she had been heedless, however, when compared to the alternative.

"Madison?" he called out as he entered the Andaluz. Only silence met his ears, but the hotel was a large place. Perhaps she was upstairs in her suite, getting things settled. She had mentioned that she planned to retrieve a few personal belongings from the shelter.

But her room was empty, and so was the penthouse suite where they'd spent several delicious nights together. Frown deepening, he returned to the ground floor. She wasn't there, either—not in the kitchen, nor in any of the other rooms.

A chill began to work its way down his spine, but he told himself not to jump to any conclusions. After all, the amount of time she'd given him had only been an estimate. Perhaps she truly hadn't known for sure how long it would take for her to transfer all the knowledge she sought onto those things she'd called "thumb drives," and so she was still back at the shelter, waiting for the process to be complete.

That would be easy enough to find out.

He transported himself directly into the shelter, for now that he had been there once, he could come and go as he pleased. Some of the lights were on—in the corridor, and in the room where the television was located. But he saw no sign of her.

"Madison?" This time her name sounded almost tentative to him, as if deep down he'd already realized she wasn't here, and he was just stretching out his search because he didn't know what else to do.

Still nothing.

He knew she wasn't here. And yet he went from room to room, checking each one, just in case. At the end of his inspection, he was forced to acknowledge that all he'd done was waste his time.

Clearly, she had been here. The computer in the one office was still on, its screen flickering through a series of glowing geometric shapes, and when he went to the access corridor that led to the outside world, he discovered that each of the heavy metal doors had been locked. Those locked doors told him that she hadn't been in a hurry when she left, that she'd been methodical about making sure the shelter had been secured.

Not wishing to squeeze himself through the final door, Qadim blinked back up to the surface and looked around the neglected backyard. He could spy remnants of the gazebo he'd destroyed, but no other evidence that anyone had been there recently.

Very well, he'd have to do his best at tracing her steps. He cast his mind back to the day when he'd first pursued her here. She'd come around the corner from a larger street just to the west. If she had taken the same route today, then he might be able to detect some sign of her.

Since he didn't know exactly where he was going, he decided it would be better to walk, just as an ordinary human might. The djinn mode of travel was very useful, but it did lend itself to missing out on small details.

When he got to the larger boulevard, that street was just as empty as the one he'd left, with the same landscape of cars slowly rusting where they'd been abandoned, weeds growing up through the sidewalks, houses growing ramshackle with no one to care for them. All in all, the scene was incredibly forlorn. In that moment, Qadim wondered if some of his motivation for remaking the city was to erase all signs of the way these people had been torn from their lives.

Something dark on the sidewalk up ahead caught his attention. His eyes narrowed, and he realized the object was the bag that Madison had said she intended to bring with her to the shelter. Next to it, another item he couldn't quite identify lay on the ground, paper rippling in the breeze.

Every muscle in his body seemed to clench as he realized the second item was her sketchbook.

Propelled by worry, he ran to the spot where the abandoned overnight bag and sketchpad lay on the sidewalk. Yes, the bag was definitely hers, and since the sketchbook had fallen open to the page with his portrait on it, he knew that it couldn't have belonged to anyone else, either.

He looked around wildly. No sign of Madison, but he also couldn't detect any signs of a struggle, nothing to indicate that she hadn't just dropped these things for some reason and continued on her way. But he knew better.

Bending down, he opened the bag and quickly looked inside. Yes, there were the things she'd said she wanted to retrieve from the shelter, along with a portable computer. In one of the bag's side pockets were a group of hard little plastic objects about the size of—well, the size of his thumb. So it seemed she had been able to collect the information she sought.

As to what had happened after that, he couldn't say for certain. It looked as if she'd disappeared into thin air. He had a suspicion, though...a terrible one. Yes, they hadn't seen any sign of Hasan or any other djinn for days now, but that didn't necessarily mean they hadn't been lurking somewhere, just waiting for the chance to come upon Madison while she was alone.

I should never have let her go to the shelter without me, Qadim thought then. *Just because something gives the impression of being safe doesn't necessarily mean that it is.*

The only thing he could find remotely reassuring was that there were no signs of violence—no blood on the sidewalk, no weeds crushed and disturbed where a person might have fallen. If Hasan had taken her, he hadn't hurt her.

Yet.

Qadim's hands knotted into fists. He knew he had to think logically, and he had to think quickly.

Hasan's territory was in a place called Chama, which Qadim knew was somewhere to the north and west of where he was now. But he would have to look at a map, because he knew very little about the state, save for the few areas he'd already visited—Albuquerque and Santa Fe and a few smaller towns located to the north of the former capitol. His connection to Hasan was not strong enough for him to immediately blink himself wherever the other djinn was holed up. That was the limitation of their travel—a djinn had to know where he was going, or he could not safely send himself to his chosen destination. The elders were not bound by this limitation, and could go where they liked, but he was not an elder, nor even an elemental of the air, who could at least hurry the process by flying to his destination.

No, he'd have to do this the hard way...and Qadim very much feared he might not be able to solve the mystery before Madison's time ran out.

She didn't know why she wasn't dead. Shouldn't she be dead? Qadim had spoken of this djinn—Hasan, she remembered—as someone dedicated to killing every survivor he'd come across. So why he hadn't immediately dispatched her, she couldn't begin to guess.

They were in a house. A nice one, from what she could tell, large and built in a modified lodge style, with vaulted wood ceilings and a big stone fireplace.

Through the windows she saw rolling, dry pasture land, and then a series of hills off in the distance, topped with tall ponderosa pines and the flaming yellow of autumn-turned aspens.

Chama, she thought. *That's where Qadim said Hasan's "land grant" was located.*

In other circumstances, she might have found the view beautiful. At the moment, however, she couldn't think of much except the djinn who stood before her.

An impartial observer would have said he was far more handsome than Qadim, his features more finely sculpted, his eyes not so deep-set and shadowed. However, all Madison could see was the fanatical fire in those blue eyes, the contempt in Hasan's expression as he studied her.

"So," he said, once his inspection had apparently concluded, "you are the reason Qadim al-Syan has chosen to betray his kind?"

Hasan's command of English surprised her. If he hated humans so much, then why would he bother to learn their language? Madison lifted her shoulders, or at least attempted to. With the way her hands had been bound behind her to the chair where she sat, her range of motion was somewhat limited. "Why a betrayal?" she asked, surprised that her voice should sound so steady when inside she felt like a quivering mess. She swallowed, then went on, "Others of your people are involved with humans. As far as I can tell, no one seems too upset about that."

A curl of the lip. "If you are referring to the One Thousand and their Chosen, well, I can say that some are not so very pleased by that state of affairs, either. However, it was the compromise that was agreed upon, and the elders have ensured the safety of those humans. But you?" He shook his head, disgust clear in his expression as he surveyed her. "You are not Qadim's Chosen. You are nothing."

"He might not agree with you on that point," Madison shot back. Her bravery surprised her, but maybe it was only that she'd been afraid of this man—this djinn—for so long that, now she was actually confronted by the reality of him, she didn't know if she was quite as frightened as maybe she should have been. She didn't know what he had planned, but if murder had been his only intention, then he could have killed her back in Albuquerque and left her body for Qadim to find. Which meant he must have something else in mind.

Her entire soul quailed at that idea, though. She could think of only a few reasons why he might have spirited her away here, none of them pleasant. But no, that didn't make any sense. He was clearly repelled by her, so she doubted her kidnapping had anything to do with sex. Then again, rape wasn't about sex. It was about power. Dominance. Her stomach churned, and she forced herself to take in a breath so she wouldn't throw up. She had to keep it together, no matter what happened.

Hasan didn't appear terribly offended by her retort. "Qadim is not always the most discriminating sort when it comes to women. And because he is seen as disgraced, he has not had many opportunities to enjoy the company of djinn women lately. It is not that difficult to understand why he might have lowered himself to dally with you when no other choices presented themselves."

Dally? Was that what she and Qadim had been doing for the past few days? Well, it was a pleasant way to pass the time. But even as that thought passed through Madison's mind, a seed of doubt began to grow there. Qadim had spoken of the trouble he and his sister had gotten into, although he hadn't provided all that many details. Maybe he really had approached her because he didn't have any alternative. He needed his itch scratched.

No, she refused to believe that. There had been a couple of highly embarrassing instances where she'd gone to bed with a man, thinking there was something to their connection...only to realize that he had no interest in pursuing anything else with her, now that he'd gotten what he wanted. She knew all too well what that felt like. But Qadim hadn't been indifferent afterward. If anything, one encounter seemed to feed off another, as if every time they made love, it only awoke a new need, rather than slaking their desire.

"Sounds like you've got it all figured out, don't you?" Madison asked. Maybe she was provoking Hasan, but she hoped he might let slip a clue as to what his plan actually was. Not that she'd necessarily be in a position to do anything about it. The past year had taught her that she could take care of herself, but going up against a djinn was not something you did lightly.

Hasan didn't reply immediately. Instead, he stood there, arms crossed, and continued to gaze at her with that highly unsettling blue stare of his. Unsettling, because Madison didn't think she'd ever had anyone look at her in such a way, like she was some intriguing new species of insect.

Then he came closer. Before she could react, he'd grabbed a handful of her hair and had pulled her head backward so she was forced to stare up into his face. She barely stifled a gasp of pain, just because she knew he wanted to know that he'd hurt her, and she wasn't about to give him the satisfaction. Those blue eyes blazed down at her. She swallowed.

"If you were a djinn woman, you might be considered passable," he said at last, right before he let go of her hair. Because her hands were tied behind her back, she couldn't even reach up to massage her aching scalp. "But a human? Qadim's exile must have turned his mind."

Madison frowned. "If he's an exile, then aren't all of you?"

"Of course not," Hasan snapped. "We have only taken back that which should have been ours all along. Our true exile was in the otherworld. No, you must see what I was given"—a sweep of his hand toward the glorious autumn vista outside the windows—"and compare it to the wasteland which is now Qadim al-Syan's. His is truly an exile, for who would ever want to live in that?"

"Well, it's better than Death Valley," she replied, nettled on behalf of her hometown. The anger felt good, actually. If she was angry, then she couldn't be quite as frightened. Anyway, she'd be the first to admit there were parts of Albuquerque that were less than scenic, but the Sandia Mountains were beautiful, and the Rio Grande valley was beautiful, and not anything close to a "wasteland."

Hasan's mouth compressed. "Do not bother to argue with me, mortal, for you have little idea of which you speak."

It was Madison's turn to press her lips together. She had to, or otherwise she feared she might say something she regretted. Yes, she'd survived trading a few barbs with the djinn, but she didn't know how long that might go on before he lost his temper. That was the last thing she wanted. She knew what he was capable of.

Apparently he saw the shift in her expression, because he smiled at her in triumph. "Ah, you are beginning to see the wisdom of silence. So you are capable of learning something."

This time it was almost impossible not to reply, but she kept her mouth shut. The best thing to do, she realized, was to avoid provoking him and hope that Qadim would be able to figure out where she was and come to rescue her. As much as she wished for that outcome, though, she worried about what would happen if the two djinn had an open confrontation. How did djinn even fight? If it were purely a physical match, then she'd say that Qadim would have the upper hand, since he was several inches taller than Hasan and had proportionally more muscle mass. But these were djinn, and so they probably had ways of fighting that involved a lot more than brute strength.

If anything happened to Qadim....

Hasan gave a satisfied nod, as if pleased by her silence. In the next instant, his hand was on her arm, and they blinked out of the living room and into another space. Judging by the wooden ceilings and trim around the window, it had to be in the same house.

A bedroom, Madison realized, looking at the queen-sized bed, the knotty pine furniture. The view through the windows here was even more spectacular, if possible.

Then it sank in. A bedroom.

She gulped in some air, hoping Hasan hadn't noticed. Apparently he didn't, because he said, "You will stay in here."

As prison cells went, it wasn't too bad. At least she could see trees and the sky, and there was an *en suite* bathroom. And the action of being blinked here had freed her from being tied to the chair, had given her aching arms and wrists a break.

Judging by the fairly modest scale of the room, she figured it must be one of the secondary bedrooms. No doubt Hasan had taken the master suite for himself.

Which was fine by her, because if he was staying there, it probably meant he didn't have any intention of sharing this room with her.

Despite her resolution to remain quiet, she couldn't help asking, "How long are you planning on keeping me here?"

A thin smile, one that didn't reach his eyes. "As long as it takes."

And then he was gone, blinking out of existence— or at least to another room in the house. It was definitely strange to watch. Now you see him, now you don't.

The important thing, though, was that Hasan was gone. At once she went to the door and tested it. Locked. She really hadn't been expecting anything else, but a girl had to try. Same thing with the windows. She should have been able to unlatch them and swing them open, but those latches felt as if they'd been permanently sealed shut.

Break the glass? There was a chair sitting up against the wall on the other side of the room that might do nicely.

And Hasan will hear it and be here in a flash...literally. Besides, maybe a djinn could fly out that window, but to a mere human, a twenty-foot drop is still a long way down.

She went to the window and looked out. Yes, because of the way the house was constructed, it probably was at least twenty feet to the ground. If she held on to the window frame and then dropped from there, she'd be cutting out some of the distance, but it would still probably be a hell of a jolt.

And that was doing a best-case scenario where a rampaging djinn didn't show up to bust her.

No, she knew the smart thing to do was wait for Qadim. He had to have missed her by now, so she knew he would have gone to the shelter to find her. And if he saw the overnight bag and the sketchbook she'd dropped, then he'd know something was wrong. It wouldn't take him very long to put the pieces together. She just had to pray he'd come up with a plan that didn't put him too much at risk. The thought of losing him now hurt almost more than the idea that she might meet her death at Hasan's hands.

Instead of hurling the chair out the window, she went and sat down on it, then stared at the sky and the trees without really seeing them.

Please help me, Qadim, she thought. *Because I don't know what Hasan is planning.*

She only knew that it couldn't be anything good.

CHAPTER FIFTEEN

To his relief, Qadim was able to find a New Mexico state map in the hotel's library. It was crinkled and somewhat worn, but still readable. As far as he could tell, the little town of Chama lay almost due north from Albuquerque, a little more than one hundred and fifty miles as the crow flies. Getting to Chama would only be the first of his problems, however. The real difficulty would be finding Hasan and—hopefully—Madison once he got there. Even a small town could have many houses, and from Madison he'd gotten the impression that the area was quite rural, with ranches and compounds on large plots of land. A search could take some time, and would be complicated by the need to avoid detection. It would never do to allow Hasan to see him coming.

For a moment, Qadim contemplated approaching the Council and telling them what Hasan had done, so he might face their justice. But almost as immediately he discarded the idea, because he knew the djinn elders would never help him. For one thing, he was far from being in their good graces, thanks to his involvement in his sister's ridiculous schemes. The real problem, though, was that they would see no reason to intercede. If Madison had been his Chosen, then she would have been protected. As things stood now, though, she was merely another human, one whom Hasan had every right to track down and kill.

Not that the situation was necessarily that dire. Hasan must have had something else in mind when he took Madison, because otherwise there was no reason for him not to have killed her the second he laid eyes on her.

The mere thought of losing her in such a fashion made Qadim's blood run cold, and he pushed the unwelcome image away. He couldn't waste his energy on imagining scenarios like that. What he needed to do now was focus on finding the woman he loved.

Loved?

He scowled. This wasn't love. He desired Madison, enjoyed her company, wanted her around him at all times, but that couldn't be called love...

...or could it?

Damn. He'd spent months or even years with women and had realized at the end that he didn't love them, but a few days with Madison Reynolds was enough for him to lose his heart?

Well, he could analyze his feelings for her later. In the meantime, he had work to do.

Although the djinn means of traveling instantly from one place to another was very useful, it wasn't infallible, especially when it involved going someplace where they'd never been before. Sometimes all that was required was a connection between two djinn, but Qadim had begun to distance himself from his old friend some time ago, as soon as it became apparent that Hasan was far too obsessed with hunting down humans for Qadim's comfort.

If he had possessed even a single picture of Chama or its environs as a reference, that would be useful and would provide him the context he needed, but Qadim had nothing. He searched the library and the offices at the hotel, hoping he might be able to find some sort of clue, even a brochure advertising that sightseeing train Madison had once mentioned, but his search proved fruitless, and he had no other resources to fall back on. Before the Heat, the world had been connected by a linked system of computers, and Qadim had heard that one could look up photographs and all sorts of other information on that system, but it was all gone now, dead as the men and women who had created it.

Which meant he would have to do this the old-fashioned way. The farthest north he had traveled in New Mexico was the little of village of Pojoaque, where he had once hidden Julia Innes at an abandoned estate in an attempt to lure Zahrias there. From Pojoaque to Chama was less than a hundred miles. In his inspection of the area while looking for a suitable place to serve as his base of operations, he had seen many horses left behind after their masters had died of the djinn-caused plague. Those horses had been skittish, but he thought he could still call one to him. Djinn naturally had a way with animals. So he would ride from Pojoaque to Chama, and then....

Well, then he would have the pleasure of squeezing Hasan's life from his throat.

If there was any pastime more excruciating than sitting around and wondering which horrible fate you were going to suffer, Madison couldn't think of one. Going by the time on her watch, she calculated that Hasan had dumped her in here a little more than two hours ago, and she hadn't heard anything from him since. She'd loitered by the window in the hope that she might see him coming or going, but apparently he was occupied indoors, or if he had gone somewhere else, he'd done so using the djinn method, and not any of the doors.

About an hour into her forced isolation, her stomach had begun growling, telling her that she hadn't gotten any lunch and that it had better get a damn good dinner. Not that Madison expected Hasan to take much care of her in that department. Maybe he planned to slowly starve her to death. It wasn't as spectacular a demise as being ripped to shreds in the middle of Menaul Boulevard, but maybe he didn't care, as long as she was dead and he'd rid the world of yet another useless human.

In usual magical djinn fashion, the indoor plumbing seemed to be working just fine. The water out of the tap was cool and sweet, and there'd been a tumbler sitting next to the sink in the *en suite* bathroom, so at least she didn't have to worry about dying of thirst any time soon. She'd filled the tumbler and brought it with her when she resumed her watch at the window, but there was nothing to see.

Well, almost nothing. She watched a few rabbits scamper across the yard, and an hour or so after that, a doe and a yearling wandered through the property, pausing to delicately nibble on the dry grass before moving on to greener pastures. A city girl, Madison couldn't help being a bit enchanted by the sight. But the deer and the rabbits certainly weren't going to help bust her out of there, so they were nothing more than a momentary distraction.

"I did say it was quite a view."

Madison whirled, almost dropping her tumbler of water in fright. Hasan stood just inside the locked door, a tray in his hands.

"There's something called knocking," she remarked caustically.

"Do jailers knock on their prisoners' cell doors?"

"So you admit I'm a prisoner."

"Of course you are. But I am not entirely without feeling. I've brought you something to eat."

Her gaze shifted to the tray he held. There was part of a loaf of bread, and some cheese. Not exactly the kind of gourmet food Qadim had prepared for her, but the meager meal at least promised that she wouldn't go hungry.

"Thanks," she said, although she knew her tone sounded anything but grateful.

Hasan affected not to notice, or perhaps he simply didn't care what she thought. He moved farther into the room so he could set the tray down on the bed. Well, that was something. If he was using the bed as a makeshift table, that meant he didn't plan to use it for anything else.

"There is spare clothing in the dresser," he said. "You should find something to sleep in. Unless you prefer to wear nothing at all?"

In answer, she just stared back at him. She could tell he wasn't being truly suggestive, but only saying what he hoped would get a rise out of her.

Since she didn't respond, he said, "Pleasant dreams," then shut the door. He must have headed back downstairs in the normal way, not djinn style, because she could hear the floor creak slightly before utter silence descended.

Madison looked at her watch. Not quite six. A little early for dinner, but she wasn't going to argue, not as hungry as she was. For the briefest second, she hesitated, wondering whether he'd tampered with the food somehow. But he was a djinn, possessing the kind of powers she couldn't possibly withstand. He didn't need to resort to something as sneaky as poisoning her. After all, she'd seen him in action on the streets of Albuquerque. Poison didn't seem to be his style.

So she picked up the partial loaf of bread and tore off a piece, then ate it slowly. Even though she'd tried to reassure herself that the food had to be fine, some part of her remained tense, waiting for the first sign of poisoning—stomach cramps? Heart palpitations? She didn't know for sure, since she didn't read murder mysteries and certainly never had any reason to investigate ways to poison people. Anyway, she kept waiting for something unpleasant to hit her, to make her realize she'd been foolish to trust Hasan even this much.

Her stomach didn't cramp. Her throat didn't seize up. She alternated the bread with some cheese, eating slowly to make the small meal seem as if it was more food than it really was. In between bites, she drank water from the tap. And when she was done, she thought she still felt fine…if one could use the word "fine" to apply to a situation where she was trapped by a murderous djinn who wanted her dead.

After she was finished eating, she went to the window and looked out into the gathering dusk. There wasn't much to see; the room faced east, and so didn't reveal much of what the sunset was doing, although the low mountains had begun to take on a faint reddish hue. Madison knew it was foolish to expect to see Qadim approaching like some sort of avenging angel, and yet that was exactly what she hoped for. She wanted him to show up and…what? Rip Hasan to shreds? Lord knows he was guilty of murder probably a hundred or even a thousand-fold. But she knew she really didn't want Qadim to be Hasan's judge, jury, and executioner. Right then she'd be happy enough if he would just take her away from here, give her some assurance that this would never happen again.

Problem was, she had a feeling that Hasan wouldn't give up until she was dead.

The house in Pojoaque looked much the same as it had when he'd left it. A little dustier, perhaps, but since barely a month had passed since he was last here, Qadim wasn't sure why he'd thought he should find it so altered.

Perhaps the alteration had been within him.

He didn't even know for sure why he'd come back here, except that it was familiar, and he needed some sort of starting point in his search for a suitable horse. If he'd been an air elemental like Hasan, he could have let the wind itself be his mount, but such an option was not allowed him. From time to time in the past he'd been aggravated by this strange limitation of his people, but never so much as he was now.

Standing here and bemoaning his inability to go directly to Madison wouldn't help him, however. He might as well get out there and see what kind of horse he could catch.

Because he had been in this area and canvassed its properties before, he did not have to walk laboriously from one spot to another, but could blink himself first to one abandoned homestead or ranch to another. He found houses with their paint beginning to peel, and rail fences starting to fall down altogether. Once he had to drive off a pack of feral dogs, although that was mainly a matter of raising his arms, as if he intended to strike out at them. That was all the situation required, for the dogs knew who was the master here.

However, if there had been horses in this area once—and Qadim knew there had, for he'd seen them for himself—they did not seem to be around anymore. Perhaps they had been rounded up by Zahrias and his people. Qadim was just attempting to decide if it was worth the risk of going closer in to Santa Fe to look for horses there when he heard someone call out to him.

"Qadim al-Syan. This is not your territory."

He turned and saw Danilar al-Harith, Zahrias' younger brother, floating in the air on the other side of the pasture. This vision was made all the more incongruous by the jeans and work shirt the other djinn wore. Air elementals did appear far more impressive when they arrayed themselves in the flowing djinn robes, which could billow nicely in the breeze they generated.

"I was not aware Pojoaque was part of your grant," Qadim said calmly.

"It is not part of yours, either," Dani returned with a frown. "We were told that you were sent to Albuquerque. What are you doing here?"

Qadim wondered where the younger djinn had acquired that particular piece of information. Perhaps the elders had passed it on as a courtesy, since the land where the Santa Fe group of djinn and their Chosen had settled was not so very far from the grant which had been given to him.

"Looking for a horse," Qadim replied.

"Do you jest?"

"No. I fear horses are in short supply in Albuquerque, but I knew I had seen some when I was here last. Unfortunately, they appear to all be gone."

"We have gathered them in," Dani said. "Our stores of fuel are dwindling, and Zahrias thought it better to have our Chosen adjust to using a more sustainable means of transportation."

"Wise of him," Qadim remarked. He had not meant the words to be taken ironically, but he could still see Danilar tense. Well, they were not all on the best of terms.

"Why would you have need of a horse?" the other djinn asked. "For that city is yours, and you can travel in it far more easily using your own powers than having to go about on horseback."

It was a reasonable enough question. It was also one that Qadim had no desire to answer. How could he admit that the woman he cared for had been stolen from under his very nose? No doubt Danilar—and Zahrias, his brother—would find it amusing to hear that Qadim, who had kidnapped Zahrias' woman, had now had his own woman taken away.

"I must travel to a place I do not know," he replied. "You know as well as anyone else the dangers of attempting to do so by our usual means."

For a moment, Dani said nothing, only watched Qadim carefully, as if attempting to glean the truth from his expression. When he spoke at last, his words were not ones that Qadim wished to hear. "I think you must come and tell my brother what it is you are doing here. This is no place for you, Qadim al-Syan, and so we require an explanation."

Damn. Qadim forced himself not to react, except to raise an eyebrow. For while he guessed that he would be able to best the younger djinn if it were to come to blows, he would also be forever invoking the enmity of Zahrias al-Harith, and indeed of all his people, if he did so. On the other hand, going to speak with Zahrias would cause an unconscionable delay. Who knew what Hasan was doing to Madison at this very moment?

"I do not think that is necessary," Qadim said, choosing his words with care. "I have done no harm here. I have not ventured into the limits of the city your people have claimed for their own. Why should I have to come before your brother like a common criminal?"

"Because you are a criminal," Danilar retorted. "Taking my brother's woman—"

"She was not his woman then."

That comment seemed to stop Dani in his tracks. He paused, as if replaying the memories of those events in his mind, then shook his head. "Semantics. You are still a kidnapper, and only free now because you realized your assistance to your sister could hurt your own chances when it came to receiving your land grant from the elders. Do you deny any of that?"

"No."

Once again Dani appeared flummoxed by Qadim's reply. Most likely he had been expecting some form of protest. Then his dark brows drew together. In that moment he looked a little too much like his older brother, although in appearance they were not all that similar, except for their coloring. "Then I fear you have no choice but to explain yourself."

"And are you going to drag me down to Santa Fe and force me to do so?" Despite the urgency of his current situation, Qadim couldn't help being somewhat amused. While Danilar al-Harith had once been a warrior of some repute, he still would have some difficulty attempting to subdue someone of Qadim's stature.

"No, because he summoned me here instead," said Zahrias, appearing from nowhere to stand next to his brother. The leader of the Santa Fe djinn did not look pleased to have had his day interrupted; his arms were crossed and his brows were knitted in a frown that was an uncanny echo of the one his brother wore.

Damn again. Qadim had been able to share that same subvocal communication with his sister—that is, until her plotting nearly ruined them both. Luckily, she could not reach from the otherworld to touch his mind here, and so he had been blessedly free of her interruptions once she had been exiled to her palace on that unearthly plane. But he had forgotten that Dani might do the same thing to summon his brother to confront their trespasser.

"Well met, Zahrias al-Harith," Qadim said politely. "Peace seems to agree with you. And how is Julia Innes?"

"Very well, although I doubt she would be pleased to hear that you are inquiring after her," Zahrias replied. His frown showed no sign of disappearing. "What is it you want here?"

"As I told your brother, I was in need of a horse."

"And there are none in Albuquerque?"

Of course there were. Not in the city center itself, but in the outlying areas were homes that had large lots, where there were barns and horses. He had made sure that the grass grew more thickly in those places, but left the horses alone. The djinn had destroyed mankind...but they had also made sure that the animals left behind would be well fed and happy. After all, they were innocents.

Without blinking, he said, "It was necessary for me to ride forth from Pojoaque."

Eyes narrowing, Zahrias asked, "To go where? Taos has been forbidden us, and to the west is Los Alamos, where I do not think you would be given a very friendly reception. And to the north, I have heard, is Hasan al-Abyad, who I do not think will be very happy to see you."

That much is true, Qadim thought, even as Zahrias continued,

"He is certainly no friend of ours, and of no one else, it seems. So I must ask again—where would you be taking this horse of yours?"

Sometimes the truth was the only way out. And perhaps al-Harith would be sympathetic. Doubtful. However, Qadim could not think of a lie that the other djinn would believe. "To Hasan al-Abyad's lands in Chama. For he has taken someone I care for, and I fear he means to do her harm. Since I have never been to Chama, nor even seen a picture of it, I can travel in no other fashion."

The two brothers exchanged a glance. Perhaps they spoke to one another's minds; Qadim had no way of knowing.

When Zahrias spoke again, his tone was dry. "So you have taken a Chosen? It seems your heart recovers quickly, Qadim."

"She is not my Chosen," he said quickly. "But she is human, and I think we all know Hasan's history when it comes to his dealings with human beings."

Another of those significant looks. But this time the al-Harith brothers appeared troubled, for they did know of Hasan's predilections, and the trail of blood he had left behind him. And because they both had selected their own Chosen, their sympathies lay with the hapless humans, not those who had hunted them down.

Dani said, "Qadim, how do you even know she is alive? For Hasan—"

"There was no evidence to show that she had been injured," Qadim replied. His throat tightened as he remembered the scene he had found, the discarded bag, the sketchbook with its pages rippling in an uncaring breeze. "I also know of Hasan's methods, and have seen his handiwork. She was alive when she was taken, which means he must have some other intention beyond simple mayhem. Else he would have killed her where she stood."

Dani nodded, and Zahrias said, "This makes some sense. And I think we can help you."

"So you will let me take a horse?"

"Better than that," Zahrias said. "For I believe one of our Chosen comes from that part of the world, and so her djinn had to find her there. He can guide you to Chama, if not directly to wherever Hasan has taken up residence."

Relief surged through Qadim as he thanked the other djinn. He had not expected assistance, only scorn—and he would have deserved it. Why Zahrias al-Harith had decided to grant him this measure of grace, Qadim did not know, but he would do his best to show that he was worthy of it.

Be safe, my love, he thought then. *For I am coming to save you.*

As Hasan had said, there was an assortment of women's clothing in the dresser of her room-slash-prison cell. Not too off in size, either; whoever had called this place home must have also been tall and slim. Anyway,

Madison didn't need a couture fit, just something to sleep in other than her jeans.

She changed quickly, one eye fixed on the door the entire time. No, Hasan hadn't shown any evidence of having that kind of interest in her—thank God— but she couldn't rule out the possibility that he might barge in here while she was changing, just to upset her, throw her off balance.

But she was able to get into the T-shirt and leggings without interruption, and folded her own clothes and put them on top of the dresser. By then it was full dark, but the electricity worked, just as the plumbing did, so at least she didn't have to sit in here in total darkness.

Under the sink in the bathroom she found a tooth-brush still in its packaging, so she brushed her teeth and used the face wash sitting on the countertop to clean her skin. All these actions felt so ordinary, so routine, and yet she knew there was absolutely nothing normal about her current situation.

Just what the hell are you up to, Hasan? she asked herself then. *Is this some kind of feud with Qadim?* But that didn't feel right. From the way Qadim had talked about the other djinn, it had almost seemed as if they were, well, not friends exactly, but at least on civil terms, even though Qadim clearly didn't share Hasan's views on human beings.

Padding quietly on the wooden floor in her bare feet, Madison went and listened at the door. Dead silence, except a cricket chirping somewhere in the hallway just outside, and a faint creak from overhead as the house settled. If Hasan was moving around anywhere in the house, she sure as hell couldn't hear him. But then, from what she'd seen of it, the home was a large one. It made sense that she wouldn't be able to hear anything.

The silence didn't reassure her, though. If anything, it only made her more nervous. Since she didn't know whether Hasan was listening to her, and the last thing she wanted him to hear was her pacing around the room, she went ahead and climbed into the bed. She'd already checked it for the ominous gray dust and hadn't found any, so whoever had lived here, they hadn't perished in this bed. In fact, the sheets were crisp and showed folds from being stored, indicating that they hadn't even been slept on. Maybe this had been someone's vacation house. It was out in the middle of nowhere, after all. In Madison's mind, the home seemed a little big for a vacation getaway, but she hadn't known any people with the means to build a second house, so her frame of reference was somewhat limited in that respect.

Well, Clay Michaels probably could have afforded it, but he'd put all his money into building a bomb shelter instead.

But even though the bed was comfortable enough, and Madison knew she should get some rest as insurance against an uncertain tomorrow, she couldn't sleep. Maybe it was only that she knew it was far too early for her to be in bed—barely seven-thirty. Or maybe it was simply that every creak, every scratch made her eyes fly open, certain that Hasan was just about to fling open the door and descend upon her.

Or worse, blink his way in. Djinn really didn't need to bother with doors.

For the fifteenth time, she rolled over and shut her eyes, praying that she'd finally found the one position that would allow her to fall asleep. The floor creaked again, and she uttered a mental curse as her eyes popped open for the umpteenth time.

Only to see Hasan staring down at her, his teeth gleaming white in the darkness. Her mouth opened—to scream, to gasp—but he was far too quick. In the next instant, he was pulling her from the bed, arms like iron bands around her chest. And then he blinked her away into the dark.

CHAPTER SIXTEEN

Going to Santa Fe felt like traveling in the wrong direction; however, Qadim couldn't refuse Zahrias' offer. He might be delaying slightly by going to that djinn stronghold for help, true. But that assistance would save him many hours on the road, hours during which anything might be happening to Madison.

The home Zahrias had taken for his own was large and luxurious. Qadim hadn't really expected anything else, for Zahrias was the leader of the colony here, and should have a house that befitted his station.

He also should have expected to encounter Julia Innes there, and yet it was still a shock to see her, to come around a corner and have her standing there, beautiful as ever, warm blonde hair falling nearly to her waist. She wore a dress in a deep blue that set off her eyes, and silver jewelry around her throat and wrists. Truly, she was stunning, but...

...but he could look on her and feel nothing, because his heart was given elsewhere. She was very lovely, but she didn't have Madison's amused mouth, or her luxuriant curls, or...anything else. Qadim could look at Julia and be glad for her happiness, and know that it did not take anything away from him.

She stepped forward as soon as Zahrias and Qadim entered the living room. "I am so sorry, Qadim," she said. Sincerity rang in her voice, and he realized that she truly was sorry for him, despite everything he'd done to her. "Zahrias told me something—"

"Only a little, for Qadim has not told me the whole story," Zahrias cut in, his tone mildly reproving.

"I do not have time for the whole story," Qadim replied. "But know that Madison managed to survive on her own for more than a year, and that when we finally met, it took some convincing to make her see that I meant her no harm. She is resourceful, and I am sure she is doing whatever she must to survive while in Hasan al-Abyad's hands. But I must go to her as soon as I can."

"I understand," Julia said. "And Sheri and Ahmar will be here at any moment. Why don't you sit down? There's a pitcher of iced water."

Qadim did sit on one of the chairs, mostly because he could tell that he made Julia nervous, looming over her. She was doing her best to be polite, but she would never forget what had passed between them, how he had attempted to use the djinn glamour on her, to claim her as his. Nor should she forget. He was embarrassed now for what he had done, but he could not change the past.

And he feared he would not be able to change the future, if he didn't go to Madison soon.

Zahrias remained standing, as did Julia. Perhaps that was only because they wanted to go answer the door as soon as this Ahmar and his Chosen appeared, or perhaps it was because, while they were willing to help, they did not feel comfortable sitting down with him as equals.

"So you are in Albuquerque now?" Julia inquired, clearly attempting to fill the awkward silence that had just fallen.

"Yes."

"That's my hometown."

"I fear you would not recognize it," Qadim told her. "I have been doing some...redecorating, as Madison put it."

Julia's elegant eyebrows lifted. "Redecorating?"

"I do not find most human architecture appealing. So...I am removing it."

Her eyes widened and she opened her mouth to speak, but was interrupted by the doorbell. At once she made her excuses and went to answer it. A human custom, but one the djinn followed as well. It was necessary to adhere to such niceties when one had the ability to appear or disappear in a house on a whim.

A moment later, she returned with a tall brown-haired djinn Qadim had never seen before, as well as a lovely young woman with long dark hair and striking blue eyes. "Qadim, this is Ahmar al-Suth and his Chosen, Sheri Hennessey."

Ahmar only nodded, but Sheri essayed a quick smile and said, "Hi, Qadim. Zahrias and Julia told me that you're looking for someone in the Chama area."

"Yes," he replied. "You are from there, correct?"

"Right. My parents were the caretakers on a big ranch up there—the owners actually lived in Denver and only came down for the summer." She waved a hand, as if realizing that information wasn't really necessary for the task at hand. "Anyway, I know Chama real well, and Ahmar knows it, too, since that's where he came to me." A pause as she glanced up at the djinn standing next to her. Something in the warm glow in her eyes and the curve of her mouth seemed to indicate that she'd been very happy to see him, and still was.

Qadim couldn't help thinking of his first encounter with Madison, how she'd bolted as if all the demons of hell were after her. He supposed that, in her mind, they really had been. She'd had no reason to believe he was going to do anything except kill her on the spot.

Whereas this Ahmar had appeared to his woman as a savior.

"Yes, I know it," Ahmar said. His voice was deep and somewhat rough, and something in its tone seemed to indicate that he wasn't overly pleased to be given this mission. Well, if he was loyal to Zahrias, then he might be puzzled by his leader's willingness to help someone who had kidnapped him and handed him over to his insane sister.

"Good," Qadim said, beginning to rise from his seat. "Then let us go."

"Not so quickly," Zahrias cut in. "I understand your eagerness, Qadim, but to go charging in without a plan is utter foolishness. Hasan al-Abyad is a hasty sort. If you startle him, he may do something that we will all regret."

Those words made a current of ice rush through Qadim's veins. Yes, he knew that about Hasan. The man was quick to anger, quick to action. If he caught wind of Madison's rescuers before they were able to gain the upper hand, things might go very badly indeed.

Although it was almost physically painful to force himself back into his chair, Qadim did as Zahrias had instructed and sat down, then waited to hear what the other djinn had to say. However, Ahmar didn't speak, but nodded toward Sheri, as if deferring to her local area knowledge.

"Right," she said. "Well, Chama itself is teeny— basically a wide spot in the road—but there are a lot of big properties around there, ranches, vacation homes, all that kind of stuff. So it's hard to say where this Hasan person could be living, because he'd have a decent number of places to choose from. But if I had to guess—"

"Please guess," Qadim told her. "Because your guess is certainly going to be better than any of ours."

Sheri looked somewhat flustered by the interruption, but then she lifted her shoulders and plowed ahead. "I'm just wondering if he isn't at the place where my parents worked."

"What makes you say that?" Julia asked, clearly intrigued.

"Well, it's a nice house, probably one of the nicest in the area." Her mouth quirked, and she added, "No offense to you djinn, but I haven't seen any of you taking up residence in someone's double-wide. You all seem to gravitate toward the million-dollar mansions."

Ahmar couldn't help smiling slightly at that comment, although he didn't say anything. And neither Zahrias nor Qadim bothered to protest, either. Qadim wondered what Sheri would think about his occupation of the penthouse suite at the Hotel Andaluz.

"So yeah, it's a big house, on a big piece of land, and the property backs up to the Chama River on one side, so it's really pretty. If Hasan was given that area for his own, he could do a lot worse."

"How protected is it?" Qadim asked. "That is, is it the sort of place with many trees around it?"

Sheri frowned. "Not really. I mean, there are trees on the river side of the property, so the view to the west is a little blocked. But on the other three sides it's pretty open. You can see all the way to Grouse Mesa from two of the guest bedrooms upstairs."

Which meant they would have to materialize on the river side of the property, since coming in from any other direction would be far too visible. Unless they could appear in the house itself.

He asked that very question, but Ahmar shook his head. "No, Sheri did not actually live at the ranch, but only worked there with her parents. Their own house—where I came to retrieve her—was more modest, and some distance away."

"I showed him the property before we left to go to Taos," she added. "But I didn't take him inside. I think I was a little shell-shocked right then." She stopped there, as if she'd intended to say more and then decided against it. Probably she knew she didn't need to elaborate on the feelings of fear and uncertainty that had enveloped the Heat's survivors, the unanswerable question as to why they were still alive when so many countless others were dead. After that awkward pause, she went on, "For some reason, it didn't feel respectful to me to go in the house. I wanted to say goodbye to the river, though, and so that's where we went."

"Which means I can take you directly there," Ahmar said. "It should be close enough, since this Hasan can have no idea that anyone still alive knows of the property and its location."

No, it was rare luck that any one of Zahrias' people had come from the Chama area at all. The djinn had gathered their Chosen from all over the state, since its population was so small, but even so, Qadim didn't want to calculate the chances of someone from Chama actually surviving the Heat. That didn't matter now, though. What mattered was that Sheri and her djinn lover were here and could help him to get to Madison.

Because she was the most important thing now. Qadim didn't want to tell himself that he would die for her; he had never believed in that kind of sacrifice, thought it foolish and wasteful.

No, he wanted to live for her.

Back in the living room. Madison had been terrified that Hasan was going to take her outside and feed her into the wood chipper or whatever other torment his twisted brain might have devised, but that didn't seem to be his immediate plan.

Instead, he sat her down on the chair where he'd first had her tied up. Something seemed to have agitated him, although she couldn't begin to guess what.

He'd tied her arms behind the chair, even more tightly than the first time. She couldn't move at all—not that she really wanted to. With the way he was pacing back and forth and muttering to himself, she thought it was far wiser to stay as still as possible so as not to set him off.

Could djinn go insane? Her only real knowledge of the race came from her research in Clay Michaels' databases and then her interactions with Qadim, and he certainly seemed level-headed enough. Well, level-headed for someone who wanted to raze Albuquerque to the ground and create a garden in its place. But she'd never gotten the impression that he wasn't playing with all the dots on the dice—he was funny and kind and loving and occasionally wicked.

In a good way, though.

She couldn't say the same for Hasan. Her fingertips were starting to tingle, a sign that the ropes which bound her had begun to cut off her circulation. But she didn't wiggle her fingers, because she was afraid he might notice even that small a movement. She didn't do anything except sit there and pray that whatever had set off Hasan this time, it would fade away and he'd turn back into the faintly sinister but at least manageable person he'd been a few hours earlier.

"How do you do it?" he said then, turning back on her so quickly that she couldn't help but let out a quick gasp, one she sucked back in and hoped he didn't hear.

The last thing she wanted was to antagonize him, but she really didn't know what in the world he was talking about. "Do what?" she asked cautiously.

"What is it about you humans that draws them in, like flies to honey? Your race is a feeble one, without powers, without long life, without anything of any note to recommend it. Your women are no more beautiful than ours. So what is it?"

Qadim had told her how the djinn would come to humans sometimes, that the myths of the succubus and the incubus had arisen from those liaisons. The djinn glamour at work, but other than that, she hadn't seen anything so strange about there being an odd kind of sexual attraction between the two races. They looked basically the same. Yes, the djinn on average were more attractive than most humans. But looks weren't everything.

"I don't know," she replied. It was the only answer she could give, but clearly Hasan wasn't pleased by it. He frowned, dark brows drawing together over his bright blue eyes, and his mouth tightened.

"You'll have to do better than that, human."

Madison's heart rate began to speed up, although she told herself that this was no time to lose her cool. Hasan was so clearly balanced right on the edge, it wouldn't take much to push him over. The problem was that she had absolutely no idea what she should say to make him calm down. "It's the truth. I really don't know. I'd never met a djinn before I met Qadim. He... wasn't what I was expecting."

"Yes, my friend Qadim al-Syan always was weak when it came to women. Oh, I will admit that they have their uses, but he is far too soft-hearted." Hasan's eyes narrowed, as if he'd just had a sudden thought. "Perhaps it is only that he was not afforded much choice, after the Council exiled him to that wasteland he must now call home. So when a human crossed his path, he decided to take her for his own, since no djinn woman would have him."

Yeah, that's exactly what happened, Madison thought, but she held her tongue. She doubted Hasan would appreciate sarcasm, especially coming from a lowly mortal. "Maybe," she said, then added, "I didn't ask."

Damn, that was probably a little too flippant. She couldn't take back the words, however, and so she only sat in her uncomfortable chair and waited to see how he would react.

A slow smile spread over Hasan's mouth. In a way it was almost impressive how someone so objectively handsome could make his face appear so unattractive. Or maybe she only saw it that way because she knew a smile like that couldn't mean anything good.

He approached her, then knelt on the floor next to her chair. Because he was tall—if not quite as tall as Qadim—their faces were nearly level. Hasan's eyes scanned her features, and Madison again had to fight to keep herself still. Being on the receiving end of that kind of up close and personal scrutiny from someone she cared about would be uncomfortable enough, but having this incomprehensible djinn doing it was a thousand times worse.

Then he reached up and ran a hand down the side of her cheek. His fingers were warm, almost uncomfortably so, and she had to fight back a shudder. "Now that I look at you, I think I can see what he saw. There is an interesting symmetry to your face."

Well, it wasn't quite the same as being compared to a Botticelli painting, but she didn't dare reply, only kept her gaze fixed firmly forward. She knew it didn't matter what she said. Hasan was going to do what he was going to do, and she'd just have to figure out what to do about it when the time came.

"And this hair," Hasan continued. He grasped a handful of her loose curls and tugged, quite hard. This time, Madison couldn't help wincing, because damn, that hurt. And then she wished she hadn't reacted, because his smile only broadened. "Was that too rough, Madison Reynolds? What if I did this instead?"

His hand moved down her hair, caressing. If Qadim had touched her like that, she would have shut her eyes in pleasure. Now, however—all she could do was hope she'd have an opportunity to wash that hair in the very near future.

And even though she'd vowed to herself that she would do her very best to keep quiet no matter what, something in her rebelled at this treatment. Yes, she doubted very much that Hasan actually wanted her. These were just more of his sick mind games. But he also was a man on the edge, and so she really couldn't begin to guess what he might be capable of.

"I'm surprised you'd want to dirty your hands on a human," she said, still not making eye contact.

Something about the djinn seemed to go still. For a second or two, he said nothing. Right then, Madison questioned her decision to keep her gaze locked forward, because she would have given a good deal to see the expression on his face.

Then he pushed himself up from the floor and came around in front of her so that she had no choice but to look at him. She'd halfway been expecting a face contorted with fury. Instead, he appeared strangely blank, as if her words had taken him past anger to a place she really didn't want to know about.

When he spoke, his voice was too soft, although there was an edge to it that made her stomach curdle. "What if I've decided I do want to? What if it just occurred to me that it could be the best way to learn what it is that can take a djinn like Qadim—who has never sullied his hands with a mortal before now—and make him thrall to a mere human?"

"He's not my thrall," Madison said. Somehow she knew she was far past the point where silence could save her. "He's—I don't know what he is, exactly, except that he's amazing." Why she'd said that, she wasn't exactly sure. Clearly, Qadim and Hasan were friends, or had been once, which meant they must have possessed qualities that the other person admired. Maybe if she praised Qadim, showed that she really did appreciate him, then Hasan would back off.

"I assume any of us would be amazing...to a human," Hasan returned. The challenge was clear in his voice. He wanted to see if she would tell him that she didn't find him amazing at all.

Giving him such a response would have been her first instinct. However, insulting the person who held you captive generally wasn't considered a very good idea. "I can see that," she said, her tone neutral.

"Ah, I am quite sure you don't." He moved behind her, and she tensed. But then she felt his hands on the ropes that bound her, loosening them. In the next moment, he had grasped her by her arm and was pulling her to her feet.

Pins and needles rushed to her abused fingers, and Madison fought the urge to wiggle them. She couldn't be relieved that Hasan had freed her hands, because she had a sick feeling he'd only done so because he wanted more access to her. That suspicion was borne out as he took her by the arms and held her tightly so she couldn't possibly wriggle free. He stared down at her, eyes flickering as he seemed to take in every detail of her features. Cataloguing her faults, or trying to convince himself that he didn't want to do this after all? She prayed it was the latter, hoped with all her being that he would come to his senses and realize that forcing her wouldn't change anything. He would still hate humans, but he would also hate himself.

His fingers felt like iron digging into her biceps. She'd known the djinn were all enormously strong, because she'd seen Qadim perform feats of strength that not even an Olympic weightlifter could achieve. But he'd been gentle with her, as if he knew he had to be careful, that he wasn't dealing with a djinn woman. Hasan, on the other hand, couldn't seem to care less. If she survived this, she'd probably have rings of bruises around her upper arms, like the world's most unwelcome tattoos.

Then he pulled her closer, his gaze fixed on her mouth. Was he steeling himself to do this? Maybe he'd lose his nerve at the last moment. Maybe he was thinking that kissing her would be like kissing a baboon. Obviously, a number of djinn didn't share his sentiments about humans, but none of that mattered right now. The only thing that mattered was what happened to be going on in Hasan's head.

Before she could blink, his mouth slammed down on hers, hard, his tongue forcing her lips open. He didn't taste bad—oddly, he tasted of cinnamon more than anything else—but revulsion rose up in her anyway. Once or twice in a bar, a half-drunk guy had gotten a little handsy with her, but never in her life had Madison been forced like this, had someone make her kiss him when she clearly didn't want to.

The kiss would only be a prelude to other things, she knew. This wasn't about sex; this was about showing who was in control.

And she couldn't allow that.

Past the sickness in her throat, past the horror that this monster with so many deaths on his hands was shoving his tongue into her mouth, a very cool, calm thought took shape.

He's a djinn, but he's built like a man. And if that's the case, then he's vulnerable just like a man. It will hurt a lot, if he's as aroused as he seems.

Because she could feel his cock pressing against her belly, hard and insistent. Those djinn pants didn't hide much. They also didn't provide much in the way of armor.

Her knee came up with every ounce of strength she possessed, driving straight into his groin. In shock, he let go of her arms, and that was the only opening she needed.

She couldn't stop to look at him, to check to see how much damage she'd done. All she could do was turn and run from the living room and down the hall, her bare feet slapping against the wooden floor. A fleeting thought crossed her mind—*damn, I wish I had some shoes on*—but she didn't let that slow her down. Maybe a blow like that would incapacitate a djinn just as long as it would a regular man, since their equipment seemed identical. And maybe it wouldn't, and he'd be raging after her in just a second or two.

The hall ended in a door, although it went to a service porch and not directly outside. But there was another door, and that one did open on the outdoors. The night was black as pitch, with not even a sliver of a moon to light her way. Yes, the stars were almost impossibly bright overhead, but they didn't do much to show her any detail.

She stumbled blindly down the steps and toward the sound of water, which seemed to be coming from her left. A sharp rock bit into her left foot, and she had to stifle an exclamation, although the pain didn't keep her from continuing to run in the direction of what she guessed must be a river or stream.

Not that it really mattered whether she'd made a sound or not, because light glared from the house, coming both from the door she'd just exited and a series of floodlights apparently mounted somewhere under the eaves, illuminating the yard and instantly revealing her position.

"I see you," Hasan called out to her from the open doorway. He sounded winded, but Madison didn't dare stop to look back at him to see if he was limping or not. "Do you really think you can run from me?"

And in the next instant, she collided with something solid and unmoving. Hasan, who must have blinked himself from the back stoop and directly into her path. His arms closed on hers, grasping her in exactly the same place where he'd held her before. A grunt of pain escaped her lips. "Let me go," she gasped.

"Oh, I don't think so. And don't try that trick again."

Air swirled around them, faster and faster, enclosing them in a spinning vortex, like being held captive in the heart of a tornado. Suddenly, Madison could no longer feel the cold, harsh earth beneath her bruised feet. She looked down, and saw that they were now hovering at least fifty feet above the ground.

"Yes," Hasan hissed. "You see, I suppose you could attempt to wound me again, but then I might drop you. I fear that soft human bodies generally don't fare very well when subjected to such treatment."

Maybe it would be better to have her neck broken by such a fall, rather than be subjected to whatever the djinn had planned next. Something in her rebelled at giving up so easily, though. Qadim was still out there, certainly looking for her, and she had to stay alive for him, no matter what happened.

"I won't," she said.

"You won't what?"

"I won't try to hurt you. Please set us down, Hasan." She hesitated, hating to sound weak even when she knew she was only doing so in order to lull him into thinking he had her beaten. But then she added, "I'm sorry. Please—I'm scared of heights."

Even in the semi-darkness, she could see a flicker of triumph in his eyes. Her arms were screaming in agony, but she didn't move, stayed quiescent in his grasp. Then he let go, and a scream rose in her throat—just before he caught her again, this time with his arms around her waist, pulling her close. She hated the feeling of him being pressed up so close to her...but she also hated the idea of dropping fifty-plus feet onto the stony ground, so she didn't resist, only stayed quiet in his arms.

And oh, thank God, they were slowly dropping toward the earth, the maelstrom around them quieting as they descended. Hasan obviously thought all the fight had gone out of her. Good. It was far from gone, but she had to bide her time. The second he let go of her, she'd bolt again. One good thing about the light glaring into the yard—it had told her that there was a line of trees not so far away, probably bordering the river. If she could just make it into those trees, then he wouldn't be able to see her very well. And maybe then she could finally get away.

Alone, and barefoot, in a landscape she didn't know. She'd still take her chances. If she stayed here with Hasan, she knew all too well what would happen.

Their feet touched the ground. Madison was just about to let out a sigh of relief when the earth below her began to shake and rumble. Caught off balance, Hasan loosened his grasp on her waist. Startled, Madison looked around her, only to see Qadim emerging from the trees, one hand outstretched.

"Run, Madison!" he called to her.

So she ran.

CHAPTER SEVENTEEN

THEY HAD MATERIALIZED IN A WOOD OF PINE TREES
and cottonwood and aspen. Directly at their backs was a
small river, or large stream; it chattered away in the darkness, rushing over a bed of smooth stone.

Ahmar pointed off to his left. "That way."

"How far is the house?" Qadim asked.

"Close. Less than a quarter of a mile. I did not want
to come in too near the property for fear that Hasan
might hear us. Next to the river like this, the sound of
the water masks most noise."

That it did. Qadim was actually surprised to see how
high the river was running, for in the more southern
parts of the state, rain hadn't fallen for many days. But
he was glad to hear the water rushing past, for it was as

Ahmar had said—it was difficult to hear much else over the sound it made.

"This way," the other djinn said, and Qadim followed him as they moved through the trees, leaves crunching under their feet. Even in the darkness, Qadim could see how the aspens here had already mostly turned, where in Albuquerque the foliage had not yet begun to shift into its autumn finery.

From somewhere up ahead and to the right, he heard a strange howling sound and tensed. He himself was an earth elemental, and his sister one who controlled the waters, and yet Qadim still knew what that noise meant. An elemental of the air had brought the winds to do his bidding, and that was rarely a good sign.

He began to bolt forward, but Ahmar reached out and grasped him by the arm. "Wait," he said, his voice an urgent whisper. "It will not do to give away the element of surprise. We are almost there. Wait until you can see what is really happening."

Wise words, and yet Qadim chafed at having to slow down. Madison could be somewhere up ahead, at Hasan's mercy, and if he had summoned the winds, most likely that meant he was using them to control her somehow.

Qadim and Ahmar reached the edge of the little wood just in time to see Hasan come to rest in the middle of an open yard that consisted of weeds and rocks and not much else. Held tightly in his arms was Madison.

She looked unharmed, but the rage that awakened at seeing her in Hasan's embrace did not leave much room for relief. Ignoring Ahmar's sudden protest, Qadim strode forward, lifting a hand so he might raise the powers of the earth against this djinn who had the temerity to take the one thing he valued above all else.

Hasan stumbled as the ground beneath his feet shifted. Madison looked toward the woods, face pale and frightened in the darkness. The sight only increased Qadim's anger, but he retained enough control to shout at her that she must run.

She didn't waste time with protests, but sprinted forward, her long legs propelling her toward the wood where he and Ahmar waited. At the same time, Hasan regained his balance and turned in her direction.

At once a wind arose, buffeting her and pulling at the heavy curls of her hair. She winced, then stumbled—for the first time, Qadim realized she was barefoot—but she did not fall and instead continued toward him, ignoring as best she could the winds that assailed her.

She was strong, but Qadim knew she could not hold out for long against Hasan's onslaught. "On your knees!" he shouted to her. "You will need to crawl, my love!"

Her eyes widened, but she did as he said, immediately dropping to the ground and moving ahead on all fours. At the same time, he sent another temblor rolling through the earth, one he made sure would crest more or less exactly where Hasan stood. The other djinn staggered, cursing, and the winds tugging at Madison's hair subsided somewhat. She didn't look behind her, but continued doggedly, as if she knew that allowing herself to be distracted would only make matters worse.

Then Hasan seemed to recover himself, and raised his arms. Not toward Qadim, but toward Madison.

A dust devil arose in the darkness, surrounding her. She stopped, choking, as the very air was torn from her lungs.

"Leave her alone!" Qadim flung at Hasan. "Your fight is with me!"

"No, I think not," Hasan replied. He did not sound angry. In fact, an incongruous note of laughter rippled through his voice, as if he was enjoying himself immensely. "For my fight has always been with these worthless humans. You are my friend, Qadim—or at least, I thought you were."

"No friend of mine would seek to wound the woman I love," Qadim shouted, and the ground roared in response, so violently that Hasan once again lost his balance, this time falling to his knees. From the house behind him came a groaning sound and a low rumble, as of rocks collapsing.

But the wind still surrounded Madison, who could barely be seen through the whirling column of dust. And then another wind arose, no tornado this time, but a cold blast that felt as if it had come straight down from the mountaintops. Qadim glanced over his shoulder and saw Ahmar standing there, face calm but focused as he brought his own powers to Madison's aid, summoning a wind that tore through the dust cloud which surrounded her and dispersed it in all directions.

Still coughing, she began to move forward again. Close, so close....

And then she was there at his feet, and his arms were around her, feeling her alive but shaking violently.

"Take her," Ahmar said. "I will hold him off while you make your escape."

"He is mine to deal with," Qadim growled. Surely Ahmar did not think that he would slink away and allow someone else to manage the man who had almost killed Madison.

"Then come back and deal with him later, after your woman is safe," Ahmar replied. Perspiration showed on his forehead, evidence of the effort he was putting forth to keep Hasan's demon whirlwinds at bay.

"Please, Qadim," Madison said, her voice a rough croak. "Take me away from here."

How could he ignore that plea? He gazed down at her pale, strained face and nodded. And then they were gone, leaving Hasan and Ahmar behind.

Every bone and muscle in her body ached. Madison sat on the bed in Qadim's penthouse suite and tried not to gasp in pain as he dabbed antiseptic on the torn and bruised soles of her feet. A first aid kit sat open on the nightstand. She wondered where he'd gotten it, but then realized the hotel would have had to keep one somewhere, if only to minister to any workplace-related bumps and bruises.

"How did you know where to find me?" she asked.

Qadim looked up briefly. The worry hadn't left his dark eyes, but he gave her a tired smile. "I knew that Hasan had been given the territory around Chama. The task of locating you would still have required much searching, if it had not been that one of the Chosen in Santa Fe was born in that area. She helped to narrow down where Hasan might be living, and then her djinn brought me there."

"You went to Santa Fe?" For some reason, that revelation surprised her. She hadn't really pried, sensing that he didn't want to discuss the subject, but she'd gotten the impression that Qadim didn't have much use for Santa Fe, or the djinn and their Chosen who lived there.

"Yes," he said briefly. To her relief, he set down the antiseptic and the soft cloth he'd been holding, then placed a pad on the bottom of her foot and began taping it in place. "That is, I went as far north as I could, thinking I might find a horse and ride the rest of the way to Chama."

"It would have to be a pretty big horse," Madison remarked, amused despite everything. Her imagination had just put Qadim on the back of one of the Budweiser Clydesdales, and she couldn't quite keep her mouth from quirking.

"True. But I encountered Zahrias al-Harith's younger brother in Pojoaque, and Danilar convinced me that it would be best if I spoke with Zahrias and told him why I had such a desperate need to go northward."

Madison nodded. At the same time, she had to ask, "But why would they even help you? You made it sound as if you weren't on the best of terms."

"No, we are not. But Zahrias—or any of his people, really—could not ignore the plight of a woman taken by a djinn with murder on his mind. Unfortunately, Hasan's exploits are well known."

A shiver went over her. Delayed reaction, probably, as the room was quite warm, worlds away from the chilly air that had surrounded the house in Chama. Or maybe it was just the memory of Hasan's harsh grip on her arms, the bruising touch of his lips on hers.

Perhaps disturbed by her silence, Qadim frowned, his gaze locked on her face. "He did not—"

"No," she said immediately. She wasn't defending Hasan, God, no, but she couldn't have Qadim thinking that the worst had happened. "He seemed more repulsed by me than anything. Disgusting human, and all that. But he did—" A swallow of air, followed by another. Why was it so hard to spit the words out? Maybe it was just that she was away now and safe, and Qadim was with her, and if she told him everything, he would go back and try to finish what he'd started. She loved him, and couldn't bear the thought of him putting himself back in harm's way like that. "He did force a kiss on me. Not to be romantic. Just to—to show me what else he intended. That he was in charge."

A long, long silence. Qadim sat there at the foot of the bed, the position he'd taken so he could minister to her wounded feet, and said nothing. He felt so very far away, and Madison wished he would move, would come to her so he could hold her and tell her that everything was going to be all right. His eyes were hooded, not meeting hers.

Then he said, "I will kill him."

"Qadim—"

"You would plead for him, when he dishonored you so?"

"This has nothing to do with him," she said desperately, willing him to listen, to not retreat behind djinn notions of honor and retribution. "I don't want you to kill him because I don't want you to take that on yourself. It's not worth it. I'm safe. I'm here. Let it go."

Scowling, Qadim rose abruptly from the bed and went to the window. What he thought he would see out there, she couldn't begin to guess, since it was black as pitch outside. "What kind of man would I be to let things lie as they are? And what makes you think that he would do the same? The two of us have unfinished business. You must realize that there is nothing to stop him from coming here and attempting to steal you again."

Those words sent a chill over Madison. She hadn't even stopped to contemplate that possibility, thinking that as long as she stuck by Qadim's side, she should be safe. But the two of them had been locked in a stalemate, and it was only that other djinn—Qadim had told her his name was Ahmar—who had been able to break the impasse and had allowed her to reach safety.

Still, she had to protest, even if she didn't entirely believe what she was saying. "I don't think he'll do that. For one thing, I plan to stick to your side like glue. I hope you don't mind." She'd hoped that comment would make him smile, but he only stood by the window like a dark, brooding god, his expression unchanging. "And also, you had one of the djinn from Santa Fe come help you. That's got to give Hasan pause as well, since he can't count on that not happening again."

"It will not happen again," Qadim said, the words flat, allowing no argument. "We are not allied in any way."

"But Hasan doesn't know that for sure."

Another silence. Qadim touched the curtains that framed the window, the dark, silky fabric flowing under his fingertips. "Do you continue to argue with me in the hope that I will eventually give in?"

"Well, maybe," she replied, then tilted her head at him. "Is it working?"

At last he smiled, but it was a weary one, barely lifting the corners of his mouth. But he did come away from the window and sit down next to her on the bed. The shifting of the mattress jarred all of Madison's abused muscles, although she didn't much care. Far more important that Qadim was here now next to her, his very presence a comfort, even if the things he'd just said certainly were not. She reached out a hand, and he took it. So warm, so strong. She'd never been the type to think she needed a man around, or someone to complete her, but right then she couldn't help but think it felt damn good to have him there, so solid, so real.

"You are tired," he said. "This is nothing that needs to be solved tonight. Tell me what you want."

"You," she said, and his eyebrows lifted, as if surprised she would have the energy for that sort of thing. "Not sex," she amended. "I just want you here next to me. I want to lay my head against you, and I want you to hold me if I wake up in the middle of the night."

"Of course. I will be here for you, my dear."

He leaned in and placed a kiss against her cheek, very gently, then helped her slip under the covers. When he'd brought her back to the hotel, he'd gotten clean things for her—a tank top and capri-style yoga pants—and had fetched a damp washcloth from the bathroom and cleaned the dust and grime from her face. So she was ready enough to get into bed, even if he wasn't. She watched as he got up and took off his jeans and T-shirt, then joined her under the covers, wearing only his boxer briefs.

At any other time, the sight would have been enough to get her blood racing. But she'd told him the truth. She was far too exhausted to even think about sex. All she wanted was to lay her head on his chest and have those wonderful muscles of his provide a far better pillow than anything the hotel might provide. His arm went around her, heavy and comforting.

She shut her eyes, and fell into a deep, dreamless slumber.

Madison slept. Qadim wished he could do the same, but despite the weariness that had invaded his limbs, he did not know if he could abandon himself to oblivion. Not while Hasan was still out there. Qadim knew that Ahmar would not have stayed to see that particular battle through to the end—he had his own Chosen to worry about, and besides, this was not his fight. He had only provided a necessary diversion, nothing more. He would have left as soon as he was sure Qadim and Madison had gotten safely away.

Whether Hasan would dare to come here...Qadim wasn't sure about that. Something in his friend's mind had come unhinged, that seemed clear enough, but he might still possess enough instincts of self-preservation to decide this fight was not worth the effort. Then again, he had devoted a significant amount of energy to making sure that every single mortal he'd encountered was wiped off the face of the earth. That he hadn't done the same thing to Madison was deeply troubling. Of course Qadim was relieved beyond measure that she had escaped relatively unscathed, but this reprieve would count for little if it only meant Hasan would make it his life's work to ensure that she, too, did not survive in the end.

Not while I live and breathe, Qadim thought then, touching her knotted curls—but gently, so she wouldn't awake. This fiercely protective instinct surprised him, for he had certainly never experienced it before. Was it only that Madison was a mortal, and so did not possess the sorts of powers that would help to keep her safe?

And yet somehow she had survived being the captive of an angry and vengeful djinn, had even managed to escape him, if only for a few brief moments. Still, that was an achievement not many humans could claim as their own.

Or perhaps it was because he had never loved any of those women from his past, and he knew now that he loved Madison, loved the sound of her voice and the way she would tilt an eyebrow at him when he said something particularly outrageous. Loved the talent in those fine, long-fingered hands of hers, loved the way her hair spread out on the pillow as she slept. Loved the long scar on her arm, where she'd told him that she'd broken a bone as a child.

He'd never understood love before. Attraction, yes, the delicate dance that brought two people into one another's orbit, culminating in an entirely different type of dance, usually horizontal. But he had always wearied of those women, or they of him, and they had parted with few regrets on either side. He had seen friends swept into passionate affairs that resulted in centuries-long commitments, and yet those relationships had never lasted for all time. Indeed, he had begun to think that love must be a construct of humanity, something they had invented to give meaning to their all-too-short lives.

He knew better now.

And he knew what he should do. He only feared he did not possess the courage to take that final step.

"Madison."

She opened her eyes, saw Qadim staring down into her face. What time was it? The place had the peculiar, indistinct blurry darkness of a hotel room with the blackout curtains pulled shut, so she really couldn't guess at the time of day. "Is it morning?"

"Yes, my dear. Quite late in the morning, and we have visitors."

That announcement made her sit up straight, heart beginning to pound. "Not—"

"No," he said at once. "Not Hasan. A delegation from Santa Fe."

"What are they doing here?"

"I suppose that is what they wish to tell us. I informed them that you were still in bed, but they said they would wait."

That comment sounded ominous. But she knew that burrowing under the covers and trying to go back to sleep was not an option. "I need to shower, and my hair is a disaster—"

He smiled. "Madison, you could never be a disaster. But I understand how you might want to feel a little more freshened up, as it were. I will offer them something to drink, and in the meantime you can prepare yourself. Just come down to the lobby when you're ready."

Then he bent and kissed her on the cheek, and let himself out of the suite. Madison pushed herself out from under the covers and got up, letting out a hiss of pain as her full weight hit her battered feet. They would heal eventually, she knew, but the interim was not going to be a lot of fun. Thank God those little jeweled sandals Qadim had procured for her were so light and open. She thought she should be able to slip them on over the bandages.

He'd brought up her things—toiletries, a change of clothes, fresh underwear. Amazing how thoughtful he could be. Once upon a time, "thoughtful" was probably the last adjective she would have ever applied to a djinn. She knew better now, though.

After peeling off the bandages and disposing of them in the trash, she climbed out of her clothes and into the shower, reveling in the sensation of the hot water beating down on her. If only she could stay in there for hours and hours. But she knew people were waiting for her, so she hurried through washing her hair and soaping away the residue of her encounter with Hasan al-Abyad. When she got out of the shower, she felt much better, if not completely herself yet.

That, she feared, would require much more than a ten-minute shower.

Fresh bandages for her wounded feet, then the world's fastest primp, with moisturizer quickly followed by some mascara and gloss. About all she could do with her hair was towel-dry it within an inch of its life, then scrunch some anti-frizz serum into it.

Qadim had also fetched a clean pair of jeans and a long-sleeved T-shirt for her. Madison hesitated over the pile of fresh clothes, then shook her head and went to the closet, hoping that he'd thought to bring up some of the djinn-style clothing as well. Sure enough, several pieces hung in the closet, so she chose a tunic and pants in deep green silk with pale gold embroidery, and put those on. There was also a pair of gold sandals sitting on the floor of the closet. She grabbed them and headed over to a chair so she could gingerly slip them on over the gauze pads on the soles of her feet.

Gold glinted from the nightstand. Madison couldn't remember seeing them there before, but when she went in for a closer look, she realized that the golden glint had come from a pair of earrings and a set of matching cuff bracelets. She slid them all on, then gave herself one last glance in the mirror. Considering everything she'd been through the day before, she didn't look half bad.

Because her feet hurt so badly, her progress down the hall wasn't nearly as swift as she would have liked. And the thought of all those flights of stairs....

But Qadim had taken pity on her, because when she got to the end of the corridor, she saw that the door to the elevator stood open. They hadn't used the elevator very much in the past, and so she uttered a silent thank-you that he'd remembered to send it to her now.

Madison got in the car and pushed the button for the ground floor. The elevator descended slowly and seamlessly, making her almost forget that it was currently powered by djinn energy and nothing else.

The sound of voices greeted her when the elevator doors opened. She'd become so used to hearing only one person speak at a time that for a second she hesitated, a little overwhelmed by the noise.

Then Qadim was hurrying over to her, his robes billowing as he approached. He held out a hand. "Madison, my dear. Is it very difficult to walk?"

"I can manage," she said.

"Then let me introduce you to our guests."

She nodded and did her best to smile, although the thought of having to meet a group of unfamiliar djinn so soon after her confrontation with Hasan was rather daunting.

There were four of them—but they weren't all djinn. The darkly handsome man with his hair pulled back from a proud-boned face...he was obviously djinn, as was the exotically beautiful woman with a fall of raven-dark hair and big striking green eyes circled in kohl. However, the Hispanic man standing next to her, while movie-star gorgeous, was clearly human, as was the blonde woman who looked up and smiled as Madison and Qadim approached the group.

Something about her seemed familiar to Madison, although she couldn't think how that could be possible. She didn't remember ever meeting her, but....

"Madison," Qadim said, "this is Zahrias al-Harith, leader of the Santa Fe djinn community, and his Chosen, Julia Innes. And this is Miguel Cervantes, their healer, and his partner, Aliyah. When they learned of how you'd been injured, they thought you could use some assistance."

"Um...thank you," Madison replied, taken aback, both by the offer and the realization that she'd heard the woman's name before. Julia Innes, whom Qadim had once hoped might be his. Madison forced that thought away, telling herself that he had moved on.

Anyway, she couldn't deny that her feet did hurt like a bitch, and she hoped she hadn't gotten anything nasty in any of those cuts, but....

"It's all right," Miguel said with a bright, flashing grin. Clearly, the djinn had made sure their Chosen were just as handsome as they were. "I've got EMT training. I just want to check and make sure everything's been cleaned out properly. When was your last tetanus shot?"

"Two years ago," she replied, thinking how incongruous that exchange had been. She might as well have been in her local urgent care center.

"Maybe if you sat down in one of those chairs over there?" Julia suggested. Her voice was low and sweet.

Again Madison got the feeling that she'd seen her somewhere before, but even though she racked her brains, she couldn't come up with a likely explanation. Maybe it was only that Qadim had spoken of her, nothing more. So Madison just nodded and hobbled over to one of the lobby chairs, while Miguel sat down on the table in front of her, carefully avoiding several glasses of water that had been placed there—for Qadim's guests, she supposed. For the first time she noticed that he had a black leather doctor's bag leaning up against that table.

"Prepared, I see," she said.

"I figured it couldn't hurt. But I'm afraid some of this probably will."

"It's all right," she told him. "I'd rather it hurt now than hurt worse later."

Miguel lifted one of her feet and very gently took off the sandal she wore. The bandages followed, while Madison did her best not to grind her teeth. As he worked away, swabbing the area with some kind of high-powered antiseptic liquid, she made herself concentrate on the conversation the two djinn and Julia Innes were having with Qadim.

"...no sign of him at all?" Zahrias inquired.

"No," Qadim replied. "It has been quiet here."

"Well, that's something," Julia said. "Isn't it?"

Zahrias' shoulders lifted slightly. "Perhaps. Or perhaps he is merely licking his wounds and planning his next assault."

"That's what I fear," Qadim said. His voice was pitched low, but Madison could still catch every word. "I have done my best to ward this place against him, but that sort of thing is not my talent."

"Which is why I thought I should come," said the djinn woman, speaking for the first time. "Hasan is my cousin, and if someone of his blood draws the wards, they will be far more effective."

Madison tried not to startle at that revelation. So this woman was related to Hasan, but would still work against him?

None of the others seemed particularly surprised by her statement, although Qadim did smile before saying, "That would be most appreciated, Aliyah."

The djinn woman nodded and headed off in the direction of the front doors. To set the wards? Probably, although Madison didn't have any real idea of what that even meant.

"Other foot," Miguel said, and once again she startled.

"What?"

"I'm done with this one," he said with another one of those white-toothed grins. "Time to move on."

"Oh, right." Madison lowered her right foot and offered up her left. As her newly bandaged foot touched the floor, she didn't wince quite as much as she had previously. Maybe the bandages he was using were thicker and softer than the ones that had come from the hotel's first aid kit.

She'd lost some of the thread of the previous conversation during that gap; as she strained her ears to hear what they were saying, it sounded as if Zahrias was telling Qadim that he should bring Madison with him to stay in Santa Fe.

"No, I will not hide," Qadim said.

"I wouldn't exactly call it hiding—" Julia began, but he shook his head.

"That is your territory. This is mine. I will not leave it."

She shot a helpless look up at Zahrias, whose mouth hardened. "It is his decision, Julia," he said. "We cannot force him."

Right then, Madison almost wished they could. This was no time to be stubborn, not when Hasan could show up on their doorstep at any moment. But it seemed obvious that Zahrias had no desire to make Qadim do something he obviously didn't wish to.

"All right," Miguel said then. "You're all patched up. Does that feel better?"

Cautiously, Madison got to her feet. Yes, the cuts and bruises still stung, but the pain was muted. She'd be able to walk around without shuffling like an old woman. "Much better. Thank you."

"No problem." He rooted around in his doctor's bag and brought out a plastic pill bottle. "You should take these, too, just to make sure nothing goes sideways."

She looked at the label on the bottle. Amoxicillin, with the prescription made out to someone named Lita Juarez. Miguel must have found it at one of the pharmacies in Santa Fe. A prescription filled for someone who would never come to pick it up.

Right then, Madison's throat felt a little tight. She'd coped with the aftermath of the Heat by trying not to think about it very much, but every once in a while it would still sneak up on her, like now.

"Thanks, Miguel," she said, forcing the words past the lump that seemed to be blocking her vocal chords. "I really appreciate it."

"Glad I could help." He snapped the doctor's bag shut.

Apparently, Qadim heard, because he looked over at them and then immediately went to Madison, offering a steadying hand under one elbow. "All better?"

"Yes, Qadim, I think so." She glanced over at Zahrias and the woman who stood next to him, and all of a sudden it fell into place. That terrible time only four or five days after the Heat had claimed her father, when Madison had hidden herself in an alley and had watched that small group of survivors pass by. Julia Innes was the woman she'd seen that day. "You were with them!" she exclaimed, and Julia's eyebrows lifted as she looked over at Madison, clearly startled.

"Excuse me?"

"I'm sorry," Madison said, aware that everyone present was looking at her. But Qadim's hand on her elbow was strong and reassuring, so she took a breath and went on, "I've been trying to place you ever since I came into the lobby. I just remembered where I saw you—it was here in Albuquerque, not quite a week after the Heat struck. You were with a group of survivors, and it looked as if you were all walking north."

"You—you saw us?" Julia's voice was incredulous, not that Madison could blame her. "But if you were there, why didn't you call out to us? Weren't you glad to see other survivors?"

"I was." Madison hesitated, wondering how she could explain her decision without sounding like a complete idiot. "But...that man who was leading you. I know it sounds crazy, but I just got a really bad vibe from him. So I decided to keep on hiding and not say anything."

Julia's expression went bleak then, and her full lips pressed together. "Well, that was probably wise of you. Richard Margolis was not a good man."

"'Margolis'?" Madison repeated, then glanced up at Qadim, whose face was carefully blank. "So the man I saw in Albuquerque was the Captain Margolis you killed?"

No one seemed surprised by her question. So they already knew the truth about what had occurred between Qadim and Margolis.

"Yes," Qadim said. For some reason, his gaze flickered toward Julia before returning to Madison. "As I said, there are few who would mourn him."

There was a quiet tension in the little group, one Madison knew she should leave alone for now. She'd have questions for Qadim later, but that could wait.

"But at least you all made it safely out of Albuquerque," she said.

"Yes, we did," Julia said. "We were in Los Alamos for some time, but now I'm in Santa Fe permanently." And she cast a look up at Zahrias, one of gentle longing as a smile curved her mouth.

Madison knew that look, because she'd worn it on her face more than a few times. Only she'd never had quite that same expression of belonging, of knowing exactly where she fit in. How could she, when she had no idea what Qadim's long-terms plans for her might be? He'd cried out the night before that she was the woman he loved, but she still wasn't sure exactly what that meant to him.

"And that is where we should return," Zahrias put in. As he spoke, Aliyah reappeared, this time coming in from the side door to the lobby, the one that opened on Copper Street. She gave him a faint nod as she went to stand next to Miguel, looping her arm through the one that wasn't carrying the doctor's bag.

"I thank you for the assistance you've given Madison," Qadim said formally.

"Glad to help," Miguel said.

They made their goodbyes, and in the next moment the group had blinked out of the lobby, leaving Madison and Qadim alone together.

"Breakfast?" he said.

"What?" Her thoughts were still far away. Maybe as far as Santa Fe. How had the djinn known to find them here? True, the Andaluz was pretty conspicuous now that all the buildings surrounding it had been torn down, but....

"I thought you might like something to eat."

She supposed she would. Last night she'd had a few bits of the bread and cheese Hasan had given her, and nothing else. Things had moved so quickly afterward that she hadn't even stopped to think about feeding herself. Managing a smile, she said, "That sounds wonderful."

Hand still supporting her elbow, he began to guide her toward the restaurant. Yes, the work Miguel had done on her feet helped a lot. They hurt, but not too badly.

But she and Qadim hadn't taken more than a few steps before a flash of brilliant light nearly blinded her. Madison stopped abruptly, arm jerking from his grasp.

Standing before them was a group of djinn she'd never seen before, five of them in total—three men and two women. And standing in front of them, his arms crossed and a smirk of triumph on his face, was Hasan al-Abyad.

CHAPTER EIGHTEEN

Qadim's entire body went rigid. The elders, here? And in company with Hasan al-Abyad?

Beside him, Madison was still as well, clearly unsure as to what she should do next.

Do nothing, he thought, knowing she could not hear him, but at the same time praying she might be able to read something from his expression. *For I must handle this.*

Fists knotted in the folds of his robe, he took a step forward. He knew he must at least do lip service to the customs a situation like this demanded, and so he bowed from the waist, then straightened and said, "Elders, you honor me by your presence." *But I cannot say the same for you, Hasan.*

"Indeed," said Ibram, eldest of elders. His voice was dryer than the desert which surrounded this town. "I believe you do not feel nearly that honored, but that is no matter. Hasan al-Abyad has a grievance to debate with you, and we are here to adjudicate."

Qadim's gaze flickered toward Hasan before returning to Ibram. From the unholy light dancing in Hasan's blue eyes, Qadim thought it clear enough that the other djinn believed he was the wronged party here. "A grievance?" he said, making sure his tones were all of wounded innocence. "I cannot think why."

At that obviously disingenuous comment, Hasan moved forward a few paces, lip curling. "Oh, you cannot think why, Qadim? Well, allow me to refresh your memory, since it appears to have failed you. I was well within my rights to take this woman and do with her as I pleased, for you have no true claim on her. She is human, and therefore prey."

"She is under my protection—" Qadim began angrily. Next to him, Madison made a brief, abortive movement, as if she'd intended to say something and then realized she was clearly out of her depth. Yes, they might have been arguing about her fate, but because she was only a mortal, she truly had no say here.

Ashtar, the elder with the fall of rich, copper-red hair, held up a hand. "Is she your Chosen?"

Trust Ashtar to get to the heart of the matter. More than once in his past, Qadim had wondered what it might be like to bed her, for she possessed a mixture of power and wry humor he found engaging, and she was very beautiful, but he never quite dared to approach her in that way. Now, he could only be relieved that he had no past with her. This was going to be difficult enough without any of those sorts of complications.

"No, she is not," he said. "But that should not matter. I found her, and I took her. She is my woman. Hasan has no claim on her."

Madison muttered something under her breath, but Qadim couldn't quite make out what it was, only that the phrase seemed to contain the word "caveman."

He was not a caveman. He could not expect her to understand some of the aspects of his world, just as aspects of the one she had once inhabited still eluded him.

"And you have no claim, either," Hasan said, the sneer back in his voice. He turned to the watching elders, his entire posture one of wounded innocence. "Was it not agreed that only the Chosen were to be protected?"

"This is true," Ibram said. Neither his expression nor his tone gave any indication as to whether he thought that was just or not. He was merely stating a simple fact.

One that Qadim knew must be subverted somehow. For yes, it was true that only those humans who had been selected by their djinn to spend eternity with them were safe. All the rest of humanity was fair game. This was what had been agreed upon during the centuries of planning and squabbling that had led up to the Heat being unleashed on an unsuspecting population. In truth, he was the one who had bent those rules almost to breaking by sheltering Madison.

"And therefore it is also true that Qadim has subverted those agreements and broken our laws by offering protection to this woman." Hasan's eyes had taken on a sly glint, as if he knew he was backing his adversary into a corner.

Qadim glanced over at Ashtar. She was watching the proceedings with the sort of mild interest that a human might have evinced at a sporting match whose outcome he cared little about. Was that truly her opinion, or was she merely shielding her feelings, since she knew she must be impartial?

"I would argue that no such law exists," he said. "Yes, agreements were made, but an agreement is not a law. Or am I misinterpreting what was agreed upon?"

A silence. Ibram glanced back at the other elders, at Nathal and Imara and Abdael, who usually were content to watch and wait to weigh in after everyone else had spoken their piece. Their faces, too, were impassive, revealing nothing of their thoughts.

It was Ashtar who spoke next. "Most would say that something agreed upon by all our people is as binding as law, even if it was not written down as such.

So that is one semantic hair we shall not allow you to split, Qadim al-Syan."

Damn. He risked the briefest of glances at Madison, saw the pure outline of her profile, the way her throat moved as she swallowed. She was frightened, he could tell, but although her face was pale, she remained still, chin up and eyes fixed forward. In that moment, he had never thought her more beautiful.

He must do whatever he could to save her.

"Very well," he said. "But was it not also agreed upon that once this world was ours and our particular territories granted to each of us, we should hold sole sway over that land and everything in it?"

Ashtar's green eyes narrowed. She sent a side-long glance in Ibram's direction, and he gave a faint nod. "Yes," she said slowly. "This was also part of the agreement."

Relief wanted to flood through him, but Qadim would not allow himself to take much satisfaction from that small victory. He still had a very long way to go. "Then if that is true, I would claim that this land is mine. Everything in it is mine. Including Madison Reynolds, for I found her here, did I not?"

"That is ridiculous," Hasan protested. "She is a human, not a necklace or a painting or a bar of gold."

Once again the elders were silent. For some time Qadim had suspected they spoke together with their minds, the way the djinn and their Chosen supposedly could, but he had never been in their presence long enough to make an educated guess. Now, though, from the way their eyes darted toward one another, and the way their mouths would move ever so slightly from time to time, he was almost certain that was what they were doing.

He would have given a lot to know what they said to one another now.

During that uncomfortable pause, Hasan stood with his arms crossed, his greedy gaze fixed on Madison. She had to know he was staring at her, and yet she never moved, never gave him the satisfaction of acknowledging his presence. And Qadim wished the elders were not there, so he might reach out with his power and shake the earth so Hasan might stumble and fall. Just one moment caught off guard, and then Qadim would have his hands around his former friend's throat. He did not even care if he damaged this building that had become his home, if it meant the threat from Hasan might be removed forever.

At last Ibram and Ashtar exchanged a nod. In that instant when their eyes were locked, Qadim realized he would never have succeeded in pressing his suit with the beautiful elder, for her heart had already been given.

"Qadim al-Syan," she said, "you pose an interesting argument. For it is true that each of us was promised our own land, and those grants included everything those lands contained."

"Well, then—" he began, but got no further, for she shook her copper-hued head at him.

"I had not finished, Qadim." Her tone was mild enough, but he could tell she would not appreciate any further interruptions.

For the first time, Madison moved. Only to shift her weight from one foot to the other, but he could see a certain tightness to her mouth. All this time standing must be paining her, undoing the work that Miguel, the healer from Santa Fe, had done.

"Before you go on, I would ask that Madison be allowed to sit down. She was injured last night, and her feet are hurting."

"I'm fine, Qadim," Madison murmured, but he didn't reply, only kept his gaze fixed on Ashtar.

"I am sorry for that," Ashtar said. She waved a hand, and one of the chairs from the conversation area lifted from the floor and drifted through the air before settling directly behind Madison. "You may sit."

"I don't—"

"Sit."

Apparently startled by the steel in Ashtar's voice, Madison settled herself in the chair. She looked much smaller seated like that, and Qadim wondered if he had made a mistake in asking that she be able to sit down.

"As I was about to say," Ashtar went on, "while it was agreed that we should all receive the lands allotted to us and everything in them, it was first agreed that all Immune who were not Chosen had no protections, and could be hunted down by those of us who took pleasure in such things." From the edge of disdain in her voice, it seemed clear enough that she had no very high opinion of those who would make prey of beings so much weaker than they.

Unfortunately, Hasan seemed not to notice, or at the very least did not care. A gloating smile lifted his lips, a smile that Qadim wanted to punch.

I would take much joy in hearing his teeth clatter against this floor. Unfortunately, I doubt the elders will allow me that pleasure.

"And so," Ibram said, picking up the thread of Ashtar's logic, "we must bow to the precedent agreement in this case. You may argue that you found Madison Reynolds here, and this much is true. But Hasan al-Abyad has the first claim, for she is human and not Chosen."

"That is ridiculous," Qadim burst out. Right then he cared very little for who he might offend. "If we are going to worship precedent here, then I am the one who found her first."

"True," Ibram said. "But you would break our compacts by keeping her as your pet, as it were. The agreement was very clear in this instance. The vast majority of our people had no interest in keeping humanity alive. Those of the One Thousand who objected were allowed their Chosen, and because of that, they must live apart. It is the fate they chose, and neither I nor any of us here will comment on that, because it is done. There is only one clear path here, Qadim al-Syan. I think you know that as well as I do."

Oh, yes, he did. He looked down at Madison, whose hands gripped the armrests of her chair so tightly that he could see her knuckles standing out even whiter against her already pale skin. She cared for him...but how much? Enough to spend eternity with him?

And did he care that much for her? He had admitted that he loved her, but he also knew that love was newly come to him, something he had barely begun to acknowledge, much less understand. His life had been composed of one conquest after another, only to be abandoned when those women no longer suited him.

If he made Madison his Chosen, he could not abandon her. They would be joined forever...and forever was a very long time.

"You don't have to do it," she said then. Her voice was low but clear, although she would not look at him, as if his hesitation had wounded her.

Neither would she look at Hasan, who still wore that hungry expression on his face. Was he eager to bed her? Kill her? First one, then the other? That would be a triumph for him, Qadim supposed, to use her body until he was done, then discard her like so much trash.

Rage filled Qadim. That could not happen. *Would* not happen. She was too brave and bright and beautiful. Perhaps it would have been better if she'd fled to Los Alamos all those months ago so she might have a normal life among her own kind, but that fate had been denied her.

No, now she must be joined forever with a sorry specimen who had hesitated when he should have marched in right away and made her his. Perhaps one day she would forgive him for his weakness.

After all, he would have eternity to seek absolution.

"She *is* my Chosen," he said then, voice strong and carrying, echoing off the high ceilings. "I choose her to be bound to me forever. She is under my protection now, and any djinn who raises his hand against her will feel my wrath."

"And ours as well," said Ashtar, moving so she stood shoulder to shoulder with Ibram. "For she is now Chosen, and protected from those who might seek to cause her harm." Her gaze flicked to Hasan, who hadn't moved, instead stood rooted in place while wearing an expression of baffled fury, as if he hadn't quite yet comprehended what had just occurred. "Hasan al-Abyad, we dismiss your grievance. You may go from here."

"But—"

"You may go," Ibram cut in, his voice a blade.

Hasan blanched. "I follow your word."

And he was gone, departing with a bang that sounded louder than usual. For a few seconds, no one spoke.

But then Ashtar said, "Our work here is done. And you, Qadim al-Syan, and you, Madison Reynolds— you must prepare to leave this place. For by claiming a Chosen, you have given up your right to this land. You must take your things, and go live with the others of your kind in Santa Fe."

Of course. He thought of all the work he had done so far, of how he had tried so hard to love this land, even if it had been given to him almost as a joke. But that didn't matter. What mattered was the woman who sat beside him, her face pale and stunned. She still hadn't quite grasped what had just happened to her.

She was his...but he was also hers, now and for all time.

They had better start making the best of it.

He turned and bent slightly so he could take her cold fingers in his and raise her from the chair. She stood, but he could feel the way her body shook.

"We will give you some time," Ibram said. "But in the morning, you must be gone."

A faint nod, and then all the elders disappeared with a wild rush of wind that set the chandeliers swinging overhead.

"Well, my love," Qadim told Madison, "it seems we might as well get started."

She sat on the edge of the bed, watching as Qadim gathered up their things and placed them in a handsome set of matched Louis Vuitton luggage. Where he'd gotten it, she had no idea. Not that it really mattered.

Her hands wouldn't stop shaking. Qadim had made her his Chosen. She would be bound to him forever, would never age, would never get sick, would never...be a true human again.

"You didn't have to do that," she said.

He paused, hands full with a half-folded robe of dark gray silk. Those deep-set eyes searched her face, as if attempting to determine whether she was serious or not. "Of course I did," he said at last. "You know that I care for you, Madison. How could you possibly think that I would abandon the woman I love to the hands of that madman?"

"I—" Well, of course she knew that Qadim would never do such a thing. Yes, there were things in his past he wasn't proud of, things he'd done and could never erase. But those few small missteps didn't make him a bad man. In this situation, he'd done the one thing he knew would save her, now and forever.

But at what cost?

With little care for the silken fabric, he shoved the robe into the suitcase and came over to her, taking her hands in his so he might pull her up from the bed. She expected a throb of pain as she put her full weight on her feet, but that didn't happen. Yes, there was a slight twinge, but so much less than it should have been.

Because she was Qadim's Chosen, and now she would heal more quickly than any normal human being ever could. She would never get sick, never grow old.

Never die.

"My love," he said, fingers tightening on hers. "I know it is a great deal to take in. Just remember that you are safe, and that we are together. All the rest— well, you will learn to live with that as time goes on. It will become easier."

"How do you know that?" she asked, unable to keep the fear from her voice. "You've never had a Chosen before, have you?"

"Of course not. But I have seen how the djinn in Santa Fe are with their Chosen. They are happy, Madison. They are learning how to share their lives. We can do the same thing."

She held on to his hands as if they were the only thing preventing her from drowning in deep water. And perhaps they were. This was nothing she'd asked for. Yes, far in the back of her mind, she'd harbored a secret hope, but that's all it had been. Hope. Not certainty. She knew she loved him, had never been with anyone who made her feel the way he did, but...was that enough?

Then he pulled her close, his lips touching hers, almost tentatively, as if he wasn't sure whether she wanted to share this sort of intimacy after what she had suffered at Hasan's hands. But as soon as their mouths met, she knew this was exactly what she needed. She needed him to touch her, make love to her, claim her again as his, now that they would be bound together for eternity.

He seemed to sense her need and fumbled with the buttons on her tunic, undoing it enough so he could pull it over her head. His hands found the clasp to her bra and undid that as well, his strong fingers closing on her breasts, stroking her.

"Yes, Qadim," she breathed. "Touch me. Touch all of me."

A low, heated growl at the back of his throat, and then they were both on the bed, his welcome, delicious weight on top of her as he yanked at the drawstring of her trousers and pulled those and her underwear down with one swift motion, just before his fingers slipped into her. She moaned, writhing against him as his mouth closed on her nipple and his strong, sensitive fingers found the places that needed his touch the most, stroking her, bringing her to the edge so she could fall over it, drowning in waves of ecstasy, her entire body thrumming with a wild heat centered in her very core.

Then his mouth was on her, and she cried aloud, knowing that the next climax was already building on the shimmering afterglow of the last, every nerve ending in her coming alive as he tasted her, making love to her with his tongue. And as she came, he slid into her, filling her, their bodies finding a new rhythm as he rocked harder and harder, his heavy hair falling around her face as she breathed him in, took him in as he reached his own climax, his warmth spilling into her, filling her.

The world spun. She clung to Qadim, knowing he was her center, the one thing she could always be certain of. He loved her enough to make her his for all time. How could she question that? How could she do anything except love him back, and know that everything was going to be all right?

They were joined, now and forever.

CHAPTER NINETEEN

QADIM HAD ASKED HER IF SHE WANTED TO RETRIEVE any of her belongings from the bunker, but she'd shaken her head. That was her old life. She didn't want to drag anything from that time of worry and fear and being hunted into this new world, this new life among the djinn and their Chosen.

The elders must have spoken with Zahrias, or informed him in some way, because he was waiting when Madison and Qadim drove into town. They'd decided that was the best way to leave Albuquerque, since they didn't know exactly where they were going in Santa Fe, and they had enough things to carry that Qadim would have been hard-pressed to take it all in one trip.

Besides, she had to be impressed with his style; Albuquerque's stores of gasoline were aging, so he'd found an electric car for them and charged it using the energy supply he'd created for their use while living at the Andaluz. And not just any electric car, but a Tesla S.

"More than a two hundred-mile range," he said proudly as he opened the trunk and loaded in their luggage.

"It's only fifty-five miles or so to Santa Fe," Madison pointed out.

His grin didn't fade. "Even better."

Zahrias didn't look all that impressed when they pulled to a stop on the north side of the Plaza, across from the Palace of the Governors. Once upon a time, you couldn't even park there, as that area used to be blocked off so that street vendors could sell their wares there, but those days were long gone.

"Welcome to Santa Fe," the djinn leader said as Qadim and Madison got out of their vehicle.

"We thank you," Qadim replied formally.

"Julia has put together a list of properties that might be suitable for your use," Zahrias continued, producing a folded piece of paper from somewhere inside his robes. He handed it, not to Qadim, but to Madison.

"That was very thoughtful of her," she said.

"We wish to see you well settled here. If there is anything you require, you need only reach out to one of us. Julia will be in contact later once you've made your decision."

"Please give her our thanks," Qadim told him.

Zahrias didn't smile. Was he unhappy that the two of them would be living here, considering Qadim's rather spotty past when it came to Julia Innes?

Unfortunately, there wasn't much he—or any of them—could do about that. They'd have to figure out a way for all of them to get along.

"We'll just take a look at these houses, then," Madison said, figuring it was best if they got on with it—and were safely out of Zahrias' orbit for a while. She applied gentle pressure on Qadim's arm, and he gave Zahrias a formal bow before they headed off to the car again.

Any worries that the djinn leader might have given them a list of sub-par properties out of spite were quickly erased as soon as Madison stepped inside the first house. Located just past the downtown area, it was enormous, easily twice the size of the two-story home where she'd grown up. Polished sandstone floors. Multiple fireplaces, including one on the covered patio off the family room. Granite in the kitchen, and the biggest whirlpool bath she'd ever seen in the master suite.

"I think I like this," Qadim said, a wicked gleam entering his eyes as he ran an appreciative hand over the granite-tiled surround. "We would both fit easily."

They probably would, even as tall as he was. "We have other houses to look at," she pointed out.

"Why? Do you think they would suit us better than this home?"

She was hard-pressed to think that they might. Secretly she'd dreamed of living in a house like this one, but she'd known that, even though she'd been doing fairly well for herself with her art, a four-thousand-square-foot updated adobe in Santa Fe's foothills would have been well out of her reach.

"No," she said. "It's incredible." She stopped there, and sent Qadim a sidelong look, complete with lifted eyebrow. "But aren't you going to miss the Andaluz?"

In reply, he stepped away from the bath and came to take her by the waist. His body was warm, and a welcome shiver went through her. She had a feeling they'd be christening that bathtub fairly soon.

"I will only miss it because that is where I fell in love with you," he said. "But we will be making a new life here. And I will confess that sometimes it was wearying to manage all those stairs."

She could only chuckle at that remark, since she knew that a djinn really didn't need to use the stairs... unless he was trying to make a human feel more at ease. "No stairs here," she said lightly. "Well, unless you count the steps down into the living room. So should we go back into town and let Zahrias and Julia know that we've made our choice?"

"No need for that," he told her as he plucked the list of houses from her hand. "I will use this to let them know." He tore off the section at the top, the one that had the address of the house they had chosen and the directions to it, folded it in half, and then—it disappeared.

"Where did it go?"

"To the home of Zahrias and Julia."

She didn't ask how he knew where that was, since he'd already told her it was at their home that he'd met Ahmar and his Chosen, where the plans had been formulated to steal Madison away from Hasan. It was still difficult to grasp that he could send objects whizzing from place to place in an instant, but she supposed if he could make himself blink from one place to another when he traveled djinn-fashion, then it was logical to expect that he could do the same thing with inanimate objects.

Madison followed him out to the driveway, where he'd parked the Tesla. They hadn't pulled into the garage because they hadn't known for sure how long they were going to be here, whether they'd decide the place wouldn't suit them after all. It turned out that the garage had been empty; she didn't know if the lack of cars and the utterly pristine state of the rest of the house was an indication that the owners had not been here when the Heat swept through the population, or whether Julia had some djinn helpers make sure all the houses on her list had been cleaned out and made ready to move in.

The enormous closets swallowed up the meager assortment of clothing they had brought, but Qadim had only smiled and said he would conjure many more outfits for her, one for each day of the month, if that would help to make things feel a little less empty. Again she could only shake her head at him and tell him she didn't think that would be necessary.

However, she had a feeling she wouldn't be surprised if she woke up the next morning and found all those closets filled—and the drawers in the dressers and nightstands in the master bedroom.

She was inspecting the contents of the kitchen pantry when she heard the sound of a large truck pulling up into the driveway. Qadim, who'd been inventorying the tableware in the cupboards, said, "That is probably Julia. Zahrias did say she would be out to bring us some necessities, once we'd decided on a house."

"Couldn't you have just blinked it here instead of making her drive all the way out to the house to see us?"

"Perhaps. But I have a feeling she wanted to come."

"And that's not going to be weird?"

His eyes met hers. "Why should it? She means nothing to me, except as someone who is part of the community we've just joined. But if you think it will be awkward, I can go outside. I've been wanting to inspect the swimming pool anyway."

"It might be better." Was that a cowardly thing to say? Maybe, but it did seem as if it would be easier to meet with Julia if Qadim wasn't hanging around.

"Of course, my dear." He let himself out the French doors that opened from the breakfast nook onto the patio, then moved out into the open area where the swimming pool was located. It was empty but clean, which meant someone must have removed any dead leaves that had been collecting in it for the past year.

The doorbell sounded, and Madison headed toward the entryway to answer it. When she opened the door, she saw Julia standing there holding two straw market baskets.

"Housewarming committee," she said with a smile.

"Wow, thank you," Madison replied, taking one from her.

"No problem." A little glint entered the other woman's deep blue eyes as she added, "I like the Tesla."

"Oh." For some reason, Madison felt herself flush slightly. "We decided that an electric vehicle was probably safer." She hesitated, then said, "I'm surprised more of the Santa Fe group doesn't drive them."

Julia didn't seem fazed by the comment. "We actually discussed doing that, but even though djinn energy may seem unlimited, it really isn't. Everyone came to a unanimous decision that we'd rather have air conditioning and electric lights than using all that power to run electric cars. That beast I'm driving"—she jerked a thumb toward the front of the house, where Madison could just barely spy a big black truck parked in the driveway—"was actually someone's project. It's been converted to run on cooking oil. We're actually thinking of doing that to more vehicles, especially if we can get some of the brain trust from Los Alamos to give us some pointers."

From the way Julia talked about that town, it sounded as if the survivors there were on fairly good terms with the djinn and the Chosen in Santa Fe. Madison hoped she'd soon begin to figure out how this strange new society really worked.

"That does sound like a good idea," she said, then continued, "Thank you so much for finding this house for us. It's spectacular."

"Oh, you're welcome." As Madison stepped aside, Julia came into the entryway and looked around with some approval. "I love how the djinn can make such short work of cleaning. One snap of the fingers, and it looks as if you've had an army in."

"So that's how you did it."

"It does make life easier."

"I was just back in the kitchen. I assume that's where most of this goes?"

Julia nodded. "We left all the nonperishable stuff but cleaned out everything else. I know that Qadim could probably bring in anything you needed, but it seemed neighborly to offer you something from our stores." By then they'd reached the kitchen; she set her basket down on the granite island, then looked around. "Is he here?"

"He's outside." Madison put the basket she carried down next to Julia's. "He wanted to look at the pool."

Julia's dark gold eyebrows lifted, and one corner of her mouth quirked. "Is that the only reason he's outside?"

"Well...." For some reason, Madison hadn't really expected the other woman to be so forthright. But if she wasn't going to dance around the issue, then Madison thought she'd better not, either. "We thought it might be a little awkward at first, so that's why he's not in here."

At first Julia didn't say anything. She lifted a net bag filled with apples from the basket she'd been carrying and placed it in the bowl on the counter. Despite her current uneasiness, Madison couldn't keep her mouth from watering at the sight of those apples. It had been a long, long time since she'd last had one.

"You really don't need to worry," Julia said at last. She turned back toward Madison and smiled. "I saw how Qadim acted back at the Andaluz. He barely looked at me. Whatever he thought he might have felt when he met me—it's gone. He cares about you, Madison. Even Zahrias knows that."

"Zahrias didn't seem very happy to see us."

"Oh, well." A shrug, and then she said, "I think he was more worried about Hasan al-Abyad still being out there somewhere."

Zahrias and the rest of us, Madison thought, fighting back a grimace. "We're not exactly thrilled about that, either."

To Madison's surprise, Julia reached out and patted her arm. "Everyone knows to keep watch. And Zahrias also let me know that the elders had contacted him, and had told him to reach out to them immediately if we catch even a whiff of that al-Abyad character anywhere near Santa Fe. It sounds like they put the fear of God in him—threatened him with banishment to the outer circles if he comes within a mile of you or Qadim."

"'The outer circles'?" Madison repeated. "What are those?"

Julia's shoulders lifted. "I don't exactly know for sure. The djinn equivalent of jail, or Siberia. It's bad. A human can't live there—well, a human can't really live in any part of the djinn world, but the outer circles are supposed to be far, far worse. It's not an idle threat."

No, from what she'd seen of those elders, they meant business. And the djinn apparently followed their edicts, so really, Madison supposed she and Qadim were about as safe as they could be. Also, while this house felt sheltered and private, it was less than five minutes to the plaza from here. They could be among friends in no time, especially traveling the djinn way.

Friends. There was an idea. She'd thought she was going to spend the remainder of her life alone in that bunker under Clay Michael's house, and yet here she was, living with a man who apparently loved her so much he was willing to spend the rest of his incalculably long lifetime with her, and living in a place where she could be part of a community again. It would take some getting used to, but she was very much looking forward to all of it.

The French door opened then, and Qadim entered the kitchen, his hair blown by the wind, looking every inch the refugee from a biker gang, what with the jeans and the boots and the brown T-shirt with the legend "Desert Mountain Distillery" emblazoned on the front. Sometimes Madison wondered if he'd adopted that look on purpose.

But she had to admit that she kind of liked it.

"Hello, Julia," he said.

"Hi, Qadim." So casual. But Madison could tell it wasn't an act. Whatever might have happened between the two of them previously, it wasn't going to affect Julia and Qadim going forward. "I was just telling Madison how the elders had put the fear of God in Hasan al-Abyad, and so I don't think we have anything to worry about."

"Good. I suppose it was too much to hope that they would put him out of his misery for his crimes."

Julia shifted her weight from one foot to the other, looking vaguely uncomfortable. "I didn't think they did things like that."

"They don't. That is, they will banish a person, which in its way is worse than death. But still...." He let the words trail off, then gave an eloquent shrug. "At any rate, thank you for that information, and thank you also for this house and everything in it."

"You're more than welcome. We're all happy to have you here. And actually, two nights from now, we'll be having a celebration at the La Fonda Hotel. We wanted to commemorate our first anniversary here in Santa Fe, and of course you're invited."

Qadim glanced over at her, and Madison nodded. A party. A real party, with people gathering together to celebrate their community. It wouldn't be like the world she'd once known, but she thought she might enjoy learning to love what the world had become.

"We'd be honored," Qadim said. "Thank you for the invitation."

"Oh, you're welcome. But I'll leave you two to get settled in. If you need anything, well, obviously you know where to find us." She flashed a quick grin at them, then made her goodbyes and headed out the front door.

After it shut, the house felt very quiet to Madison. Qadim watched her carefully, as if attempting to discover what might be going through her head. After a moment he said, "So...what would you like to do now?"

"I think—" She stopped there and then looked up at him as she felt her mouth curve into a smile. There were so many things they needed to do—finish inventorying their food, find a cover for the pool, winterize the house against the coming cold. November was approaching fast. But one thing overrode all else. She knew the best way they could make this house truly theirs, bond with it just as they had bonded with one another.

Eyes glinting, she replied with a grin, "I think I'd like to try out that bathtub."

THE END